M

# Cherokee Warriors:
# The Loner

Black Fox carried the pan of cool water to the bedside and went to the corner cupboard for washcloths and towels. The Cat didn't look tough and strong enough to be a deputy, though, especially not without her shirt. She looked soft and temptingly feminine and she felt fragile beneath his hands.

He didn't want to know that and he didn't want to see the delicate wings of her collarbone beneath her smooth skin or the hollow in one beautiful shoulder and the bloody wound in the other one. He didn't want to touch her again, or open her shirt, or let his hand brush against her hair. All because he didn't want to think of her as a woman.

How could a woman be his prisoner? It just wasn't right. Nothing about this was right and the whole situation unbalanced him somehow.

Small, beautiful girls weren't supposed to have big, ugly wounds or be headed for jail. They certainly weren't supposed to be on the way to be hanged. It wasn't natural.

*Other* **AVON ROMANCES**

# GENELL DELLIN

# The Loner

## Cherokee Warriors

AVON BOOKS
*An Imprint of HarperCollinsPublishers*

This is a work of fiction. Names, characters, places, and incidents are products of the author's imagination or are used fictitiously and are not to be construed as real. Any resemblance to actual events, locales, organizations, or persons, living or dead, is entirely coincidental.

AVON BOOKS
*An Imprint of* HarperCollins*Publishers*
10 East 53rd Street
New York, New York 10022-5299

Copyright © 2003 by Genell Smith Dellin
ISBN: 0-06-000147-X
**www.avonromance.com**

First Avon Books paperback printing: May 2003

Avon Trademark Reg. U.S. Pat. Off. and in Other Countries, Marca Registrada, Hecho en U.S.A.
HarperCollins® is a registered trademark of HarperCollins Publishers Inc.

Printed in the U.S.A.

10 9 8 7 6 5 4 3 2 1

fazed. He kept running, dashing through the flying bullets on a straight line without zigzagging or hesitating, headed for a horse standing saddled at the east edge of the store property.

More shooting sounded, this time from the west. Black Fox gave it a glance and saw three riders arriving at a gallop with big, powerful Tassel Glass in the lead. His fringed turban and white old-style shirt made him unmistakable, as did his huge bay horse. Tassel Glass, chief of the bootleggers, fired his handgun as he came.

Even so, the boy was still running unharmed, even though the hail of bullets came from two directions now. He was nearly to the horse.

It must be The Cat. Though only a few had ever seen him—and those for no more than a glimpse he was fleeing the scene of one of his exploits—they all said he was a young boy, afraid of nothing, riding a lightning-fast yellow dun.

Well, that horse would have to run like wildfire faster than the boy was on foot.

And The Cat was as brave as he was fast. The fight raging around him might as well be a dance, for all the fear he showed.

Cat vaulted from the ground into the saddle, the dun already moving out. Dashing the small rider drew his handgun from the his hip, twisted in the saddle, and fired Glass and his men. They were riding into without slowing at all.

# Chapter 1

*Cherokee Nation West*
*April 1877*

Gunfire tore the heart out of the sweet spring afternoon. Spooked by the sudden noise, Black Fox Vann's young horse tried to bolt out of the woods. Black Fox put a stop to that foolishness while he listened with his practiced ear.

Six or seven rounds, at least. By two different guns. On the edge of the town or just outside it.

He settled Gray Ghost Horse back into his long trot and moved him on out, even though the colt no longer wanted to go in that direction. He finally did it, though, and without the comfort of a murmur or a soothing word because Black Fox was still listening.

Nobody was in the trees just ahead of him, not running toward him to attack, anyhow. Nobody was coming at him from behind.

Despite that, he squeezed the gray with his legs and sidepassed him off the trail and into the trees. A lawman was always a target, and half the population of the Nation, good men and bad, recognized him on sight. He'd been a Cherokee Lighthorseman for too many years to travel incognito ever again.

The fusillade erupted in earnest, sounding much closer now. More guns than two and more rounds fired than he could count. So. It had nothing to do with him or his presence here on the outskirts of the town of Sequoyah. It was just some trouble that had burst out into the open.

He glanced at the sun and then urged the gray into a short lope. He needed to see the situation and decide whether to take care of it before sundown or stay hidden to keep trailing The Cat.

A grim smile lifted the corners of his mouth. Nobody actually *trailed* The Cat, not for more than a short distance at most. What he was doing was trying to guess where the boy might be and get there at the same time.

The nagging regret pulled at him. It was a shame The Cat had turned killer. Until then, Black Fox had been willing to cut him some slack in his

Robin Hood thievery of giving to the poor, since there were so many, much worse men to hunt and bring to justice.

The shooting, sometimes sporadic and sometimes nearly solid, kept up for a minute or more. Then it paused for a second, resumed, and seemed to go on forever without stopping. Black Fox saw the flashes of firing muzzles as he reached the edge of the woods, and when he did, he realized that all the action was taking place at his destination, Tassel Glass's general store.

He rode up to a spot behind a thick-trunked ol' sycamore tree on the side of the road into [S]quoyah and sat his horse. Hudson Becker, a w[hite] man, and his mixed gang (white, black, [and] Cherokee) of thieves and bums were shoo[ting at] Glass's store. A small war between boo[tleggers, it] looked like. Tassel Glass was a rich, [powerful] Cherokee who was commonly called [one of the] bootleggers—maybe Becker was tr[ying to take] over the title from him.

Window panes lay shattered [across the] porch, glinting in the low sun's r[ays. A barrel of] pickles that sat just outside the [door leaked] rivers of juice from the bullet h[oles.]

The screened door burst op[en as a boy] flew out of the store. He rac[ed] into the yard on feet that [...] Black Fox watched him w[ith curiosity] greater than his alarm, [...]

The dun horse bounded across the road like a scared rabbit with the boy lying low over his neck. The two of them disappeared, crashing into the woods not a hundred yards from where Black Fox sat.

"Go, Ghost!"

His horse leapt in pursuit as if he'd been a lawman's mount forever and the last thing Black Fox saw, on the very edge of his vision, was blood blossoming on Tassel Glass's white shirt and him tumbling from his horse. He could've been shot by anybody there. Or he could be The Cat's second killing.

Or he might not die after all.

The Cat was plowing through the trees, clattering over the rocky ground with reckless abandon and Ghost stayed on the trail of the noise with a vengeance, but Black Fox never got another sighting after he saw his prey enter the woods. He searched ahead, scanned the trees and the shadows mercilessly as the gray plunged forward but The Cat had vanished.

The noise of his flight was fast growing fainter and fainter. Finally, Black Fox had to stop and listen for a moment. He headed to the northeast, which was as good a guess as he was going to get.

He clenched his jaw. The direction he picked had better be right, because he'd have to catch the boy before dark or lose him entirely. That child was fast.

Black Fox bent low in the saddle and urged the big horse on, letting everything fade completely away from his mind as his instincts took over. He opened every sense he possessed to protect himself. Limbs reached to snatch him from the saddle and rocks and sudden drops and rises in the forest floor waited to make the gray's feet stumble. He couldn't afford a mishap. This was the only chance he'd had at The Cat during the entire two weeks he'd been looking for him and he wasn't going to let him get away.

In a way, though, he wished he *could* let him go. He'd already dreaded the sickening chore of taking a young boy in to be hanged and now that he'd seen how small he was, and how unfalteringly brave, it would be worse. If only it hadn't been a deputy marshal The Cat had killed, and a white man to boot, he could've taken him in to a Cherokee court. But any crime in the Nation involving a white man fell under the jurisdiction of the U.S. federal court in Fort Smith, and Donald Turner had been deputized by Judge Parker himself.

Besides, a Cherokee court would hang him for shooting somebody in the back just as fast as Parker would.

Black Fox knew this kind of thinking was death to a lawman and a lawman was all he was. He hadn't earned his reputation by going soft on criminals just because they happened to be young and he wasn't going to start now.

He rode for another mile or two without hearing a sound from the forest up ahead. Dusk was falling, and deep in the woods it got darker even faster. The gray was proving his mettle by moving among the trees like a silent fog—the reason Black Fox had named him Gray Ghost Horse—but still there was no Cat in sight.

Black Fox strained his ears but he heard nothing. Even the night birds were silent. He hoped it was because their peace had been disturbed by The Cat's passing. Or by The Cat's presence somewhere nearby.

He was trying so hard to see into the twilight ahead that he barely had time to duck when the gray carried him beneath a low-hanging branch of a maple tree. It slapped him in the face. With wet leaves. They hadn't had rain for a week.

At that moment, he smelled the coppery scent of blood. When he wiped his fingers across his cheek, they came away smeared and when he held them up in the fading light he saw the tint of red.

Every nerve in his body went on alert. He bent from the saddle to search the ground just ahead of his horse and rode that way for a dozen yards. The gray jogged out of the trees and into a small clearing that lay at the foot of a short limestone bluff. A creek burbled over a rocky bed.

A stone's throw ahead stood a horse, his heaving sides catching glimmers of the dying light. With one wide glance, Black Fox saw that it was the little dun standing over a small figure lying on the ground. The Cat wasn't moving at all.

Black Fox dismounted, led the gray a little closer, then dropped the reins and left him. He drew his gun as he ran to The Cat, but he needn't have bothered. The child had passed out—from loss of blood, no doubt. He'd been shot in the shoulder and he was bleeding all over the grass.

Black Fox pulled his bandana from his pocket and staunched the blood as he took in a long, ragged breath. At least he'd found the kid in time to save him.

An ironic smile twisted his lips. Yeah, in time to save him so he could take him in to be hanged.

He moved The Cat out of the puddle of blood and laid him on some dry grass nearer the bluff, then started quickly gathering wood for a fire. The kid was small-boned and lightweight. He had his hat tied on as carefully tight as a cinched saddle. He was clean-cut and clean-shaven, and his well-worn clothes were much cleaner than those of most outlaws who lived in the woods and were always on the run. How had such a boy gotten himself into such a dangerous business?

He didn't appear to be Cherokee, but he might be from a family that had intermarried for a long time. Many members of the tribe no longer showed much Indian blood.

Black Fox made himself quit thinking. This was just another bad man, no matter his race or his size or his age, and now he was caught and all Black Fox needed to consider was how to get him from here to Fort Smith. That couldn't happen until the kid could ride, so he'd better get enough light to see by and examine that wound.

He went about building the fire quickly, close to the creek because he'd need water, and if he got into digging out the bullet he might need more and wouldn't have time to carry it far. When he took his camping things from his saddlebags, he filled both the cooking pot and the coffeepot because a person who'd lost a lot of blood needed warm liquid to drink.

Bringing the still unconscious boy into the flickering light, Black Fox laid him down and untied the bandana. The Cat moaned and he worked faster, hoping to get the bullet out—if that had to be done—before he came to.

The bleeding was slowing down. Good sign. The wound was in the flesh near the armpit and might be a clean one. He needed to look at the other side of it to see. Quickly, he unbuttoned the boy's shirt and peeled it back. And froze.

His slender body was already wrapped in a bandage, around the chest. The only blood on it was what had come from the new wound. Black Fox grasped the tucked end of it and started unwinding the wide strip of cloth.

The Cat was already hurt before he got shot? He had made that incredible run to his horse with an old wound in his chest and then had ridden this far with another one added to it?

The binding fell away and Black Fox stared, trying to get his mind around the shocking sight. The Cat had beautiful, white breasts tipped with rose nipples. The Cat was a *girl*?

Heat surged up his neck, embarrassment that he'd invaded her privacy like that, and he pulled her shirt back over her. But his jaw set hard.

The little vixen. What kind of a deal was this? How in the *hell* could The Cat be a girl?

But there was no mistaking those beautiful breasts. She must've fooled everyone by cutting her hair short like a boy's.

He started untying the hard-knotted hat strings, seeing for the first time by the firelight that long dark eyelashes curled against her cheek. Damn!

Why hadn't anyone ever mentioned *those* before? At least then he'd have had a notion he was chasing a girl. He'd never seen a boy with lashes like that.

He reached for his pocketknife and cut the stubborn leather strips so he could take off her hat and wad it up under her head so she could rest more comfortably. The minute he pulled at the hat, a mass of curly red hair spilled out.

*The Cat was a girl who hadn't even worked very hard to conceal it. She had fooled everybody in the Nation without even trying.*

That truth rocked him back on his haunches to

stare some more, willing it not to be so. But it was. And she was beautiful, even though her face was pale as milk in the firelight. As if to make up for that, her hair grabbed the glow from the fire and gleamed a darker auburn.

"Dear God," he muttered. "It'll be even worse to take a young *girl* in for Judge Parker to hang."

To his shock, she answered him.

"Ride away," she muttered thickly, "and you won't have to worry about that anymore."

He looked into her half-opened eyes.

"And you'd die right here," he said. "You nearly bled to death already."

"No skin . . ." she said, then stopped to get a breath, ". . . off your nose."

Her eyes closed completely.

Black Fox went back to looking for a bullet exit hole, throwing the binding loosely over her breasts while he began taking her blood-soaked shirt off her. Woman or not, he was the only one here to take care of her.

Cathleen needed to jerk away from him and jump up and run but she couldn't even lift her hand. She needed water but she couldn't say it and she needed to get away from the burning pain in her shoulder more than she needed air but she couldn't even turn her head.

What blood was left in her veins was rushing to her brain, screaming danger, yelling for her to escape, to get to her horse, to do something. She needed to think what to do and do it because this man was taking her shirt off. He must be either a lawman or a bounty hunter.

"Who . . . are you?" she mumbled.

Dear God. She barely had the strength to move her tongue with her mouth so dry.

"Black Fox Vann," he said.

*Dear God.*

She was as good as dead right now because everybody knew about this Lighthorseman who never gave up. He was relentless. He did what he had to do.

But wait! What was that he said about a hanging? Wasn't that a bit severe just for robbing Tassel Glass, who had a hundred times more possessions than she could ever carry away in a whole train of freight wagons?

Probably he was going to take her in to hang because she *intended* to kill Glass. But no. Her brain must be a little weak, too, from the loss of blood— even Black Fox Vann couldn't know her *planned* crimes.

Even Judge Parker couldn't hang a person *before* they committed murder.

Her mind spun out of control, like in a nightmare, and she tried to get it back so she could gather her strength and escape. Then he lifted her shoulder and the pain swept through her like a prairie fire burning everything else out of her brain.

She clamped her teeth together. He wasn't going to make her scream or cry. She hadn't cried since the day Tassel Glass killed her mother and she wasn't going to start now just because she was in the hands of the law.

No. She would watch for chances and she'd get free soon enough.

Black Fox left her for a minute and she hoped he'd gone away but he was back in a heartbeat with a clean shirt. He slipped it onto her good arm and covered her chest with it.

"Good thing you had this cloth wrapped around you," he said, as he started washing her wound. "I'd have had to tear up my only other shirt for a bandage and you'd have been left naked."

Would Black Fox Vann be the kind to take advantage of a woman? She'd never heard anything like that about him. She thought not, and her mind really was working better now that the pain was easing some.

"Don't even think about it," she said, as fiercely as she could. "I can wear a bloody shirt."

Her voice was so weak she could barely hear it. She must've used up all her strength as well as her air when she was trying not to scream.

"Don't worry," he said, although his voice was still gruff. "Your virtue is safe with me."

His fingers touched her gently, so gently, as he washed around her wound. But that made it hurt like crazy again. And he didn't need to try to lower her defenses by saying something kind.

"But my life isn't, is it?"

When she said that, she forced her eyes open so she could see him. So she could challenge him with a look. He didn't need to think he had all the power. She might as well try to dent his confidence a little. What else could she fight with but words?

He looked right into her eyes but he said nothing and showed nothing in his face. He was a hard man. And she could not believe he was the one who'd finally caught her.

The thought was nearly more than she could bear. She wanted to scream then, not from pain but from fear. There was no one to help her. She'd been completely alone for nearly a year and there was no one to come to her aid.

And here she was, weak as a newborn kitten, *so* weak she was helpless.

That thought scared her worse than what he'd said about hanging.

She clamped her teeth together and stared out into the darkness. Her head was going around in circles. She should get up from here and make a dash for her horse. But she couldn't even sit up without help and she knew it.

"Leave me alone," she said. "Go away."

He gave no indication he heard her and continued washing the wound. When he finished, he dried it with the tail of the shirt he'd halfway put on her. A thought skittered through her mind: what other man would think of drying her skin before he kept the air off it with a bandage? What man would even know that that might make it blister or petrify the wound?

For a breath or two, he left her alone and the pain went away.

Then he started winding the cloth around her shoulder and up over her collarbone on the other side of her neck and back under her arm, winding it very tightly, and the pain started up again with a devilish vengeance—it kept grabbing her lungs and squeezing every drop of air out of them.

Over and over again it did that until finally he was done and he laid her back down and let her be still. She forced words out of her mouth just to make him talk so she'd have something to think about besides the pain.

"I asked you a question," she said through her clenched teeth. "Why is my virtue safe with you if my life isn't?"

He was standing up now, with his face far, far above her. He jerked his head around to look at her.

"I'm not that kind of man," he snapped, his voice filled with scorn for the very thought.

He walked over to the fire, poured a cup of coffee into the tin cup he carried, and started back to her.

"Water," she said, though her tongue was so thick and dry she hated to try to move it again. "Cold water."

Oh, how it galled her to have to ask him for a drink! She could hardly bear it but she had to have water or she thought she would die right there and then.

"All right," he said, "but then you'll have to take some of the coffee."

The pain wasn't slowing down any at all that she could tell.

"You're not . . . the boss of me," she said.

He was going for water, she could tell. She couldn't see him now but she could hear the creek. This place had been one of her favorite haunts.

Then she caught herself. It still *was* one of her favorites. She might be down but she wasn't beaten yet. She wasn't going to let him take her out of the beautiful country that she loved.

"Yes, I am," he said, his voice low and sure. "I'm the boss of you until you walk into that jail."

A moment later he was walking back up the little slope to her, a cup in each hand. He went down on one knee beside her, set one cup down and brought the other to her lips. To her consternation, she couldn't hold up her head, so he propped it up with his big hand.

It was so weird to be touched. No one had

touched her for months and months, not since she'd hugged her little half-brothers good-bye.

And no *man* had ever touched her. Except for Tassel Glass.

The water lapped cool and wet and wonderful onto her lips and she drank it with Black Fox Vann's long, strong fingers in her hair and burning into her scalp. She could still feel the shape of them after he'd laid her back down. Even through the pain she could feel them.

Black Fox Vann could be a very gentle man, along with being a hard one.

"I'll let you rest a minute," he said, and somehow the tone of his rich voice soothed her, "then I'll give you the coffee."

She had to fight that soothing. It could get to be too much. She had to keep her guard up.

"I don't want it."

"I know," he said, and now his tone was even more peaceful.

The cool water was in her stomach now and the pain was bad and the two things were making her chill inside. She clamped her jaws together and tried to hold her body still. She had to think about something else or she would start to shake on the outside, too. That would make her more helpless than ever.

"Has Judge Parker started hanging people for stealing?" she said, her teeth chattering in spite of her.

Black Fox Vann bent over her immediately, propped up her head the way he had before, and held a spoonful of hot, fragrant coffee to her lips.

"All judges—and juries—hang horsethieves," he said.

Then he took the coffee away and blew on it, to cool it. Was it breath or saliva that the Cherokee believed held the essence of a person? She couldn't remember. It had better not be breath because she didn't want Black Fox Vann's essence in her.

The chill was making her tremble in earnest now, even her head shook in his hand. He held it a little more firmly. Somehow that made her feel more secure than anything else. More secure than caught.

"You've got to take this," he said. "It's cool enough not to burn your mouth."

She let him spoon the coffee into her and, on the fourth or fifth time, she felt its warmth begin to spread through her body. He must've dipped the spoon and held it to her lips a hundred times, at least it seemed that many, before the shivering lessened and finally stopped.

"Enough for now," he said, and was gone.

She glimpsed him building the fire a little higher and then he was out of sight a while before coming back to her with a horse blanket in each hand.

"I'm going to put one of these under you," he said, "and the other on top."

He laid one out beside her, knelt down and picked her up, just picked her right up as easily as Mama had picked up the boys when they were babies. She landed on the blanket as lightly as a feather and the pain didn't kick up again at all.

"I *know* all judges hang horsethieves," she said.

He chuckled as he covered her with the other blanket. He was so careful with it that her pain did not intensify.

"Good," he said. "Outlaws need to know such things so maybe they'll keep their necks out of the noose."

"If you're trying to scare me with all this talk of hanging and nooses and Judge Parker," she said, "you can forget it. I've never stolen a horse."

He squatted there on his haunches and looked straight at her in the light from the fire.

"All judges hang murderers, too," he said.

She felt her heart slow down. Inside, she grew even warmer.

"Well, then, you can turn me loose," she said, "because I never killed anybody, either."

*Yet. I haven't killed him yet. And when I do, it won't be murder.*

"Except for Deputy U.S. Marshal Donald Turner," he said, in a tone that was flat and oh, so sure. "You shot him in the back down by PawPaw a couple of weeks ago. Have you forgotten about that?"

She felt her eyes go wide with the shock of it.

He really believed that, she could tell by the way he spoke. And the way he looked at her.

"I was down by PawPaw a couple of weeks ago," she said, and swallowed hard. She really did need another drink of water. "But all I did was rob Tassel Glass's whiskey-selling friend Johnny Burke of his ill-gotten gains."

He looked right through her and into her soul. He had the darkest, most piercing stare she had ever seen in her life.

"Are you The Cat?" he said.

She didn't hesitate. He looked like St. Peter on the Great Judgment Day.

"Yes."

"You use the sign of the track of the mountain lion?"

"Yes."

"You left it on a blackjack tree above Donald Turner's body."

That one wasn't a question. Which was the most fearsome thing of all.

"No!" she cried. "No! I didn't shoot him."

"Did you put your mark on the tree?"

"Yes. That's where I waylaid Johnny McGill."

"Did you shoot him?"

She smiled at the memory.

"No. I didn't have to shoot one round. He just threw me the money sack and rode off as fast as he could."

She leaned up on one elbow and stared at him

narrow-eyed, fighting the panic that was trying to take her. She couldn't let him see it, she couldn't let him know that she was so scared.

Gentle or not, water and coffee or not, bandage or not, this man was her mortal enemy.

"I didn't even steal his horse," she said.

He looked at her for a long, long time, searching her entire self very, very thoroughly.

Finally, he spoke. "I want to believe you," he said quietly. "God help me, I want to."

His jaw hardened.

"But I don't."

# Chapter 2

**B**lack Fox tried to make himself stand up and walk away. He needed to see to the fire. He needed to get some more water into her. But he couldn't stop looking at her—as if somehow that would help him absorb the truth.

Who would've thought that The Cat was a woman? No, a girl. She was very much a girl, probably no more than sixteen or seventeen years old.

He got up and went to pour some more water into the cup. Then he knelt beside her and held the drink to her lips with one hand as he supported her head with the other. She had a beautiful, full mouth. And her hair felt like silk between his fingers.

"Did you think you could go on forever and not get caught?" he said, when she'd stopped drinking. He laid her head down and folded his jacket to go under it. "What were you doing, anyhow?"

"Getting ready to call Tassel Glass out," she said. "Just as soon as I got good enough with my handgun."

Astonished, he stared at her. He lifted her head and slipped the makeshift pillow beneath it.

"I'm good with a rifle," she said, in a matter-of-fact tone, "but I never had used a six-shooter very much."

His mind raced, trying to understand.

"So you went to the store today for a shootout with him?"

Her eyes blazed.

"Maybe. Maybe not. I was testing him," she said impatiently.

"That's usually what a shootout is," he snapped, irritated by her tone. "A test to see who can draw faster."

She narrowed her eyes at the sarcasm.

"This test was to see if he recognized me dressed as a boy. To see if he knows that The Cat is me. To see if he knows I'm back in the Nation and after revenge. That's why I use my sign—he knows my family nickname is Cat for Cathleen."

"Revenge for what?"

"He trapped my stepfather by giving him a job,

supposedly to work off all the money we owed at the store. Instead, he shot him dead. He raped my mother and then killed her by setting fire to our house."

Her jaw clenched, although it trembled along the line of the delicate bone.

"Why?"

"To try to bed me," she said. "And I am going to kill him."

Her tone was low and even. Every word came out fierce and sure.

Every word proved he'd been right not to believe that her lawlessness ended with thievery.

"Oh," he said, "and will you steal his horse, too?"

She sagged back against the ground. She knew what he meant by that. It didn't make her waver one bit.

"No," she said. "And I won't kill and I *didn't* kill anybody *else*, either. All I want is that son of a bitch out of business and off the face of the earth."

Black Fox sat back on his heels and took a long, deep breath. He'd better quit thinking about her as a girl and think of her as a prisoner who would escape if he gave her half a chance.

Yet the thought of her being tormented by Glass's lecherous intentions, maybe even touched by his hands, made him want to kill the man, too. *To try to bed me*, she had said. At least old Tassel must not have succeeded, which was a miracle, given his known ruthlessness.

"Glass has a lot of enemies," he said, "and you or one of Becker's bunch shot him today. He may be dead right now."

"If he's not, he will be," she said.

"But not at your hand," he said, in the same ungiving tone she had just used.

It was for his sake and not for hers that he was arguing with her. It'd make it easier for him if she were convinced there was no reason to try to escape.

Which was a stupid way to be thinking when he'd already told her she was on her way to be hanged.

No, it wasn't. She cared more about Glass's death than her own life or she wouldn't be planning to call him out. And that was a sad comment on life in the Nation when a young person, much less a woman, felt she had to impose her own justice. It made him feel derelict in his duty.

He turned away from her and stood up. Then he looked down at her, hard and straight.

"The reason you took such a risk as to go openly into Glass's store," he said harshly, "is that you're wishing all this mad wildness was over with. Well, now it is. You're on your way to the Fort Smith jail."

Cat gave him her best defiant glare for as long as she could, then she closed her eyes and turned her face away. He might as well have stabbed her in the heart.

*You're wishing all this mad wildness was over with.*

He was right, and that chilled her mind worse than her body already was. How could he know that about her? He really could look into her soul with those dark eyes of his. When she got ready to escape, she'd have to be careful not to let him see her thoughts.

Because he'd said that, her weakness reached even deeper into her and called up her loneliness. It pulled at her until she wanted to turn loose and fall into it, to let it take away her will.

But if she did that, she would never get to her goal. What she needed to do was rest up and drink every bit of water he gave her and sleep. He wasn't going to take her anyplace tonight. He had already unsaddled the horses to get the blankets for her and now she could hear him over there in the dark somewhere, moving the tack around, judging from the small sounds of the bits and the cinch buckles clinking.

Yes, she would let herself sleep so her strength would come back. She took a deep breath and told herself that by relaxing, by sleeping, she was not giving in to the weakness. Instead, she was gathering strength.

However, many months of outlawry had ingrained the habits of survival deep in her. The minute she tried to give in to exhaustion, sleep escaped her. She listened to the faint sounds Black

Fox made walking around and she knew when he pounded a stake into the ground to tie the horses for the night.

They weren't going anywhere tonight. They were staying right here until morning and she had believed him when he said her virtue was safe. She needed rest. She would go to sleep, she would *will* herself to do it.

A rough hand clamped over her mouth and held her head against the ground. For one terrible instant she thought it wasn't Black Fox and she would go mad from being so helpless, so limp from pure fear. Then she caught his scent and his voice, low and quiet as breath in her ear.

"Somebody's out there," he murmured. "I'm getting you away from the light."

Then it scared her that she hadn't heard anything. She wouldn't last long like that.

He pulled the blanket she lay on far enough into the dark that he wouldn't be silhouetted by the fire when he stood up, and then he gathered her up into his arms and started moving fast up the incline of the hill. The pain stirred and spread through her whole body again but Black Fox clasped her tight against his chest and the warmth of his body spread through her, too.

It nearly made her forget the pain.

"There's a cave up here," he whispered.

His mouth brushed her ear. She wouldn't have

believed her overwrought feelings could've let one more sensation in, but a thrill tingled her all over at the touch of his lips on her skin.

"You just stay quiet," he said. "I'll take care of whoever it is."

The sound of a branch snapping underfoot rang in the night like a shot. Then Cat heard the creak of saddles and the snuffling of horses.

"There's more than one of them," she whispered, although, for some reason, she could hardly get breath to speak.

"I know," he said.

Then she wondered why she warned him. If he got shot, she wouldn't be a prisoner anymore. She was crazy for feeling safe in his arms.

She had to do something to drive that feeling away.

Black Fox laid her down. "You're in the mouth of the cave," he said, bending over her. "Don't move from here."

"Hey! Hello the camp! Is that The Cat there? We're ridin' in. We want to join up with you!"

Chill bumps stood up on her skin and she tried to think who it was. She had spent so much time eavesdropping and spying on the bootleggers in this part of the Nation that she should recognize the voice. She finally did, just before he announced himself.

"This here's Hudson Becker," he called, and she heard the slur of his tongue that told her he'd been sampling some of his own wares. "I got a deal for you, Cat Boy, 'cause you been doin' so much harm to Tassel Glass."

"I've been doing harm to him, too," she muttered. "He probably wants to kill me."

Terrible images flashed through Black Fox's head, images of The Cat, helpless and female, in Becker's hands. Thank God the bootlegger thought she was a boy, or he'd be even bolder.

"You've got the wrong camp, Becker," Black Fox called back. "We're Lighthorsemen here."

It galled him to say that, with every muscle in his body aching to stay silent and get out of there, to drift through the night in a big quarter-circle and get behind them, to surprise them and take them all prisoner before they had a clue he was there. The bootleggers did a lot of harm to the Nation, sometimes as much as the murderers, but it seemed he never had time to go after them.

He couldn't do it, though. Working alone, he'd never be able to keep them away from The Cat on the long journey to Fort Smith, or even to the Tahlequah jail.

A long silence reigned.

Then there was a rustling in the edge of the woods, and Becker yelled again, his voice sounding closer this time.

"I don't believe you. Which Lighthorsemen?"

"I'm Black Fox Vann," he said. "Ride on in and we can meet face-to-face."

More silence.

"Get him in here and turn me over to him," The Cat murmured sarcastically, "and you won't have to go through all that upset of taking a girl in to hang."

Hot fury stung him. Ungrateful little wench.

"Careful what you wish for," he snapped. "I ought to be out there rounding them up instead of protecting you."

"I can protect myself," she said. "Go . . . ahead. Arresting them would stop a whole lot of meanness in the Nation and capturing me only stops good deeds. You . . . know that."

She was nearly too weak to talk. Or else her pain was that bad.

It made him mad at himself that he even bothered to think about which it might be.

"Save your breath," he said. "You're gonna need it."

He set his jaw against his anger, went to the saddles he had piled to one side of the cave's entrance, and slid his rifle from the scabbard on his saddle.

"I'm climbing to higher ground," he said. "If I have to drive them off I don't want them shooting toward you."

"No, 'cause they might kill me and you want Judge Parker to do that," she said.

"Don't move," he said.

"I'm helpless," she said bitterly. "Remember?"

"Don't feel sorry for yourself. You could already be dead."

He left her.

"You're bluffin'," Hudson Becker yelled drunkenly. "You're just some longrider hiding out on your lonesome. You ain't no Lighthorseman."

"Come on in and see for yourself," Black Fox yelled back.

"I will. I need another horse. I've got a man here riding double because his mount took a bullet."

"Stop auguring and try us," Black Fox said. "We'll empty some more saddles for you and then you won't need our horses."

He was glad his eyes were getting adjusted to the night. If they started shooting, he would have to move quickly and silently from one place to another to make it seem more than one man was shooting back at them. Damn his luck, anyhow! How could this happen at the only time in his life when he had a wounded woman as his sole responsibility?

Somebody in Becker's gang shot off his gun, apparently into the air. Black Fox held his fire. No sense letting them see where he was until he had no choice.

"We know you're on your own and by your lonesome. We tracked you."

Black Fox laughed.

"Then you couldn't track a herd of cows across

a muddy barnyard," he said. "Come on in here
and count us. Then we'll take you up to Tahlequah to see the jail."

"You oughtta take a long walk tomorrow so's
you can think about all that lying you're doing tonight," Becker said righteously.

He was slurring his words even more.

"Come ahead," Black Fox called. "Stop flap-
ping your jaws and try us."

He moved the instant he said it, and it was a
good thing he did. Two of Becker's men shot at
him, sending one of the bullets whistling past his
ear. Black Fox shot back, then scooted fast away
from that spot along the rocky ledge. Somebody
yelled in pain.

Nothing would be easy if they actually worked
up the nerve to storm the camp. He didn't know
how many of them there were, and one of them
could get to Cat while the others were keeping
him busy. Somehow, he had to make them want to
go on their drunken way.

"I'll take you," Becker said. "Even if you *are*
Lighthorse. That'd be a feather in my cap. Yep, we
might just kill us a Lighthorseman."

Black Fox fired toward the sound of the rough
voice. A second later, while he was moving to a
new location, another rifle—not far from him—
did the same.

He nearly jumped out of his skin. His mind
raced crazily. Had one of them gotten around

him? But if so, why would the man be firing at his own gang?

The other rifle barked again and he caught a glimpse of its flash at the mouth of the cave. Quickly, Black Fox fired, too, so it'd be positively clear that there were two of them. How in the world had The Cat recovered enough to pick up a rifle, much less aim and fire it?

The moon was rising. It caught the glint of the rifle barrel and the gleam of red that was always in The Cat's hair. She was sitting or kneeling behind a rock and steadying her long gun across it.

Flame flashed at the muzzle. She sank down so her head would be behind the rock in case of return fire.

"Hey," he called, keeping his voice low, "get into the cave. *Now!*"

"Keep firing," she said, her voice shaking. "I can't do this much longer."

They each took two more shots at Becker and his men. On the last round, they scored another scream of pain. Several coarse shouts rang out, somebody's horse started thrashing around in the woods, and Becker called to his men to head home.

"Hey! We'll be back before daylight," he yelled. "Then we'll see who you really are."

The sound of glass breaking, probably a thrown bottle, shattering against the rock wall of the bluff completed the threat and farewell. The Becker gang tore off through the woods then, making enough noise for a hundred men.

Despite that, Black Fox stayed in the shadows as he ran to Cat.

She sat slumped against the rock as if trying to hug it, her rifle hanging crazily across her lap. Black Fox laid his long gun down, took hers, breached it open and reloaded it. Then he picked her up.

Instantly, she sank back against him as if his arms were a refuge. A fierce protectiveness surged through him and his grip on her tightened before he could stop himself.

Quickly, he laid her onto the blanket where he'd left her to begin with and put the rifle beside her.

"How d'you . . . know . . . I won't shoot you?" she said.

"You'd have done it already if you were going to do it tonight," he said.

"I should . . . have," she said, drawing in deep breaths of exhaustion.

"I'm glad you didn't," he said grimly.

He needed to remember this, now that she *hadn't* shot him dead and he would live to transport other prisoners. It was something he'd already known well, and he had foolishly let the fact that she was a woman make him forget: a lawman should never, ever assume a prisoner was too weak to drag himself—or herself—to a weapon and use it.

"I'm glad . . . I had the strength . . . to shoot," she said. "I'm not . . . hurt as bad . . . as I thought."

"Stop talking," he said, as he slid the makeshift pillow under her head. "You barely have the strength to get your breath."

"I could've . . . saved myself . . . from hanging if I'd shot you," she said. "Instead, I saved you 'cause you were outnumbered."

He covered her with the other blanket and then stood over her, shaking his head. This girl had sand in her craw and nobody could deny it. She never quit fighting, whether it was with guns or with words.

"Don't try to make me feel obliged to you," he said. "You helped me out because you were too weak to escape and you knew that you'd be safer with me than with them."

"Not . . . true," she said.

She had the faintest trace of teasing in her voice.

"You're the stubbornest woman I've ever known," he said, and heard the same light tone in his own voice. He stiffened. What was happening here?

He wasn't going to let her make him put his guard down.

"You could've ridden off and left me to them," she said. "I told you. It would've saved you from worrying over taking a woman in to hang."

"The Cat's an even bigger catch for me than Hudson Becker would be," he snapped. "Besides,

I'd have had to find some help if I tried to haul you *and* that whole bunch to Fort Smith."

The moonlight fell across her face. She looked up at him, looked at him straight as a man would do, with the power of absolute resolve in her eyes.

"You're just trying to make yourself more famous by taking me in," she said. "But you'll never do it, Lighthorseman. I'll get away from you before we ever see Fort Smith."

Her eyes closed and her head fell to one side. She had passed out.

Panic struck him. Had she lost more blood or simply overdone her strength? She must've started bleeding again—how could she not, from the recoil of the rifle?

He fell to his knees and looked at her shoulder. She'd bled through the shirt since he'd bandaged her, but the stain didn't seem to be spreading. If it wasn't, it was best not disturbed.

And it was best he not disturb himself by glimpsing the proof of her womanhood again. He was going to treat her like a man from now on or else he'd wind up wounded or dead.

While he kept watch for more blood, he found his bedroll and spread it out for her—nearer the fire but in the shadows—then moved her onto it. All night long, he sat beside her, trying not to think.

He put on his other jacket and leaned back against the wall of the bluff, keeping watch, listening to the birds and the rustlings of small animals in the woods, feeling the night all around them, looking at the moon. And trying not to think.

Especially about this girl who swore he wouldn't take her to jail. All he had to do was his job and he knew how to do that. He'd been doing it for seven years.

His job, those of the other Lighthorsemen, and those of the Cherokee sheriffs and their deputies were the only way to save the Nation, the only way to keep it sovereign for the Cherokee and not let it fall under the control of the United States. The Americans would take over and impose their own government if lawless men from everywhere continued using the Indian lands for a refuge.

Lawless women were another matter.

No, they weren't. A killer who would shoot someone in the back was still a killer, woman or man.

When the chill of the early morning came down into the hills, he added the second saddle blanket to The Cat's covers and punched up the fire. She was just like any other prisoner to him. He'd been a little taken aback, that was all, because she was the first woman among all the wrong-doers he'd ever caught.

If she'd shot Tassel Glass in the back he might be able to understand—she certainly had reason enough to want revenge on the man. But she had done it to Donald Turner instead—ironically, when he carried a warrant in his pocket for Glass's arrest.

Black Fox got up, poured himself a cup of coffee, and went back to hunker down in his spot against the bluff where he could see in three directions when the sun came up. The Cat had shot Donald Turner in the back, yet she was waiting to get good enough with a handgun so she could call Tassel Glass out in an honorable fashion. Did that make sense?

Thoughtfully, he sipped at the hot, strong brew. Could she be telling the truth about drawing her sign on the trunk of the tree *before* Turner was killed at its foot?

He considered that while he drank his coffee but he found no answer.

She seemed not to be a liar, considering that she had told him straight out and honestly what she planned to do to Tassel Glass, but her sign had been on the tree above Turner. No other evidence had been found.

On the other hand, she *must* be a liar, by the very fact that she was an outlaw. That breed was all alike—untrustworthy to the core.

Except for Charley Burntgrass, who'd been one of the most dangerous men in the Nation when Black Fox had first been sworn in as a Lighthorseman. Charley had picked up Black Fox's wallet, fallen unnoticed out of his pocket in a skirmish when the young lawman was posing as the newest member of the Hickory Mountain Gang in order to gather evidence against them.

He could still see the wry grin curving Burntgrass's thin lips as he handed the flat leather packet back to Black Fox.

"I may be the meanest son of a bitch north of the Red," Charley had said proudly, "but I ain't no snake-bellied thief."

That honesty had saved Black Fox's life, for in that wallet was the folded paper that was his authorization as a Cherokee Lighthorseman. And now, here, tonight, The Cat had been honorable enough to shoot that rifle she could barely hold level and make a show of force that may have saved his life again.

But that didn't mean she wasn't a liar.

Black Fox leaned back against the rock wall and looked toward her. She was breathing slow and steady, as if she were completely, soundly asleep. Unlike Charley, she *was* a thief, and she'd admitted it. But she claimed not to be a killer.

His pulsebeat stuttered a little, with hope. Maybe she was as honest as old Charley had been, all those years ago.

He set his cup down on the ground and shook his head. That thought was as naïve as any he'd had as a greenhorn beginner of a Lighthorseman and now he was a seven-year veteran and a captain. He was forgetting everything he'd learned in those long years—all because his prisoner tonight was a beautiful red-haired girl.

"Better get a handle on it, Vann," he muttered to himself, "you're acting as foolish as an old man."

Restless, he shifted his position to sit cross-legged, what the whites called Indian-style, and look down to the moonlit creek chattering over the rocks below. It had been a wild ride, these last ten years, and if he could live them over, he wouldn't spend them any other way.

His fate had been irrevocably decided that long-ago day when the drunken band of outlaw Intruders had invaded his parents' farm and killed his parents before his eyes. All he'd wanted from that day forward was to rid the Nation of dangerous scum like them.

It still chilled his blood to remember watching from the persimmon thicket as his mother and then his father had been shot dead as they worked in the garden. And then from the ground, running, as he raced to help his parents.

The lead man, who was turning his horse toward the screaming little boy, deliberately aimed at him and shot him, too. After that, he'd watched them through slitted eyes as he played dead.

Black Fox turned his head and looked out into the night, seeing it all again against the black sky: the raucous riders shouting that they were taking the place, that the Indians had to give up their lands to white men, while they rode, charging, at his astonished, unarmed father. They mercilessly shot him three times so that he finally fell into the rows of corn while still struggling to get to his wife, whom they shot in the next instant.

He could still feel it all, too. The stinging pain as the bullet slammed into his shoulder and the rage and terror that fought inside him with the sorrow that was already welling up into his throat. He'd known his parents were dead the minute they fell.

Well, he wasn't that horrified, helpless boy anymore. He was known throughout the Nation, and over the United States border in Arkansas, too, as a fearless, ruthless bringer of justice, the most famous Cherokee Lighthorseman of them all.

Black Fox's fame came from several jobs he'd done that people still talked about. He had trailed William Emmit, who never robbed a man he didn't kill, all the way to Klo Kotcha in the Creek Nation, and had brought him in alive. He had tracked James Morley, a notorious horsethief, for thirty days, long after the posse and the federal marshal from Fort Smith had given up, and he had caught him alive, too. He had faced down Mose Fourkiller as he openly boasted of his treachery in killing his neighbor and had shot the man dead.

But the exploit that had sealed his reputation and made him the most prominent Lighthorseman of all had happened when he'd stopped the jailbreak at the old Tahlequah jail. He had rushed Buckskin Adair knowing the murderer held a smuggled gun and had already freed two other prisoners to overpower the guard. All three of them had been giving him the turkey-gobble death threat and coming at him, Adair shooting, when Black Fox had hit two of them with his first two shots and the third had thrown up his hands in surrender.

He shook his head in wonder as he remembered. God had been with him, and Adair had been a lousy shot or he would not be here tonight.

Black Fox got to his feet and stretched, walked to the edge of the woods where he could stand in the shadows and look out across the vague outlines of the wooded hills. All that was past and he must think about the present.

Now he had captured his first woman outlaw and she was wounded. What was he going to do with her?

She was not able to ride and she would not be able until that wound had healed sufficiently. She'd lost so much blood that she'd be weak for quite a while before he could start on the long trail to Fort Smith without killing her.

He wasn't carrying enough supplies to stay here for the days it would take before she was near normal strength again. He couldn't leave her long enough to hunt for food, not so much because she might try to escape—in her weakened state, she wouldn't be up to hiding her tracks and he'd be able to track her—but because she might overdo herself and start the bleeding again. She'd already done that once.

Black Fox felt his mouth curve at the memory of her and the long gun she'd fired at Becker. She had enough spunk for two people her size.

There was no place else to take her but to his home, where Aunt Sally and Uncle Muskrat would be on hand to help if he needed it. Though he really didn't want to get them involved if he could help it, it would be good to be close to them in case The Cat's condition should worsen, because Aunt Sally was an herb doctor who had treated many a gunshot wound and many a fever.

But Aunt Sally was also very admiring of The Cat, and for that reason Black Fox didn't want her to know that he had the Cherokee Robin Hood in custody. He grinned at the thought of the brisk, bossy woman who had raised him. It was amazing, come to think of it, that he had become a Lighthorseman wanting to enforce the law, because Sally had her own very definite opinions about right and wrong, justice and punishment. She didn't see one thing wrong with The Cat's stealing from the rich to give to the poor.

Yes, he would take her home with him. It'd be a fairly long ride, but he had no choice. Cathleen had too much courage to let herself die on the trail.

And she had the same sorrow he did, having seen her people murdered before her eyes.

# Chapter 3

**B**lack Fox still hadn't closed his eyes when the first streaks of pink tinged the sky. And he still hadn't figured out what to believe about the guilt or innocence of this woman/child he had in his care. It wasn't his job to figure it out, he must remember that. It had to be left to a jury to decide.

Yet, he always wanted to believe that the prisoners he took to jail were guilty. It was a crime on his part to rob a person of even one day of freedom if he or she was innocent.

Finally, he tossed the remains of his dozenth cup of coffee away and stood up. Time to get going.

His movement disturbed The Cat's sleep.

"Wa-ter," she mumbled.

He got her a drink of cold water and held up her head so he could pour some of it down her throat. He tried to talk to her but she only moaned in response.

Black Fox laid her back down and walked to the edge of the camp. Nothing as big as a man or a horse was moving among the trees. The sun was bringing a stronger light each minute.

Becker could very well make good on his threat to return come sunrise, so they needed to get out of here now.

He went back to The Cat and stood over her. She was shifting restlessly in her sleep and muttering. He touched her forehead and his heart sank. She was hot, and running a fever.

Black Fox tried to get her awake and get some coffee into her but she clamped her beautiful lips together and refused to take even a sip. She wouldn't open her eyes, either.

For several minutes, Black Fox knelt beside her, trying to prepare her to ride. He could see through her shirt that the bleeding had not completely stopped and he bound the bandage tighter. Then he tried again to get some liquid into her but she wouldn't take it.

Finally, he realized he would have to carry her because she couldn't hold her eyes open for more than a heartbeat at a time, and there was no way, short of being tied in the saddle, that she would be able to stay on a horse. He couldn't do that to her.

His heart twisted inside him. He wanted her gone and off his hands and he wished for her to be somebody else's responsibility more than he had wanted anything for a long, long time. But he had to take her home with him. There was nowhere else to go and get there with her still alive.

He brought the horses up and saddled them, put his gear back into his packs, then ran the little dun horse's reins through his own saddle ring and knotted them. Only then did he kick dirt over the fire, hoping The Cat could stay warm as long as possible. Fever made a person feel cold and soon she might be chilling. He had to get her to shelter and into a real bed.

His bed.

Black Fox gathered The Cat up into his arms, bedroll and all. That would keep her warmer.

And it would keep her curved, soft body from resting right next to his.

That thought shocked him. She was young. It was unworthy of him even to let such a sensual consideration as that cross his mind.

Dear God, and she was sick into the bargain. But she settled into the curve of his arm with a natural ease that said she trusted him.

"No," she mumbled, starting to thrash around a little, "leave me alone."

She kept her eyes closed.

"I know it hurts," he murmured soothingly, "but I have to hold you tighter while I'm mounting my horse so as not to drop you."

He stuck the toe of his boot into the stirrup, managed to get a grip on the horn with one hand, and stepped up with her in his arms. It would be the perfect moment for Becker to shoot at them.

The thought must have leapt from his brain to hers.

"What . . . about Becker . . . ?" she muttered.

He swung into the saddle and found the other stirrup without jostling her too much.

"Becker's sleeping it off," he said, hoping it was true. "Didn't you hear the firewater in his voice last night?"

"Um," she said and went even more limp in his arms.

She leaned her head against his shoulder as if he'd asked her to lay it there. He glanced down at her pale, pale face as he turned the horses.

The Cat was looking at him with her eyes wide open. They were as green as still water in the early morning light and they seemed to look straight into his soul.

"Are we going to Fort Smith?" she said.

Her voice faltered on the last word and that small sound was like a knife to his heart. God in Heaven, she was only a kid.

A kid who had good reason for the things she did.

He set his jaw and wished he had never set out to hunt The Cat.

"Not right now," he said. "In the shape you're in, the trip would kill you."

She gave a sharp little laugh that made his skin crawl.

"Oh, yeah," she said. "I keep forgetting you want the hangman to do that."

He looked away, to guide his horse. There was no way he could think about that hanging now. She was only another prisoner. He must forget that she was a woman.

She made a noise so that he met her eyes again and she held his gaze with her strong, green one as if for reassurance that he was telling the truth.

"We're going in the opposite direction of Fort Smith now," he said.

She closed her eyes and let her head go into the curve of his shoulder, let her whole weight rest in his arm as if she believed him. As if she knew she was safe.

And last night, he had laid a loaded gun by her side. As if he'd known she wouldn't shoot him.

A seed of trust had been born between them. Now it was his job to rip it out by the roots.

Black Fox stayed off the worn trails and made his own path through the woods, riding with every sense and every nerve alert for a warning of danger. He held both the reins and The Cat with his left arm—she had passed out again, as far as he could tell—so his right one would be free to draw his gun from the hip holster. Their two horses seemed to be making enough noise for twenty.

But a few squirrels, a red-tailed hawk sitting on a stump and a startled yearling deer were all that saw their passing and before noon he pulled up on the edge of the yard that surrounded his home-place—cabin, barn, and outbuildings. For a minute, he held the horses in the shelter of the trees, so he could see whether Uncle Muskrat or Cousin Willie, who farmed the place, were any-where around.

At the edge of the bedroll, where The Cat's face lay against his arm, the heat of her skin burned through to his, even though he wore a jacket. The fever had gone higher than ever, despite the fact that he'd washed her face several times with the bandana wet in cool water from his canteen.

A team of Uncle Muskrat's work horses munched grass in the back pasture and cattle grazed there, but no people showed themselves. Nothing indicated that someone might be in the barn, either.

Black Fox squeezed the Ghost with his knees, so the gray and the little dun started toward the house at a walk while he kept on scanning the place with his searching gaze. It'd be for the best if no one knew The Cat was there. His family could be trusted to keep a secret, yes, but Sally was a talker and if word accidentally got out, folks would ride for miles to see the heroic Robin Hood who'd been helping the poor people all over Sequoyah district, and sometimes in Flint and Goingsnake, too.

At the front door, he stopped the horses, dropped the reins and carried The Cat into the house and straight to his bed. She moaned when he laid her down, and when he touched her face, it burned his fingertips. He needed to do something about that fever, and do it now.

But first, the horses had to be tended, and it would only take a minute to get them out of sight.

He left the room with one glance back at her still face, pale as death. At least this was one time he knew she couldn't escape. The thought made his jaw harden. Why had she put herself in the middle of a firefight, anyhow? A young, pretty girl like her should be at home with her mother learning to cook or wandering the spring woods looking for poke salad and picking the first wildflowers.

Guilt stabbed him. She was in this mess because the lawmen of the Nation had done nothing about the evil deeds of Tassel Glass. It made him feel guilty as a representation of them all, even though he'd been busy chasing killers and hadn't known that Tassel Glass fit into that category. The man was widely reputed to be a bootlegger and a merchant hard on collecting debts owed him, but this was the first Black Fox had ever heard of his being a murderer, too.

It was a sad state of affairs when little orphan girls had to seek their own justice.

Moving swiftly, he led their mounts to the barn, stalled and unsaddled them, filled the water buckets and threw them some hay. At night, he would turn them out to graze and he'd keep them up during the day, so as not to attract attention.

That thought seized him with a stark dread. How long would they be here, with him responsible for her—nursing her back to health before he took her to her doom?

He picked up his saddlebags and The Cat's, threw one over each shoulder, and ran for the house. Then he wished he could turn around and run back out again. She was really sick, and she might have to stay here with him for several days. It bothered him more than he was willing to admit that, after only a few hours, he was thinking about her far too much.

She was tossing restlessly, muttering and groaning, her eyes moving back and forth beneath her closed lids. For a long, paralyzing moment, he watched her. Maybe he should get his Aunt Sally to come and take care of her.

Maybe he should put that thought right out of

his head. This was his responsibility and he would deal with it.

Black Fox turned, went to the kitchen, and started building a fire in the kitchen stove. As soon as the kindling caught, he added a couple of sticks of wood and blew on the small flames, willing them to grow. Then he went out onto the back porch and pumped some cool water into a pan.

Yes, he would take care of this girl himself. Not only was it his job, but Aunt Sally would be so upset that he was holding The Cat prisoner she would probably demand that he set her free. Sally and lot more people, too, held the view that The Cat was a hero and should never be punished for doing good for poor people and especially not for harassing Tassel Glass.

The last time he saw her, Sally had remarked that Tassel Glass deserved to be robbed since he always robbed everyone else with his high prices. Sally hated all bootleggers, too, since her son Willie was one of their best customers.

The fact that The Cat was a girl, and a very brave one, would cinch the deal and Sally would try to talk him into letting her go. His aunt judged everyone by the heart and she would deem The Cat's heart in the right place. Why, when The Cat healed, Sally would probably ride into town with her to help give old Tassel his just due.

That image made him smile as he set a pot of

water on one of the stovelids to boil for the sumac tea. Aunt Sally and The Cat would make a team that could terrorize bad men all over the Nation. Maybe he should go ahead and introduce them, then deputize them both.

Black Fox carried the pan of cool water to the bedside and went to the corner cupboard for washcloths and towels. The Cat didn't look tough and strong enough to be a deputy, though, especially not without her shirt. She looked delicate and temptingly feminine and she felt fragile beneath his hands.

He didn't want to know that and he didn't want to see the fragile wings of her collarbone beneath her smooth skin or the hollow in one beautiful shoulder and the bloody wound in the other one. He didn't want to touch her again, or open her shirt, or let his hand brush against her hair. All because he didn't want to think of her as a woman.

How could a woman be his prisoner? It just wasn't right. Nothing about this was right and the whole situation unbalanced him somehow.

Small, beautiful girls weren't supposed to have big, ugly wounds or be headed for jail. They certainly weren't supposed to be on the way to be hanged. It wasn't natural.

He began by bathing her face, then slipped a towel beneath her and began unbuttoning his shirt that she was wearing. Her hot skin felt like melted satin every time he grazed it with his fingertips. That water had better be boiling soon because she needed medicine, and she needed it now.

Her eyes fluttered open and Black Fox saw that she had to make an effort to keep them open. But the look she gave him was lucid.

"*Stop it*," she said, her voice raspy in her throat, her hands weakly pushing at his.

"I'm cooling you off," he said. "Your fever's way too high, and I'm going to wash you with this cold well water to try to bring it down."

"No," she said, snatching the cloth out of his hand. "I'll do it."

Her gaze darted away from his as embarrassment stained her pale cheekbones—pink streaks appeared above the flush of fever in her cheeks. She scooted back to prop herself up on the pillows in spite of the fact that she was trembling.

A streak of fear shot through him.

"Your fever's getting higher by the minute," he said carefully. "I need to help you out of your clothes, at least."

"No. I'll do it."

Quickly, she held the cloth to her forehead, then began moving it over her face with one hand while the other held the front of the shirt together.

Touched by her maidenly wariness, he turned away to give her some privacy, yet he could hardly let her bathe so slowly while her temperature rose. He tried to think what to say because she didn't have a lot of strength to waste on being upset. Or on washing herself, either.

"You let me take care of you last night," he said calmly. "Why not now?"

"Now I'm able to do it myself."

To prove it, Cathleen forced her shaky arms and hands to work, to move the cool cloth over her upper body beneath the loose shirt. He had touched her so gently when he'd bandaged her out there by the cave that she had liked it. She had liked it a lot. Even the awful pain hadn't been enough to distract her from liking the feel of his hands taking care of her. That was what scared her.

Yet, she certainly hadn't liked it so much that she wanted him to strip her off and *bathe* her! She'd never been naked in front of a man and she wasn't about to start now.

He reached to undo the buckle to her belt.

"Leave it," she said, forcing strength into her voice. "I'm *not* taking off my clothes."

"Oh, yes, you are," he said. "If you're able to bathe yourself, fine, but either you have to do a good job of it or I'll have to carry you outside and dunk you in the watering trough."

He turned his back to her and, to her chagrin, reached for her feet and pulled off one of her boots. She tried to kick, struggling hard to hit him with her sock foot, but it was like kicking a rock. He took hold of the other boot with both hands.

"I won't look at you if that's what you're afraid

of," he said. "I'll just help you get your jeans off and I'll go straight out of the room."

"No," she cried. "I *can't* take off my boots and jeans."

She bit her tongue. It might be best not to warn him again that she would escape as soon as she could. And, she had to admit, before she could even hope to run from him she did have to get rid of this fever. This minute, she felt way too weak to ride.

She gathered all her strength and began bathing herself more vigorously.

"Don't be thrashing around like that," he said. "You'll make that wound bleed . . ."

His big shirt slipped off her shoulder and she saw that the wound already had bled through the bandage. More than it had done at the cave during the night. He saw it, too.

"All right," he said, "be *still*."

He took the cloth from her, folded a dry one, placed it in her hand and on the wound, pressing down.

"Hold it right there. I'm going to get something to put on it. Don't move."

She didn't. The stain was bigger than the square of cloth she held against it.

She could hear him moving around in the kitchen, clanking the stove lid, pouring water, opening the creaky door of a pie safe or something. Her hand shook, with weakness more than fear, as she kept pushing down hard on the wound the way he had showed her.

But she did feel fear, too. She thought about her mother, who had spent so much of her life afraid—first of starving, then of her children starving because Roger drank too much to really make them a living. Her frail, sweet, scared mother whom Tassel Glass had raped and killed.

The memories steadied her, hardened the core of her.

She, Cathleen Nuala O'Sullivan, was not going to die here as a captive. And she was not going to hang. Even Judge Parker couldn't hang a person for shooting someone who'd been honorably called out to a gunfight.

As far as the Turner killing went, she would prove herself innocent. Yes. She must make a plan.

She would escape, she would call out Tassel Glass and kill him, then she would find out who shot the deputy federal marshal in the back. To do all that, what she must hold in her heart was not fear but determination. She would become more determined than she was weak, she would become more determined than she was afraid.

Black Fox came back into the room. He carried a small cloth tobacco bag and another pan of water.

"What is that?" she said.

"Herbs. What my Aunt Sally used to stop the bleeding the last time I got shot," he said. "Cat-paw bush."

"You made that up," she said.

It made her smile, in spite of her wound, in spite of her anger and grief and pain and exhaustion. It felt very strange to smile, as if moving those muscles would crack the skin on her face.

He glanced at her as he went around to the other side of the bed and she thought she saw a gleam of amusement in his eye though his expression was as serious as ever.

"I'm surprised it helped you," she said, "if she didn't use fox-paw bush."

He did smile then, slowly, unwillingly, while he was looking straight at her, and a bolt of lightning went right through her. This was the first time she saw him smile, and the effect on her was devastating.

Black Fox Vann didn't look like a stern lawman when he smiled. Maybe she could make friends with him and cause him to let down his guard. Maybe a true chance to escape would be worth putting her pride aside.

While she modestly held the shirt over her breasts, Black Fox began to work, unwinding the bandage he'd put on the night before, soaking it loose where it had stuck to her skin. It was making her sick at her stomach to see how much blood she'd lost but he didn't tell her to look the other way. She appreciated that acknowledgement of her strength.

She did need to distract her mind, though.

"How long has it been since you were shot?" she asked.

He was silent so long she thought he wasn't going to answer.

Finally he said, "More than a year ago."

"Have you been shot many times?"

"Three," he said.

She lay there with her wound exposed and tried not to look at it or think about it.

"And how long have you been a Lighthorseman?" she said.

"Ten years."

"That's not a bad average," she said.

Black Fox flashed a scornful glance at her, as if to say he should never have allowed himself to be shot even once. He dipped the cloth in water and started to wash her skin.

She gasped from the pain.

"Once was when I was only a boy," he said quickly, as if to divert her from the hurt. "Once in an accident. Once in a firefight."

She forced herself to think about what he said instead of what he was doing. Definitely she would *not* think about the pain that was trying to make her scream.

"When you were only a boy," she said slowly, setting her jaw against the hot misery in her shoulder and in her bones from the fever, "that shot wasn't the accidental one?"

His hands stopped moving, just for an instant. She looked at him.

"No," he said, "it wasn't."

And the way he said it, she knew that he wasn't going to talk about that anymore. She tried to imagine who would deliberately shoot a child.

Someone as lowdown and cruel as Tassel Glass.

Black Fox finished cleaning her wound and laid the sack of herbs against it.

"Hold this," he said, "while I find a bandage."

He went to an old cabinet in the corner of the room, took out a ragged piece of cloth, and started tearing it into strips. He came back to her and sat down on the side of the bed.

"Take your hand away," he said. "I'll bind it now."

She let her arm fall to her side. She felt so exhausted she didn't know if she could move it again, but when the shirt slipped lower on her breasts, she managed to pull it back up and hold it there.

"It's not easy to staunch the blood because that's an awkward spot for a tourniquet," he said, "so I'm going to pull it tight."

"I'm tough," she said. "Just stop the bleeding, that's all."

He did wind it tighter and tighter, under her arm and up over her collarbone on the other side, then around her neck and back again. When it was done, the pain was less but she didn't have the strength left in her to even hold open her eyes. She lay there, against his pillow, and wondered if a person could get too weak to breathe.

"Don't go to sleep yet," he said. "You have to drink something to bring that fever down. I'm making sumac tea."

She tried to do as he said, but she drifted helplessly in and out of awareness until his weight sank her bedside again and the warm metal of a spoon touched her lips.

"Drink," he said. "This will help break the fever."

He fed her the liquid over and over, and then did it some more until she couldn't swallow anymore. With her eyes still closed and her whole body so enervated she couldn't talk, at last she shook her head in refusal.

So he left her alone and she let the sleep take her.

A wash of panic woke her. She started up in alarm, trying to get away from the thing holding her, wild to get out of the trap. She jerked her leg, hard, but still it held her.

Pain tore at the top of her head as she strained to see through the dark to know which of her hideouts surrounded her.

"*Don't*," Black Fox said. "You're tightening it."

She almost jumped out of her skin. It took a

few seconds for her to recognize this man beside her, for no one was ever in any of her hideouts but her. Black Fox Vann. She was his captive and in his bed.

And he was in it with her! Her arms started shaking and her head hurt worse.

He was sitting up, touching her caught leg. She jerked it again and he slapped his big hand around her calf and held it hard against the bed. The sting of a rope burned her ankle.

"Stop it, I said," he growled. "I've got to get loose and get out there."

Only then did she hear the rough voices outside the open window. Fright roared in her ears like a storm.

"Who's there?" she cried. "Where's my gun?"

Light blazed in her face.

"What the *hell*?"

She couldn't even think enough to consider whether or not she knew the voice. It seemed the light was talking.

It was also moving erratically up and down in the air with a life of its own.

"Set the lantern down, Willie," Black Fox said. "Over there, on the chair, set it down before you drop it and set the place on fire."

Here she was, weak as a baby, her leg in a trap, and the room was being invaded.

She was Black Fox's prisoner. He'd waited until she went to sleep and tied her to him.

The panic came back in a huge wave and awakened what was left of her wits. How could she ever get away from him if he did this every time he slept?

# Chapter 4

**F**uture escape aside, she still couldn't stand it. She was *tied* to him and even though she trusted him not to thrust his hand under her clothes the way Tassel Glass had done, she had to get loose. She had to get free.

Or as free as was possible at the moment, with her head roaring like a freight train, pounding with pain and not only Black Fox, but some other man in the room.

He got the rope untied, swung his feet to the floor, and stood up. At that moment, she realized he had also stripped her of her clothes. She wore a big nightshirt, and that was all. Her fear exploded. The pain in her shoulder screamed

65

louder and slammed her back against the pillow.

The light swayed harder.

"You got a *woman*?" it said. "Black Fox?"

"Hey, Willie!"

That yell was from further away, outside the house.

"Willie, let me in there, you billy goat."

That gruff order was moving nearer, almost inside the room.

"Who's there?" Black Fox asked. "Willie, who's with you?"

As he spoke, he stepped forward into the circle of light, averting his face a little so it wouldn't blind him.

Her heart was beating like a bird's wings in a cage. Her aching head screamed for her to get up and run while she had the chance, to scramble away now while he was distracted.

Foolishness.

She could crawl across the bed and go out the window and run off into the dark. Where had he put Little Dun? The horse would come to her low whistle.

Insanity.

Cat had a dozen crazy thoughts but not one muscle in her body responded to those desperate mental urgings. Not one. All the movement she could manage was the smallest of bitter smiles.

What a dreamer she was—she couldn't even lift her head away from the pillow.

"We . . . we're just gonna sleep it off . . ."

"*Who? We who?*"

That tone of voice would take the bark off a tree, much less sober up the lushest drunk.

It seemed to work on Willie.

"Swimmer and Tall John," he said clearly. "And Bras and me."

Calmly, Black Fox took another step toward the lantern. He looked as big as a giant with the flickering light throwing his shadow onto the wall. It grew up and up and spilled over onto the ceiling to loom over her.

"Cousin Willie," he said, "as you see, I've got somebody here. Yes, a woman. You all need to move along."

"S-sorry," Willie said.

Black Fox took the lantern from Willie and set it on the chair as another young man of about the same age—eighteen or so—pushed his way into the circle of light.

"Swimmer," Black Fox said, "you boys have to sleep out tonight. Move on."

"We'll go t' the barn," Swimmer said, his words slurred by drink. "You got a woman in here."

He didn't even look at Black Fox, he was so busy looking at her. Cat met his stare in the dim light, helpless even to look away.

"Howdy, ma'am," he said, and tipped his hat.

"Out," Black Fox said.

But Willie, too, had drunk enough to be as emboldened as Swimmer. She felt Willie's eyes on her now, although his face was in the shadows.

"Howdy," he said. "I . . . I ain't seen you in town for a long time, Cathleen."

She remembered him then. An awkward, talkative boy who, a long time ago, had helped her unset the stubborn brake on her parents' farm wagon. She'd been stuck out in front of Tassel Glass's store with a load of supplies bought on credit, as usual.

Swimmer shuffled closer and put his hand on the high footboard of the bed so he could lean toward her.

"That your yellow dun horse out there with Black Fox's gray?" he asked. "Anybody ever tell you he looks just like The Cat's horse?"

Black Fox said, "Where did y'all ever see The Cat's horse?"

Willie said quickly, "Swimmer, we gotta go."

But Swimmer was already answering.

"Down at PawPaw," he said. "That little yellow dun can run like a deer. I thought it *was* a deer when it came busting out of the woods right in our faces . . ."

Willie tried to interrupt but Black Fox was ahead of him.

"What were you boys doing at PawPaw? When?"

"Aww, *Swimmer*," Willie said. "How come you have to be such a blabbermouth?"

"The day that deputy out of Parker's court got killed down there," Swimmer said, still holding onto the bed while he turned to look at Black Fox with a wise nod of his head. "You oughtta seen it. The Cat rode right through our bunch like . . . uh, well, like a cat with his tail on fire."

He guffawed at his own joke. The lantern light showed the slack mouth and glazed eyes of a man who'd had way too much whiskey to drink.

"Johnny McGill was mad as a nestful of hornets when we got to the rendezvous and . . ."

Willie grabbed him by both shoulders and pushed him toward the door.

"Out," he said. "Didn't you hear Black Fox? We gotta sleep somewhere else."

"In the barn," Swimmer said again.

"Not in my barn," Black Fox said, following them with the lantern in hand. "Y'all are in good enough shape to ride on."

Their voices faded into the other room and then out of the house. The screen door slammed.

Cathleen lay without moving, barely breathing. The argument continued intermittently, floating in through the open window in bits and pieces. Then it must've become a regular conversation because the tones got lower and lower until she couldn't catch a word at all. Finally their saddles creaked and their horses' hooves pounded against the ground.

A short time later, Black Fox came back into the

room. Her fear rose, strong as a storm in her pitifully weak body.

"Don't you dare tie me to you again," she said. "I won't stand for it."

Maybe tough talk could cover up the fact that she wouldn't be able to raise a hand to stop him. As if she ever could, since he was over six feet tall and she was no more than five feet two.

"How do you know Willie?" he said.

"It's none of your business," she said. "How do *you* know him?"

Black Fox answered promptly, as if to show that she should do the same.

"He's my cousin," he said. "He farms this place for me."

He waited but she didn't speak.

"When he helped you with your wagon brake that day, was your dun horse there?"

"You should've asked him that when you were questioning him about me. Obviously, y'all were standing around out there discussing me."

He ignored that and repeated the question in a flat, merciless tone that demanded an answer.

"Was your dun horse there?"

"*No*," she said. "Why?"

"I'm wondering if the boys will realize you're The Cat when they sober up."

That piqued her interest enough to make her forget everything else for a moment.

"So what if they do?"

"Word will get out that you're here. People will come to see the brave outlaw who's been doing all the good deeds."

"Hardly anyone knows about that," she said.

"You'd be surprised. You've been the talk of the district for months."

"*Really?*" she blurted, genuinely surprised.

She thought about that while he set the lantern onto the chair again and blew out its light.

"Well, then," she said, "you must be afraid they'll come here and say you should turn me loose."

Black Fox didn't answer. He came back to the bed, sat down on the side of it, and looked out through the window.

"That wouldn't matter," he said absently, "I do my duty no matter what anyone says."

Her blood was still pumping from the fright she'd had and all the fierce feelings. Her mind raced to understanding in a moment. It *would* matter if people came there. They might help her escape, if not here, then on the road to Fort Smith. Her heart opened to embrace the hope.

Black Fox turned to look at her as if he'd read her thoughts.

"Don't worry," she said quickly. "Willie and Swimmer will be so busy telling everyone they saw a woman in your bed they won't think about my horse again."

He groaned.

"That's all I need," he said. "Maybe they'll be too drunk to remember."

"You should've told them I'm a prisoner and wounded, and then you wouldn't have to worry about your reputation."

"I'm not worried about it."

He was bothered a little bit, though, she could tell. Black Fox Vann was a loner, she'd heard that plenty of times. A woman in his bed would be news.

Her spirits lifted. Maybe someone would come to see his woman, even if they didn't know she was The Cat. And it would provide her an opportunity to escape.

Black Fox leaned back against the headboard of the bed, stretched his legs out beside hers. He was so close she could feel his warm breath.

She made her own breathing even, willing herself to be calm. Nothing had ever made her feel more frantic than being tied to him, except for Tassel Glass's wandering hands.

"Don't think you're going to tie me to you again," she said, holding her voice completely steady by the sheer force of her will, "because you're not."

"I'll do whatever I have to do," he said sharply, but absently, too, as if his thoughts were far away.

"How could I run off? I can barely even lift my head I've lost so much blood. You knew I couldn't get out of this bed by myself, much less out of the house. Why did you tie me to you?"

"I've seen you rally before," he snapped. "I was taking no chances. Your fever had finally gone down and I had to get some sleep."

"You won't have me in custody very many nights," she said, forgetting her new resolve to stop challenging him. "You can sleep when I'm gone."

He gave a surprised little bark of a laugh.

"Tall talk when you're flat on your back," he said, shaking his head. "You've got sand, Cat. I'll hand you that."

Her shoulder was hurting and her head was heavy and her patience was spent. He still hadn't said he'd not tie her again.

"It was either get sand in my craw or lay down and die," she said.

She stared straight ahead, seeing her home in flames and her mother dead.

"How long have you been living in the woods?" he said.

"Since late last spring."

"When your home burned?"

"First I took my little brothers to Fort Smith," she said, "to my mother's cousin. I knew from the minute Mama drew her last breath that I'd never rest until I brought down Tassel Glass."

"You knew then he was a bootlegger?"

"Everybody knows that," she said scornfully. "Roger, my stepfather, was one of his best whiskey-drinking customers."

Black Fox nodded.

"And besides helping people get stinking drunk," she said, the old anger rising in her in a wave, "Glass charges more for every item in that store than it's worth to put people in debt to him so they have to do whatever he says."

"Who was your mother?" he said. "Was she Cherokee?"

Cathleen hesitated for a minute. Would it help her if she answered yes?

No. She had heard that Black Fox Vann had delivered many a Cherokee involved in a crime with a white man to Judge Parker's court and Donald Turner had been white. Besides, she would not suffer the indignity of lying.

"No. We were Intruders," she said. "That's why I didn't come to you Lighthorsemen for *justice*."

Bile rose in her throat with that word.

"There is no such thing," she said bitterly. "The white man's law wouldn't do anything about my mother's murder, either."

She had to speak through clenched teeth to keep from crying.

"You reported it to the authorities when you went to Fort Smith?" he asked.

"Not only that, but I begged them," she said. "I went to the federal marshal and to the prosecutor and when they wouldn't help me, I even asked for a meeting with Judge Parker himself."

"Did you get it?"

"No."

Her lips were trembling now but she couldn't stop talking.

"Not one of them cared or valued my mother's life," she continued, and her throat filled with fury that nearly choked her. "All the murdering and burning happened over in the Nation and I was accusing a rich, powerful Cherokee. We were Intruders and they weren't about to lift a finger."

She drew in a deep, ragged breath.

"By the time I was through, I hated every lawman there nearly as much as I hated Tassel Glass."

Then she bit her tongue and held her rage inside. What was it about Black Fox Vann that loosened her tongue so foolishly?

She had just given him, this Cherokee Lighthorseman who already believed her guilty, a perfect reason for her to have killed Federal Deputy Marshal Donald Turner.

Black Fox was surprised by a quick sinking of disappointment that weighted his heart. Why should he care? He'd been thinking she was guilty all along, hadn't he?

So why did he feel as if he'd just taken the first swallow of the Black Drink at the Medicine Dance?

He'd never felt this let down before because of

*anything* a prisoner said, especially not an admission that would help prove he'd been right in arresting them. It proved just how much he wanted Cathleen to be innocent.

The Cat. His prisoner. He ought not think of her as Cathleen. Every time he did, it only emphasized the fact she was a woman, which he was trying to forget.

Without glancing toward her again, he got up off the bed and walked to the window, where he leaned against the frame with both hands and stared out into the night. Over there, near where the cleared farmland met the woods, a lighter shadow moved through the dark grasses. A small animal, most likely a young possum, going about his night business into the trees.

The sweet spring breeze moved through the grass, too, and the nightbirds called back and forth. Beside the barn, the horses grazed, the sounds of their movements muffled by its thickness. This was a good spring, with just the right amount of rain.

The Nation needed that. It needed good crops this year and it needed freedom from the outlaws that were keeping it in turmoil. Arresting this girl was his job.

Black Fox closed his eyes and tried to breathe in rhythm with the whispering leaves. The roaring, sleepless aching in his head didn't belong in a night like this.

And neither did a hanging for a girl who'd suffered such an injustice.

*Get a grip, Vann. You already had evidence she was at the scene of the murder. What difference does it make that she had reason to kill that deputy?*

He opened his eyes and tried to put his mind in some other place but it kept jumping back to The Cat. She lay quiet now, her breath coming lightly as if she'd fallen asleep. She probably had. She was bound to be exhausted after losing so much blood.

*He* was exhausted and there wasn't a nick on him. He was certainly too tired to suffer any interference or to think what to do about it if it occurred.

It was a rotten piece of luck that Willie and his friends had picked this night to come to his house to sleep off a drunk. And even more rotten that they'd seen The Cat's horse.

Maybe they'd not make the connection that she could be The Cat. Maybe they'd forget, not think of it again, and not mention it to anyone. Maybe he'd be able to get her to Fort Smith without anyone's noticing them on the trail. *That* should be his focus now, not whether she could possibly be innocent in spite of her mark on the tree.

In spite of her hatred for lawmen.

It would be a miracle, though, if no one paid them heed. People—people who were sober—were bound to see them and notice the little dun horse.

A girl showing a mass of red, curly hair would never make anyone think of The Cat, but the horse would. Its size and speed were invariably mentioned in every tale of The Cat's bravery.

He needed to take Cathleen to Fort Smith on a different mount.

He would like to haul her in a closed-up buggy, but there was no chance of that. To stay off the beaten trails, they'd have to go horseback.

And he'd have to watch her every second. No matter how much she objected, he'd have to tie her to him when they slept.

*Don't you dare tie me to you again. I won't stand for it.*

That thread of panic in her voice, just under the surface of the bravado, had been truly pitiful. It had torn at him to hear it, for she was a helpless creature, caught in his trap, and she knew it.

He whirled on his heel and left the room. Sometimes, because they were stretched so thin over so many large, turbulent districts, a Lighthorseman had to serve as arresting officer, judge, and jury. But this time, even if the case hadn't been the murder of a white man, and a federal deputy marshal at that, he would do no more than arrest her and take her in.

How could he judge her? His mind knew she was guilty and his heart would not stop hoping for proof she was innocent.

He'd never been like this before. He felt as if

he'd turned into two people living in the same skin.

The sunshine pouring in through the open window woke Black Fox with its heat. He opened his eyes to its light, dancing brightly in the auburn curls of Cathleen's hair.

As always, he was instantly awake and alert, so without thinking he knew who she was and why she was there. Yet he didn't move. She was lying very near him, with her head turned so that all that cloud of red/gold hair glittered only inches from his face.

He took a deep breath of its scent. It smelled of sunshine and cedar trees after a rain. And a little of dust and gunpowder.

Sometime during sleep he had unknowingly slung his arm across her pillow above her head. Some of her hair spilled onto his blue sleeve, some appeared to be under it.

Still, he didn't move.

It was a strange thing to wake with a woman in his bed. There was an unfamiliar companionship in it. Even though she was under the covers and he was on top of them, they lay on their sides, spoon-fashion, as if ready for their bodies to come closer and fit together. His free arm lifted and reached to brush back her hair so he could see her face.

So he could touch her. The urge was so powerful it was hard to ignore.

He jerked his hand back and rolled away from her, swinging his feet to the floor all in one motion. He was Black Fox Vann, Lighthorseman. He didn't caress a woman prisoner, he did *not*.

Even though before this was all over, half the Nation would be thinking that he had done so. Willie and Swimmer were bound to tell Tall John and Bras they'd seen a woman in his bed, and four rowdy boys, drunk or not, were way too many to keep such a secret. There was no hope of escaping some curious visitors before Cathleen was able to ride. He heaved a long sigh.

Then he set his jaw in rebellion against his own resignation. He was still himself. He was still Black Fox Vann, whose life was the law. One quick kindling of desire for his captive didn't change that and neither did her sleeping in his bed, no matter what anyone said about it.

He reached for his boots, grabbed them both in one hand, and stood up.

"Black Fox?" she said, her voice soft as a mist in the warm air behind him.

"Here," he said.

"Thanks for not tying me."

The gratitude in her voice made him feel like a lowlife longrider for *ever* having done such a thing.

"I . . . intended to stay awake," he said, without turning around.

"But you slept?" she said drowsily.

"I dozed."

Which was a big, fat lie. He'd slept so deeply he was rested.

Eager to get away from her questions, he walked in his sock feet around the foot of the bed and headed for the door into the kitchen. But before he reached it, he glanced at her.

She lay on her back, looking up into his face with her green eyes as soft as her voice. Her hair blazed against the white pillow.

"Dozed so hard you snored," she drawled, her eyes twinkling and her luscious mouth curving into a faint smile.

Even with his habitual dignity threatened, he couldn't help himself. He felt a smile ghosting over his lips, too.

"That must've been the horses snuffling in the pasture that you heard," he said.

He'd meant it as a teasing reply, but his voice took on more warmth than he'd intended. A camaraderie.

She laughed. The low, sweet chuckle reached out and wrapped around him.

"You can't blame it on them," she said. "That was enough noise for a whole *herd* of horses."

She scooted up against the pillow then, wincing from pain. A fine sheen of sweat broke out on her forehead.

"Do you still hurt as bad as you did?" he asked.

"No, but I still feel like I've been bucked off and

stomped," she said. "You can quit watching me. Right now I couldn't jump up and run away if you took after me with a gun."

"Don't try to fool me, now," he said lightly. "I know you're a tricky one."

She smiled weakly, then the smile faded and for a long moment they looked at each other without saying a word. He wanted to go to her and wipe the sweat away from her brow. He wanted to say something else that would make her smile again.

He wanted to lie back down beside her.

Cathleen found herself looking up at Black Fox, wondering at the look in his eyes. It made her feel like another person, a girl without a care in the world, a girl who wished he would come closer. It made the other half of the bed feel hollow beside her. It made her wonder what he was thinking about her.

Because he *was* thinking about her. That much was clear.

It might be distrust, with him trying to see into her mind and find out if she planned an escape or not. It might be a trick to get her to say something.

Yet it didn't seem to be.

It might destroy all her defenses if she didn't watch herself every minute because right now it was making her realize how dismally lonely she was. How alone she had been for many, many months now.

It was a friendly kind of look.

She slammed that thought away and tried to pull her thoughts together. She *wasn't* some other girl. She was The Cat, an outlaw, and this man was a Lighthorse. He was her enemy. He had captured her and he believed she'd killed a man. He was not going to turn her loose, no matter how he looked at her or how she felt when his eyes searched hers this way.

She needed to make him go away.

"I told you I'm not able to get out of this bed," she snapped irritably. "You don't have to stand there and watch me."

"I will if I want to," he said.

He didn't say it mean; he spoke absentmindedly, as if he weren't quite aware of what he said. The searching had turned to a faraway look in his eyes—he was looking through her, all the way past her now, thinking about something else entirely. He might as well be trying to read something written on the floor beneath the bed for all he saw of her.

She wondered what had taken his attention from her. She wanted him to look at her, really look at her again.

And that thought scared her more than anything else. It was insane. All she needed to know of his thoughts was what he might do to prevent her escape.

When she pushed up to sit higher against the pillows, the nightshirt bunched into a hard knot under her bottom. She couldn't pull at it without starting the pain again.

"I told you not to undress me," she said, feeling her color rise—along with her temper—as she imagined him doing it. "I told you not to take off my jeans and boots. You're a *man*. You had no *right*."

*That* brought his thoughts back to her. He looked at her, really looked at her again, his eyes full of surprise and then as much anger as a nest of hornets.

"Don't be ridiculous," he snapped. "You've got bigger things to worry about than who sees you naked."

"It's more who *handles* me naked that concerns me," she said stoutly.

She did feel embarrassed, yes, but mainly she felt scared. She was used to the hard, sharp edges of anger and revenge turning around and around inside her. Or the high, hot flares of excitement and intense concentration pushing against cold fear when she made a raid or ruined a bootlegger rendezvous.

Now she had strange, turbulent feelings attacking her and no names for them. They were growing stronger by the minute as she looked at Black Fox Vann.

Drive him away. What she had to do was drive him away and put the wall between them again.

"You can rest easy," he said, his tone filling with

sarcasm. "All I've handled is your wound—when you were *bleeding* to death."

"Just keep your hands off me," she said, her voice trying to taper off from exhaustion.

"Don't worry," he said, in that same sardonic tone. "I'm no Tassel Glass. All I wanted was to save your life."

"You have no *right* to save my life," she said, sudden new anger pushing strength into the words. "You're the one trying to take it. I'd rather bleed to death than hang."

A terrible look sliced across his face, as if her words had cut him like a blade.

"*You're* the one who took your own life when you killed Donald Turner," he said. "And you'd better remember that, Cat."

"I didn't kill him, Black Fox," she said. "And *you'd* better remember *that*. You'll be the death of an innocent person if you take me in to Judge Parker."

She thought she saw a glimmer of doubt in his eyes before he turned away.

"I did not kill Donald Turner," she said, from between her teeth, clenched now against the pain in her shoulder. "And if you're anywhere near the kind of lawman that people say you are, you'll go looking for whoever *did* kill him."

He refused to reply to that. In fact, he spoke quickly, as if to change the subject.

"You say you're not able to get up," he said

sharply, as if calling her a liar, "but you surely have to. I can help you use the ... accommodations under the bed so you won't have to go all the way to the outhouse."

"No, thanks," she said, just as sharply. "I can manage."

"I'll help you stand up ..."

"No," she snapped. "Just go and close the door."

That, apparently, made him mad. He strode across the room and into the kitchen, closing the door behind him with a smart slap.

Narrow-eyed, Cat stared at it. Now they were enemies again.

And she wasn't quite sure how she felt about that.

# Chapter 5

〜❦〜

**S**he threw back the covers and, moving slowly, sat up, swung her feet off the side of the bed, felt underneath the edge for the lidded chamber pot, and pulled it out. By being very careful with every movement she made, and using the edge of the bed as support, she managed to use and replace it without causing a great deal more pain in her shoulder. At least not unbearable pain.

It was true that she was sore all over but it actually made her feel better to move around. She needed to be as active as she could so she'd be ready when the time came to escape.

An idea hit her. Maybe she should annoy Black

Fox as much as possible so he'd be wanting to get away from her. Surely she could make him leave her alone for a little while, from time to time. If he could get into that habit, then one of those times he'd come back and find her gone. This new, hopeful scheme made her smile to herself.

Besides, she desperately did need to wash up. It galled her to ask him for any help at all, but it would serve both those purposes if she did.

"Black Fox?" she called.

She thought she hadn't spoken loudly enough, but he heard her and knocked on the door.

"Cat?"

"Come in."

He swung the door wide and left it that way.

"Would you please bring me some water to wash my hands and face?" she said. "And some elm twigs so I can make a toothbrush?"

Instead of the annoyance she had hoped for, she caught a glimpse of sympathy across his face.

"You're suddenly full of plans," he said speculatively, as if wondering just how helpless she really was.

"I feel dirty," she said. "After breakfast, maybe you'd help me take a bath."

The shock in his eyes came and went as quickly as the sympathy had, but she saw it. He shrugged and leaned back against the doorjamb in a sure, careless gesture that, for some reason, made her heart skip a beat.

"For somebody who's so loathe to have a man touch her that she can hardly bear for him to save her life," he said wryly, "you're bold as brass. Have you forgotten that *I'm* a man?"

The question was so preposterous it made her laugh.

"No," she blurted, "I couldn't forget *you're* a man if my mind left me completely."

Then she turned red as a summer sunset.

"I . . . I mean, uh . . . I *meant* help me by bringing water and towels," she stuttered. "I can wash myself."

She could barely talk and she could hardly think at all because her imagination had leapt to life, making whole scenes of Black Fox bathing her. She could see him bending over her, his broad shoulders blocking out the window light and making a small part of the world for them alone. His dark gaze fixed on hers while he caressed her with those big, strong hands, his rough palms slipping over her soapy, wet skin.

"Will you not need any soap?" he drawled.

Cathleen pushed the vision away and really looked at him again, standing there leaning against the doorjamb with his gaze resting on hers. Honestly, though, that didn't help a bit.

"Well . . ." She had to stop and swallow hard. ". . . yes. I will . . . need soap."

Her breath caught in her throat. Her blood surged faster through her veins.

Those dark, dark eyes of his were looking right into her mind and seeing what she was thinking. She would swear that was true.

His beautiful mouth curved up on one side in a lazy half-smile.

"Good decision," he drawled.

He was teasing her again, and it made her feel strangely warm inside. No one had talked to her very much, much less teased her, in a long, long time.

She narrowed her eyes in mock anger.

"Are you saying I *need* soap?" she asked.

And then she smiled at him in that same, slow, lazy way. She didn't intend to, but she did.

"I'm saying you look like the best thing that ever happened to that old nightshirt of mine," he blurted.

Shocked, she stared at him, the blush rising in her face again. He stared back, looking as startled as she felt. Yet his gaze lingered on her an instant longer, as if he were memorizing her face.

"I'm going to the smokehouse," he said, and without another word, he turned and left her.

Cathleen tried to leave him, too, in her mind. She needed to start thinking about the best way to escape when she got strong enough, but she kept smiling to herself and remembering what had just passed between them. Black Fox had said more than he meant to say, which she was sure didn't often happen to him. For an instant there, he had looked as astounded as a dismayed little boy.

Because he was lonely, too, she thought. The insight struck her like a lightning bolt. He was no more accustomed to talking to women than she was to talking to men.

Somehow, that touched her. And so did what he said.

*He didn't mean to say it, but he thinks I'm pretty.*

A little thrill of happiness ran through her. She pushed it away.

They needed to forget about this attraction between them and go back to acting like what they really were, which was enemies. *Mortal* enemies. At least on her side of it, the situation was mortal.

She had to stop this smiling and teasing with him and hold onto her plan to irritate him so much that he would want to get away from her as often as he could. There was no question that she could do that if she set her mind to it.

If she didn't pay attention and keep her eye on what was reality instead of what her imagination could conjure up, she wouldn't even live to regret it. Her mother had warned her that a handsome, sweet-talking man could lead a girl down the road to perdition.

If she didn't get a grip on her feelings right now, this handsome, diffident lawman with the rare and mysterious smile would lead her, not down the road to perdition, but straight to the hangman's noose.

Cathleen barely managed to keep that attitude all through breakfast, since Black Fox behaved in a totally un-enemy-like way. He did everything her best friend could've done——if she'd ever had a best friend——and he did it all without being asked.

He brought her a twig toothbrush and water to clean her mouth both before and after the meal, he put honey on her hot, cooked oats (the only food he had to go with the smokehouse bacon) for her. She was glad that they ate mostly in silence, she in bed and he at the kitchen table.

However, when he remembered about her bath and started preparations for it without her even reminding him, her resolve began to slip away. Never, since she'd been big enough to help herself, had anybody taken her desires to heart.

It had been hard enough to think of him as her captor when he brought her food and smiled when she said how good it looked or when he came back to take away the empty dishes and remarked how glad he was that she'd been able to eat. But now, with him heating water and bringing her soap and towels, a clean shirt of his and the soap she told him was in her saddlebags, she lost her resolution completely.

Her plan to annoy him was failing, since she

didn't even have to ask him to do anything. And he wasn't irritated in the least to help her, only solicitous of her needs. He even carried in a small table from the parlor and put it beside the bed to hold the pan of water.

"This is very near a dream," she blurted. "I never had anybody wait on me hand and foot before. Much less a man."

"Gotta get you well," he said, "so then you can do the work and I can lay around in bed."

The light, easy way he said it sounded as if they'd been friends forever. It sounded as if he liked her.

Then he put a hand behind her good shoulder to help her sit up. For some reason, the gesture made a hard, quick lump form in her throat.

"Can you manage for yourself?" he asked. "If you tear that wound open, it'll set the healing back a long time."

"And we can't have that, can we?" she said, but the bitter bite she tried to put in the words wasn't there. She just sounded sad and tired instead. "We've got to get on the trail to Fort Smith."

He didn't reply to that. He simply helped her the rest of the way as she carefully sat up and swung her feet off the side of the bed. She was dizzy. Not a whole lot, but definitely dizzy.

"If I spill that pan of water, it'll be a terrible mess," she said. "I'm not going to try to wash my hair."

"Go ahead and bathe," Black Fox said, "then I'll help you with your hair."

He paused at the door just before he closed it.

"Put that shirt back on until we're done," he said, the teasing grin playing on his lips again. "I might accidentally get your fresh one wet."

She narrowed her eyes at him and said, "Is that a threat? Are you wanting a water fight?"

"Depends on how good you feel," he said. "I wouldn't want to take advantage of a wounded woman."

He closed the door behind him and she smiled in spite of herself. At that moment, she decided to give up her plan altogether. She might as well enjoy his company until she escaped.

But when she was clean and lying across the bed on her back with her hair hanging off, when Black Fox was pouring fresh, warm water through it into a bigger pan on the floor, bending over her just like in her imagination, "enjoy his company" was too weak to express what she was feeling. He was sweeping her against her will into an even better dream.

He leaned over her and reached for the chamomile soap she liked. It felt almost like an embrace as his big body surrounded her.

It felt almost like a safe, warm place.

"Hmm, smells good," he said, and drew in a deep breath of the soap's scent.

He started rubbing it between his strong, wet

hands and she watched him. She couldn't help it. She couldn't help wondering what it would be like to have his hands on her.

"Nice soap for a girl on the run," he said wryly.

"If you're asking where I got it, Mr. Glass furnished it to me."

He raised his eyebrows. "Good of him, wasn't it?"

"Would be if he knew about it," she said.

"Now I'm compromised as a Lighthorseman," he said, "using stolen property right here in my own house."

"Think of it as Tassel's charity to the poor," she said. "It's the only luxury I ever took for myself."

"Did you take luxuries for other people?"

"Sometimes," she said defensively. "Mostly for children."

She could hardly remember what or for whom now, though. Her old life was beginning to feel like a dream and this dream was beginning to feel real. Black Fox's nearness was filling her senses and stilling all her memories.

He lifted her head in his hands in a gesture that ran all through her and made her take a deep, deep breath. Then he began to work the soap into her hair.

Every move he made was rhythmic and gentle, yet every one sent his touch flowing into her blood and along the length of her limbs. Even her wound somehow felt better.

"Tell me if I'm too rough," he said.

"No," she murmured, "you're not."

*You're wonderful, this is heavenly.*

Then his big palms moved in and cupped her head and his strong, calloused fingertips found her scalp. He began to move them, slowly and surely, making small, tantalizing circles all over her head. He began to loosen every muscle she had and soon she was melting into the bed.

Her eyes drifted closed in spite of her wanting to keep looking at him, even though he wasn't even meeting her gaze anymore. The breath she had slid right out of her body and she wasn't sure if she could take another.

"Have to get you clean," he said, beginning to pull the soap through the length of her hair. "Might even be a bird's nest in here, who knows?"

She meant to giggle but all she could do was smile.

"More likely to find a stray bullet," she said lazily, "judging from the smell of gunpowder in it."

His hands were mesmerizing her. No one had ever washed her hair but her mother. And no one had touched her in so long a time.

Tears sprang up behind her eyelids. She had forgotten what it was like to be touched— gently—by another person.

Even as she had the thought, though, she knew

it was a false comparison. This was nothing like her mother washing her hair when she was a little girl. This was nothing like any other person's touch to her.

A heat was starting to build and spread throughout every inch of her body. Was this desire?

"You'll do," he said. "No wonder your hair smells like powder. I couldn't believe it when you started firing." He was referring to the gunfight at the cave.

She looked up into his dark eyes.

His fingers slowed in their circling, but they seemed to reach for her more.

"I was scared they would kill you," she said.

He brushed some soap from her temple as she closed her eyes. For one long heartbeat, he let his hand linger against her cheek. At least she thought he did.

She couldn't know anything for sure or think about it, either.

All she could do was float beneath Black Fox's hands.

"Why would you care if they killed me?" he asked.

His tone was idle but there was something in it that made her open her eyes. He met her gaze and held it as if he really wanted to know.

"Like you told me out there, I knew you'd protect me," she said seriously.

They couldn't seem to look away from each other.

Finally Black Fox picked up the pitcher of rinse water and moved to the side so he could pour it through her hair without splashing it onto his legs. Gently, he sat on the bed and leaned over to cradle the back of her head.

His face hovered close, very close, to hers. She wanted to touch his cheek like he'd just touched hers. No, she wanted to trace the aristocratic shape of his cheekbone with her fingertip and draw it down along the hard, chiseled line of his jaw.

She wanted to touch the pulse beating hard in the side of his throat.

"But what really made my decision," she blurted, "was how handsome you are."

Surprised, he glanced at her and the blood rose to flush his skin even darker. He looked suddenly shy as a boy. It was so endearing that she lifted her head and kissed him.

Right on the mouth. She put her hand on the back of his neck and kissed him before she even had a scrap of a thought about what she was doing.

He froze, as if he were as surprised at her action as she was, then he dropped the tin pitcher, clattering, into the pan on the floor and held her head exactly there so she couldn't move.

Not that she wanted to. His mouth was hot and

sweet and the taste of him spread through her like a fire.

What had she done? What was this?

This was kissing a man, which she had never done before.

This was a man kissing her back. How could she have known that it held such power?

But soon she realized there was more. At first it was a light kiss as she'd begun it. His lips were soft and gentle, as if fearing to hurt her, but then he held her closer, sliding one big hand beneath her wounded shoulder to support it, and he deepened the kiss until it grew stronger somehow, much stronger, and he trailed the tip of his tongue along the seam of her lips, demanding entry.

The heat in her blood deepened, too. Her lips were burning so beneath his that she couldn't have denied him even if she had tried.

His mouth tasted of honey and spices and coffee and there was a mastery in it that made her want more.

But she couldn't stand any more because this was such an assault on her senses, such a scent of Black Fox, clean and masculine in her nostrils, such a feel of hard muscles beneath her palm, such a sound of his sweet breath and the safe, close sensation of the way he clasped her close to him. She clung to him.

A slow yearning began somewhere in the center of her, not just in her body but also in her mind. A need for this to go on and on, a wish that she could always stay here, just here, in the strong circle of his arms.

This taste of what might have been would only make what had to be that much worse to bear.

Hard as it was to do, she turned her head and broke the kiss.

She opened her eyes and looked into his dark ones, waiting for her. They were glazed with the aftermath of the kiss and it made her heart beat even faster to know that she had this kissing power over him, too. He looked exactly the way she felt.

Cat couldn't help letting her gaze drift to his mouth again. His marvelous mouth.

"I'm sorry," she whispered through lips that were aching to kiss his again. "I didn't mean to start something like that."

He still hadn't put her back down on the bed.

"What *did* you mean to start?" he asked, with the ghost of a smile hovering at the corners of his mouth.

His delicious mouth.

It was her turn to blush.

"I . . . I didn't . . . don't know. I . . . never had done it before."

Quick regret flashed in his eyes and stayed there.

Her dripping hair pinged water onto the pitcher.

"I'm the one who's sorry," he said harshly. "You're just a kid. I won't take advantage of you. It won't happen again."

Apparently he realized for the first time that he was still holding her and he turned her around lengthwise on the bed to lay her down.

"The towel," she cried. "My hair! Don't get the pillows wet."

He reached for it and wrapped it around her head. Finally, way too soon, he let her go. She sank back into the pillow.

*It won't happen again.*

His jaw set, he went down on his haunches to mop up the water from the floor with another towel.

She felt as weak as when she'd first come to after being shot—that moment when she'd first seen him bending over her.

She felt hot inside, still, from his kiss and everything that it did to her.

She felt cold as if she'd waked from a nightmare all alone in one of her hideouts with the echo of those words in her ears, the words, *It won't happen again.*

Which made no sense whatsoever, considering that she'd come to that same conclusion or she would never have had the strength to stop kissing him when she did. He was a lawman. She was an outlaw.

He was going to take her to jail. To the hangman. She was his prisoner.

But what was pulsing on her own tongue, still savoring the taste of him, was *Please let it happen again.*

He was gathering up the wet towel and the pan of water and the pitcher, getting ready to take them all into the kitchen, his wide shoulders set as hard as his jaw. Clearly, he was blaming himself for this new, wild desire that she could still feel vibrating in the air between them.

"You need to rest," he said gruffly, as he stood up and turned to go.

Suddenly, she couldn't let him.

"Will you come back and dry my hair some?" she asked. "I can't use my wounded shoulder—I can't raise both my arms."

"In a while," he said.

Tiredness tried to take her while he went outside to throw the soapy water out and refill the pitcher but she didn't want sleep. She wanted Black Fox.

The thought went through her like the blade of a knife. If that were true, she was in bad trouble.

Maybe it was that she didn't want him to look so grim and feel so guilty. She liked it when he smiled.

Things might as well be pleasant between

them. They would be each other's only company for several days to come.

It would take that long for her to regain strength enough to escape. When she managed to get her freedom again, she'd forget all about that kiss.

And so would he. There was no use in him taking things so seriously.

She was dozing when Black Fox returned and came to the bed. Even though she looked up at him, he dried her hair without saying a word.

His hands on her felt so right, even through the towel. When he took it away, she shook her head to spread her hair out over the pillow so that it would dry.

"Thank you," she said.

"Rest now," he said.

"First I need to tell you something so your head won't get too big for your hat," she said, her old impishness coming over her for the first time in ages. "What I meant about you being handsome is that you are, compared to Hudson Becker."

He stared at her.

"Compared to *Hudson Becker?*"

"Yes," she said, "you know how he has that little bitty head, like a chicken. Behind his back, his men call him 'chicken head.'"

The beginnings of amusement sparked in his dark eyes. Then it grew and he grinned. When she laughed, so did he.

"Thanks," he said wryly. "That makes me feel a lot better. I was getting scared you'd be embarrassing me with compliments all the time."

"No," she said, using her eyes and her voice to make him—and herself—know she really meant it. "Don't worry, Black Fox. It won't happen again."

He stood there by the side of the bed for a heartbeat or two, looking down at her with a face she couldn't read.

*It won't happen again.*

Finally, he touched her hair, lightly, where it spilled over her shoulder. A curl caught around his finger and clung to it as he pulled his hand away.

That night, long past midnight, Black Fox lay awake. His whole body thrummed as if he'd never sleep again, because Cathleen lay in the bed beside him. He was on top of the covers, yes, but that didn't help any.

It was the kiss that had done him in, which was truly stupid. She herself had told him that she hadn't known what she was doing and even if she had, it didn't mean a thing.

Except that now he wanted another one.

Restless to the point of walking the floor, he rolled off the bed and paced to the open window. He wanted to leap through it and run from here to Muskrat and Sally's place and back. He needed to run until he dropped, wet with sweat and tired to the bone.

Even then, though, he'd be longing to reach out and roll Cathleen into his arms, desperate with the desire to taste her again. He felt his mouth curve in a smile as he stared out into the night.

To taste her and to laugh with her. No one had been silly or laughed with him for ages. He wanted that almost as much as he wanted to kiss her.

He had been lonely for a long, long time. Maybe all his life.

That thought hit him like he'd been pole-axed.

*Well, too damn bad, Vann. You've been a lawman for a long time, too, and you'll go on being one. It's your life.*

He should have taken her straight to Aunt Sally's and damn the consequences. He should have never let himself be alone with her.

She was a very young woman. He was twenty-seven years old.

She was an outlaw, a killer. He was a Light-horseman, a captain.

He turned on his heel and strode out of the room. If he so much as looked at her, sleeping there in his bed with the moonlight streaming in to fall across her, he would not be able to resist touching her again.

# Chapter 6

❧⁓⁓❧

**C**at woke with a start from her nap—a restless doze too light to be really called sleep. The air was too hot and too still to breathe, much less be able to sleep. She sat straight up and swung her bare feet off the bed, pulling her shirt away from her sweaty skin.

Her wound didn't hurt so much as it had the first couple of days she was here. Sitting up, even using her left hand to fan her shirt tail, didn't pain her shoulder nearly so much as it had. It was still sore and achy, very sore very deep inside, but the sharp, stabbing pain had turned into a dull, slow one.

And, for the first time since she'd been shot, she

didn't feel dizzy when she stood up. She stayed still for a minute, waiting for the swirling feeling to come to her head, but it didn't. She started for the door.

Cat marveled at how fast her strength was coming back. Black Fox urged water on her all the time to help rebuild her blood supply and he'd been feeding her soups he made from cured venison and hams, wild onions, and cattail roots which tasted like potatoes. He always had meats hanging in his smokehouse, he told her, and supplies of flour and meal and other staples in his kitchen because he never knew when he'd end up at home for a few days.

Besides the food, she'd been sleeping more than she ever had in her life. Every afternoon she took a long nap while Black Fox stayed outside doing chores at the barn. So far, Willie and his friends must've kept their mouths shut, because no one had come around and it had been just the two of them for several days. She wasn't sure, but she thought about a week had passed since they'd been at the cabin.

Pushing her hair back from her hot face, she left the bedroom and walked across the small parlor to the front door of the cabin. A person could hardly breathe inside the house, the air was so heavy and close.

She pushed open the screened door and stepped

out onto the porch. It wasn't much better out there.

"You didn't sleep long," Black Fox said.

She turned toward the low, rich sound of his voice, something deep inside her already reaching for him, making her feel shaky all over. Today, instead of being at the barn doing chores, he sat on the shady end of the porch hunched over a small table littered with tools and pots of color, feathers and bits of leather, doing something that absorbed him completely. He had spoken without looking up.

Cat walked the short distance to him while taking in the surprising sight of such a big man bent so intently over all those little objects. Was it some kind of game?

"What are you doing?" she asked.

"Painting," he said.

She was close enough now to see what he had in his hands.

"On a *feather*?"

She leaned over to see better. He was, indeed, daubing paint on a large white feather whose color changed to speckles and then a shaded warm brown at the tip. On the wider, solid-white part, he had painted two horses running through a field of grass. Each horse was no bigger than his thumbnail.

He didn't answer, just laid down his brush and picked up an awl to use on the tiny spots of orange paint he had just applied. Before her eyes, they became infinitesimal flowers scattered among the shades of green grasses. Black Fox cocked his head and looked at them critically while he wiped off the tip of the awl with a rag.

Then he picked up the feather and held it for her to see.

"Do you know them?" he asked.

The horses were a yellow one and a taller gray, galloping single file through a grassy meadow, heads up proudly, manes and tails flying like flags.

"Little Dunny and your Ghost," she said, in amazement.

He even had the black points on Ghost's legs come to exactly the right height.

"Whoever heard of painting a picture on a *feather*?" he said wryly, voicing her exact thought.

"Is that what everybody says when they see this?" she asked.

"Nobody sees it," he said, picking up a brush and dipping it into a pot, beginning to concentrate on adding some trees to the edges of his imaginary meadow. "Only Aunt Sally and Uncle Muskrat and Willie ever saw one—and that was when I first started doing it."

A knife-edge of recognition sliced through her that brought a quick pleasure. Black Fox didn't show his surprising creations to just anybody. This was a secret he was sharing with her.

"When was that?" she asked.

"When I was ten. When I first went to live with them," he said.

When his parents were killed. As hers had been murdered, too. But, for the first time, the past seemed long gone and dead. It had no power to touch this moment.

A sudden breeze rustled the leaves on the trees bending over the house and Cat lifted her hair off her neck with both hands. The slight coolness caressed her skin. Time stood still. Nothing existed besides this quiet homeplace nestled deep in the wooded hills.

Black Fox's hands moved with small, sure gestures. He didn't look at her. He was focused on his creation.

"It looks tedious to do," she said.

"No-o," he said, slowly, as if thinking about that, "it's making a new world. Like a dream."

She smiled at his intensity.

"Looks like a nightmare to me," she said, teasing him. "Have you noticed you've set us afoot? How come we're not riding them?"

That made him glance up at her, as she had hoped it would, and they shared a grin.

"I'm no good at painting people," he said. "Don't worry, these two horses love us. They'll come if we whistle."

"I don't think so," she said. "They look too happy to be free running in that meadow."

"But we're right there in the trees, waiting for

them in the woods," he said, still not breaking the look that held their gazes locked. "And we're going to step out and offer them some wild apples."

"I thought you said they'd come because they love us," she said.

His eyes twinkled.

"It never hurts to have a backup plan," he said.

"Oh," she said.

They couldn't look away from each other.

Black Fox's broad shoulders called to her hands and his shiny hair glinted blue-black when a glimmer of sunlight passed over it. But it was his mouth, his beautiful mouth, that filled her with the most longing.

What would happen if they kissed again? Would it only make her want more kisses with an even deeper longing than the one she had been feeling?

His kiss had wakened her to the secret magic that could exist between a man and a woman. Her whole body was awake now. Black Fox was right here, so close she could smell his light sweat and his coppery skin.

"Cathleen," he said.

At that moment, she thought he was going to reach for her, pull her head down and kiss her. She saw it all in his eyes—the desire, the intent, the urge to move toward her—as he let his gaze drift down from her eyes to linger on her lips.

Then he went very still and shook his head, as if

telling himself not to do it. As if he had made the same vow she had made to herself after he had washed her hair and they had shared that soul-shaking kiss. She had sworn not to let that happen again and he must have done the same.

So she took a step back from his small work-table and leaned against the porch post. She lifted her head to draw in a long, ragged breath.

"Do you smell the storm?" he asked, tearing his gaze from her face to go back to his work. "There's one coming."

He made one more dabbing of green paint and then began to clean his brushes.

A stronger breeze rose and swirled the yard dust at the foot of the steps. A storm was coming and she had shelter. She even had company.

But her limbs were trembling and her insides felt hollowed out. Would this be the way she would feel forever, if she couldn't have Black Fox's kiss?

"I like storms," she said. "Let's sit out here in the swing and watch it."

He gave her a slanted glance as he began cleaning up his mess.

"What if it brings a dancing devil? A tornado?"

She grinned at him and spoke before she thought.

"Then I'll jump into your lap and hang onto you," she said playfully. "Will you save me from blowing away?"

He looked her up and down.

"You're fattening up right nicely," he said. "I'd judge you're too heavy to blow away."

"I'd judge you'd better get in the house right now and latch the door before I take my heavy revenge for that remark," she said, pretending to advance on him.

He held out the painted feather as if in defense.

"Take this in and put it on the mantel to dry, will you?" he said. "Otherwise, it'll catch dust in the paint. I'll bring the rest of this mess."

Carefully, they transferred the feather from his hand to hers. Their fingers brushed together, and she could not have said which one of them caused them to linger.

And she did not know which one of them caused them to part.

Somehow, then, he was propping the door open with his foot so he could move the rest of his things into the house and she was holding the shining feather up against the blue-gray sky, watching the tiny horses running through the grass and flowers with their heads held high. She had to think about it, she had to think about anything but touching Black Fox again.

"What kind of feather is this?" she asked, as she followed him into the room.

"An eagle feather," he said. "I picked it up over on the mountain."

She let it go reluctantly, savoring the feel, however spare, of his fingers skimming hers. He noticed.

They gazed at each other for a long, slow heartbeat.

Finally, she turned away, went back outside on the porch, walked to the swing, and sat down. She was attracted to him on a level somewhere deep inside her where even words couldn't go.

Already, she longed for him to be beside her. She wished he would sit down, put his arm around her, and kiss her.

Yet she didn't. If she had one grain of sense left in her addled head, she didn't wish it.

That would only stir up the longing that had tormented her since the first kiss. Since he had taught her to want—no, to need—another one.

When he came out and sat down in a chair, though, instead of beside her in the swing, it was frustration instead of relief that filled her until she thought her skin would burst. He was watching the sky. The least he could do was talk to her.

"How did you ever think about painting on a feather?" she asked.

He shrugged, as if to say he didn't know.

"Eagle feathers are sacred, so I always gathered the ones I found. And I didn't have anything else to paint on."

"How did you know you *could* paint?" she asked.

"A traveling artist came through Sequoyah," he

said. "I watched him paint my grandfather in his turban and I knew that I could do that, too."

But Black Fox kept looking at the sky instead of at her. Once she might have thought that he, too, was just wanting to stay away from the specters of the past, but now she knew that it was this terrible yearning that made him turn away.

She knew. She understood. If he turned right now and looked at her the way he had done when he sat at his worktable, she would leap up and run to him, throw herself into his lap, into his arms. She was becoming totally shameless now.

A blast of cooler wind sent the dust flying high and the squirrels scurrying into their nests in the trees. For a long moment, neither of them spoke.

"Look at the sky," he said finally, nodding toward the southwest where the clouds were building faster than the eye could watch them. "Do you want to change your mind and go inside?"

Cat glanced at the sky, then turned to watch it. She shook her head.

"I can stay here as long as you can," she said.

If only she could. If only they both could stay here as long as they wanted. Her heart twisted in her chest as thoughts of the future came roaring into it. She was Black Fox's *captive*. She mustn't let him capture her feelings, too. She mustn't let herself want to be close to him, ever again.

\* \* \*

Late on the afternoon of the next day, just before sunset, Black Fox left the house to turn the
horses out for the night. It was a still evening,
close and humid, with everything about it prom-
ising yet another storm.

He stood in the doorway of the barn for awhile
to look at the sky. Clouds banked dark in the
southwest, all right, but they didn't seem to be
moving much and the horses had been housed up
all day. Being stalled day and night wasn't natural
for them and he hated to do it, especially considering that it might be a useless precaution since
the dun had been seen already.

They whinnied at him. They wanted out.

Finally he turned and went to unlatch the stalls.
He'd let them run free until he could tell what the
weather would do. The last thing he wanted was
for them to get hurt in a storm and not be able to
travel, because he intended to hit the trail at
dawn.

They needed to get moving before word got out
and curiosity seekers arrived. He'd decided to go
ahead and use the dun horse because trading it for
a different one might arouse more suspicion than
would a girl riding it when everyone still believed
that The Cat was a boy. And, incredibly, there was
another, even more urgent need to get going: he
was beginning to think of Cathleen as someone to
take care of instead of someone to take to jail.

He had to get her out of his house and off his

hands and out of his mind as soon as was humanly possible.

As soon as the stall doors swung open, both horses left the barn at a fast trot, heads up, smelling the air. Once in the pasture, they bucked and ran and kicked up their heels. Few things were as exciting as a change in the weather.

Black Fox watched them for a few minutes, then he turned to the work of cleaning their stalls. He forced his thoughts onto the packs he had readied for the trip to Fort Smith. The medicines he would carry in case Cathleen's wound should begin bleeding again should be sufficient. They had plenty of food to take and he had enough grain to give the horses some each evening.

Cat had been sleeping quite a lot, but she had been walking a little inside the house, too, so she was probably able to sit in the saddle for a long ride. No matter if she was or wasn't, they were going anyway. He'd stop frequently or hold her on his horse with him if he had to. He'd do anything to be rid of her.

Rid of this prisoner. *She was his prisoner.*

Never in all his twenty-seven years had he dealt with such an inner turmoil. Not even when those Intruders shot him and his parents and his world had come to an end. The feelings he had right now—all roused by the girl in the house, napping in his bed—were tearing him apart.

The worst was wanting to touch her creamy

skin and shiny hair. He had loved the silky feel of it in his hands as he helped her wash it. No, the worst was aching to kiss her a dozen times a day. That memory was another thing he had to be rid of.

He never should have done that in the first place.

He never should have even washed her hair.

She'd been so glad to be clean, though. She'd thanked him twice for warming the water because she was accustomed to bathing in the creeks and rivers. *How* had she lived in the woods for so long without being discovered?

She had braved more loneliness than most women could stand. Or most men.

He drew in a long, deep breath. Yes. She had to go. And now.

All last night, he'd been wanting constantly to be near her, to take in the fresh, wild scent that was hers alone. He'd spent the whole sleepless night wishing he could turn in the bed and take her in his arms. He felt a hundred times more worn down from fighting the desire than he did from not sleeping.

Wanting her made him feel like a lowdown wretch. Desire for her was not only unworthy of him, since she was hardly more than a child, but it was a betrayal of himself, since she was an outlaw. She was part of the scourge that was damaging the Nation at its very core.

Black Fox tried to hold that thought uppermost in his mind as he tossed the last forkful of straw and manure into the wheelbarrow and rolled it out the door. He was only thinking about her all the time because he hadn't held a woman in so long.

But, to be entirely honest with himself, these feelings torturing him were not all desire. They went way deeper than that—he had never noticed how lonely he was.

He dumped the wheelbarrow, took it to its regular place, and upended it against the wall. Then, slowly, he walked toward the house.

There was no doubt that if he didn't get the girl off his hands pretty soon, he'd be hard put to recognize himself. Every time they found themselves laughing together, he actually felt that they already were friends. Bluntly put, he was losing his mind.

On the porch, with his hand on the screened door's handle, he paused to listen.

Hoofbeats. Someone was coming across the fields from the direction of Muskrat and Sally's. Quickly, he went inside and saw that Cathleen was asleep, lying across the bed on top of the covers.

He couldn't help but smile. She had grit. Since her clothes had dried from the quick washing he'd given them, she had insisted on staying dressed. She was modest above all.

Closing the door between the bedroom and the

kitchen, he went back to the porch to wait. It was probably Willie and he didn't need to be talking to her anymore. If it was Muskrat or Sally, maybe it could keep them from seeing her at all.

It was possible Willie had kept the news of a woman in Black Fox's house to himself. He had been very drunk that night.

As it seemed to do now, all the time, Black Fox's mind stayed on her and the picture she'd made in there on his bed. She trusted him or she wouldn't be sleeping so much. Her will could keep her awake a great deal of the time—he had no doubt of that, even with her exhaustion from the loss of blood—because he'd never known anyone with as strong a spirit as she had. If she didn't hang, she'd be a formidable woman some day.

If the jury found her innocent. He had the thought again despite willing it away.

If only they would.

Willie rode around the corner of the barn on a nice paint horse Black Fox hadn't seen before. He was using his father's best saddle and had several colors of yarn braided into the sorrel and white gelding's flaxen mane. That made Black Fox notice that Willie himself wore a brightly printed dress-up shirt with big sleeves that swayed in the wind.

He must have a girl he was courting, although, up to now, he'd always been too shy. Good.

Maybe that would settle him down from drinking so much.

"Where're you going?" Black Fox asked with a smile, as the boy rode up to the porch. "Is there a dance somewhere?"

Willie didn't smile back. He swung down from the saddle.

"I see the dun horse is still here," was all he said.

Black Fox ignored that. "Want something to drink?" he asked.

"Whiskey," Willie said, "but I know you don't have it."

Black Fox waited.

Willie dropped his reins. "Water will do," he said.

Black Fox started for the door. "I'll get it," he said. "Have a chair."

Willie made as if to follow him instead.

Damn! Black Fox did *not* want him talking to Cathleen again. Now that he himself had foolishly told her that she had lots of sympathy among the people, she was liable to tell Willie she was a prisoner and beg his help to escape.

"Sit right here," he said, turning one of the cane-bottomed rocking chairs.

At last, Willie obeyed.

Black Fox went to the kitchen, keeping an eye and an ear on the bedroom door as he pumped fresh water into two tin cups. He could hear nothing. The Cat hadn't had a good nap yesterday, so she'd probably sleep deeply today. Thank God, her body was healing.

When he returned to the porch with the two full cups, Willie was pacing the floor instead of sitting in the chair. Back and forth, back and forth, in front of the door, peering inside every time he passed it.

He grabbed the screen when Black Fox got there and looked into the house as he opened it.

"Looks like we'll get another storm," Black Fox said, and led the way to the chairs.

Willie didn't answer, but he did finally come to sit in the other chair. When Black Fox sat down and held out his cup to him, he took a sip, then glanced over his shoulder toward the bedroom window.

The boy was looking for Cathleen. Black Fox held back a sigh. They were about the same age and Willie probably fancied her.

"Your folks are well?" Black Fox asked.

As he waited for the answer, he realized that he was hoping, for the first time ever, for one of Willie's tirades that he apparently always saved only for his Cousin Black Fox. A tirade about anything: Uncle Muskrat's farming methods, Aunt Sally's rules of the house, the lack of deer in the woods, anything but mention of the young woman in there in Black Fox's bed.

Willie looked at him over the rim of his cup,

met his eyes, then dropped his gaze as he turned the cup in both hands.

He muttered into it, "I have something to say to you, Cousin."

"Then look me in the eye and spit it out," Black Fox said.

Slowly, Willie lifted his head. His broad face looked truly surly—and very young.

It took him a long time to speak. Clearly the "something" was very hard for him to say.

"If her horse is still here, then she is, too," Willie finally burst out in a tone that came out suddenly loud. "And I aim to see to it that you make an honest woman out of her."

A fast fury shot through Black Fox. But then, just as quickly, it faded into amusement. Here was the kid, worrying about the morals of his elder cousin.

"Who are you talking about?" he asked. "Does she have a name?"

Willie's eyes flared hot. They searched Black Fox's face to see if he was making fun of him.

"I *said* the dun horse," he snapped. "I mean Cathleen and you know it. How many women you got, anyhow?"

The poor boy was really riled up. This was probably the first infatuation he'd ever had and it was all based on one brief meeting months ago. Willie didn't know Cathleen. This was nothing but the sap rising in him because he was besotted by her striking good looks.

"That's none of your business," Black Fox said. "A young whelp like you should have all you can do to mind your own women."

"You don't know nothin' about it," Willie barked.

Black Fox captured the boy's gaze and wouldn't let it go. He kept his expression serious in spite of a strong wish to smile. It wasn't that hard to remember how tender a boy's pride could be, especially in matters of the heart.

"And *you* don't know nothin' about Cathleen," Black Fox said. "Or what she's doing in my house. If talking about her is the only reason you rode over here, get up now and go on home."

His tone shook Willie up a little, as he had intended it to do, but the kid was tougher than he'd thought.

"I ain't goin' home until you get this through your head," Willie said. "If you don't marry her, I'll do it myself."

His voice cracked a little on the last word and pity stabbed through Black Fox. It was a sad and pathetic thing when a boy got his heart broken for the first time.

"Son," he said, more kindly, "forget about Cathleen."

Willie hung in there, though. He kept on meeting Black Fox's hard glare with a matching one of his own.

"I seen her in your bed," Willie said. "And I

wasn't so drunk that I seen you right there with her."

Black Fox started to tell him then that she was a prisoner. A wounded prisoner. But he couldn't make the words come out. Something stopped him.

Well, it was good sense that stopped him. If he told Willie Cathleen had been shot, sooner or later the boy would put two and two together—a gunshot wound and the little dun horse—and add them up to get The Cat.

There was no other reason he would pretend he was Cathleen's lover.

"I aim to see to it that you treat her right," Willie said. "She's a nice girl."

He was getting so worked up that he was denting the tin cup with both hands, nearly crushing it. Taking a deep breath, he steadied his voice. And strengthened it until Black Fox was afraid he would wake Cathleen and she would hear.

Then he realized that it was Willie's intention to speak to her. He didn't quite have enough nerve to try to force his way past Black Fox and into the house.

"I want her to know that if you won't marry her, I will," he said loudly. "You ain't doin' her right, ruining her reputation like this, Cousin Black Fox."

Black Fox stood up.

"Willie," he said, "I appreciate your opinion.

One of these days you'll understand this situation but until then you'll just have to trust me."

Willie got up, too.

"I'm trusting you for seven days," he said. "You can count them."

Black Fox's patience was worn thin. Enough was enough and he didn't want Cathleen to wake and get mixed into it.

"There's your horse," he said. "Get on it."

Slowly, reluctantly, Willie did as he was told. He thrust the battered cup at Black Fox and thumped his heels loudly on the boards as he went down the steps.

Black Fox stood and glared at him while he gathered his reins and stepped up into the saddle. Willie looked straight at the bedroom window again but he pretended to speak to Black Fox.

"If she leaves, you tell her to follow the trail north on the far side of the pasture," he said loudly, "and take the east one when it forks."

"Go," Black Fox growled.

Willie went. The steadily rising wind blew his long hair around his face as he turned the horse and whipped it straight out as he rode—slowly—across the yard and around the corner of the barn.

Black Fox shook his head as he watched him go. Willie didn't know anything about heartbreak now. He'd have to wait until the day he would hear that Cathleen had been hanged.

Of course, Willie would know about her troubles long before then. Word that The Cat had been arrested, once it got out, would spread like wildfire and Willie would have the shock of his life when he discovered that The Cat was Cathleen.

No doubt, the boy would be one of hundreds of her admirers who would go to see the trial. Thank God, it'd be the U.S. authorities in charge of keeping order then, and not just one lone Lighthorseman.

The images that flashed before his eyes then sickened him to the core, so he blotted them out. Turned his thoughts to something else. Ignored the future and filled his mind with chores to be done now.

That's what he'd always been able to do with the horrible happenings of his life, wasn't it? He'd better start praying he would always be able to do it.

He turned to take the cups back into the house. The rain—and it was a cold one, considering how hot the day had been—was just starting to come in on the storm wind and he needed to close the west windows. He would let the horses stay out awhile longer.

Black Fox took the cups to the kitchen and set them on the table. Still not a peep out of Cathleen. If the low thunder rumbling in the west didn't come closer and wake her soon, he'd do it himself so she'd eat something for supper. He'd snared two rabbits that morning and made soup for the noon meal out of them, some wild onions, and the rest of the potatoes stored in the root cellar. He would warm some of it for supper and they'd take the rest with them.

But first, he would look through the medicines in the packs for the trail one more time.

He closed the kitchen windows against the rain, driving hard against the glass now, and stood there for a long time looking out into the blurry green side yard where the woods grew up close to the house. Poor Willie would get soaked on the way home but maybe that was good.

Maybe it would cool off his obsession with Cathleen.

Finally, he turned away from the glass. The storm would pass and sunup would be here before he knew it. Everything had to be ready so they could make as many miles as possible before tomorrow night. He must get Cathleen out of this area where the horse was known so well before they slowed their pace.

He needed to stop calling her Cathleen. Even in his mind.

She was The Cat and she was an outlaw.

And he might as well wake her now. She needed to get up and move around for the rest of the day to prepare for a long day in the saddle. He wasn't going to tell her that, though; he wouldn't give any indication that they would be taking to the trail in the morning.

Crossing the room with long, quick strides, he knocked on the door.

"Cathleen?"

He bit his tongue. *Why* couldn't he stop that?

"Cat. It's time to wake up or you won't sleep tonight."

He waited but there still was no answer.

A cold fist of foreboding squeezed his stomach into a knot. Had she passed out? Had her wound started bleeding again? Oh, God, had she been bleeding for a long time?

He laid his hand on the knob, turned it, and stepped into the room with his eyes already searching for her bright hair rioting over the pillow.

The bed was empty.

# Chapter 7

Something crashed in the woods somewhere not far behind her, and Cathleen looked back. By now, Black Fox would have discovered she was gone and come this far in pursuit. She had taken too much time to saddle her horse and even now her shoulder was throbbing like mad from the effort and sending pain all the way down her arm. She rode with her arm tucked against her belly and her thumb in her belt loop to hold it there.

She tried to stare through the thick rain while she pulled her hat down tighter. If she lost her hat, she'd be done for because, even with it on, the overhanging tree limbs snatched at the ends of her hair and when she took to the woods she was liable to hang her self by her hair.

Hanging was what she'd better remember, instead of recalling riding on Black Fox's horse with him holding her in his arms. How could she have felt so safe there? How could she possibly be wishing to feel those arms around her again?

It was hard, because she felt so miserably sore and cold from being soaked through by the rain, but she had to think what to do. Surely Black Fox wouldn't be thrashing around in the woods back there if he could see her on the road.

Or maybe he would. Maybe he was hurrying ahead to set up an ambush. Maybe he was trying to stay out of sight while he caught up with her.

When she heard even more noise, she whipped her head around to face front again and urged her horse to go faster. Somebody or some animal was back there. It very well might be Black Fox.

Should she take to the woods or not? From his pasture, she had cut through the woods to the trail—really more of a road, since it was wide enough for a wagon—that ran from Sallisaw up to Sequoyah and then on to the northeast, eventually reaching all the way to Swimmer. Normally, she avoided roads and trails, but this time she was in a terrible hurry. Rushing through the woods and underbrush was terribly jarring, sometimes not too fast at all, and here in the road, the rain was washing out her tracks. In fact, it was faithfully doing that as it quickly created a sloppy kind of mud.

But on the road, she could be seen from a long way back. A long way in either direction, actually, in spite of the rain.

No matter how much she was hurting, she'd better take to the woods.

She'd almost reached the downhill slope into a long, angling valley called Takatoka. Along the top of it ran Rattlesnake Ridge. She could follow it for miles and come out at the far end very near one of her hideouts—the one she'd been trying to reach when the wound dropped her from her horse and Black Fox caught up with her.

This time, her situation wasn't nearly that dire. If she would think about that, it would help her be thankful for this pain instead of the horrible weakness she'd felt then. She could make it to safety if she didn't panic.

"Come on, Little Dun," she said, even though the wind blew her words right back into her mouth, "let's get off this road."

At least being in the trees afforded a little bit of protection from the weather. And being high on the ridge gave her an advantage in case someone should approach from below. At least it would be a help for as far as she could see through the woods and rain.

As the wind and rain died down, she heard noises again. Same direction. Coming closer.

Up ahead, to the left of the narrow trail, there was a thicket of blackberry brambles. She couldn't ride into it because of the thorns but she could hide behind it.

Her insides were in turmoil, with one instinct urging her to ride on as fast as she could and another sending her for cover as the loud noises came closer. It wouldn't be Black Fox. How could she have ever thought that? Even in a rush to get ahead of her, he wouldn't make this kind of racket. This sounded like an invading army.

Her heart was crowding up into her throat in her haste to get out of sight and she was gasping for breath by the time she finally reached the thick cover and eased Dunny in behind it. This wasn't a good spot, since she couldn't see very well, but she didn't dare move now.

She listened. When she heard the snuffling and rooting sounds, she slumped in the saddle with a deep relief.

Hogs. It was a herd of wild hogs. They might be rooting for food along the ridge beneath the many oak trees, but they seemed to be moving fairly fast. Maybe they were simply going to another range.

Her heart began its drumming again. These were dangerous animals, and besides that, she needed to know whether there were men nearby, either hunting or driving them. Carefully, slowly, she eased her mount out to where she could see.

Most wild hogs were dangerous creatures and would attack a horse if cornered and, many times, a person on foot whether they were cornered or not. She didn't intend to try to hunt them, but she made every effort not to draw attention to herself or Dunny. Their long tusks were lethal weapons and more than one good horse had had its belly ripped open by them.

There were at least fifty or sixty head of hogs, traveling along at a brisk pace, as if they'd been spooked by something. Maybe the lightning and thunder. A few slowed to root around for an acorn or two as they passed within a stone's throw of her, but they didn't lose much time.

They were ugly and they looked mean, with their long snouts and long tails, long bodies, and long tusks. They even had a long squeal, as some of them demonstrated as they passed her by. She jumped, afraid that the noise meant they had seen her, but they gave no sign of it.

She watched the woods closely, but even as what appeared to be the last of the hogs came into view, she saw no people, mounted or otherwise. This was truly a wild bunch, foraging entirely on their own.

Or was it? Until they were gone way past her, she didn't dare move. She kept watching for people somewhere around—that could have been the reason they were trotting along so fast—although her nerves were screaming for her to run. Black Fox could be close behind her.

But she waited, mostly for fear that one of the old boars would hear her and turn back. Finally, when she was sure that they were gone and no drovers or hunters followed them, she left the cover of the bramble bushes and started riding west along the ridge.

Almost immediately, she came up on a high spot that didn't have many trees and when she twisted in the saddle to look back, she could see all the way to the road. The rain had lessened to a sprinkle.

There the hogs were, spilling out of the woods into the muddy road. And there was a man on a tall gray horse coming down it. Black Fox. Even from this distance, she knew him and not just from the horse he rode, either.

She'd never even seen him ride, she realized with a shock. But it was Black Fox and he was right out in the open with the razorback hogs pouring into his path.

Her breath caught in her throat. They were all over the place, swarming around his horse. If they attacked, he'd be helpless.

Then his horse reared and the blood turned to ice in her veins. If Black Fox was thrown, the hogs would kill the man, for sure.

Far down the hill, too far for her to get there in

time to help in any way, the gray horse stood frozen with Black Fox clinging to his back. All she could do was watch and wish she could turn away. All she could do was pray.

They were like a tiny statue set in the muddy road.

The gray horse came down to earth again and he must have had the bit in his teeth because he began to run, heedless of the hogs, heading into the woods on the opposite side of the road from where she was. Black Fox bent low over his neck and stayed on him. The hogs in the back of the herd began slowing to roll in the mud and some in the front of it turned back to join in.

For a foolishly long time, Cat watched the spot where Black Fox had disappeared. Finally, she turned Dunny's head and started west.

It was the hardest thing she had ever done. What she wanted, more than she could believe, was to ride *to* Black Fox instead of away from him.

Black Fox made himself smile at the desk clerk and respond to the man's chatter when he checked into the Talking Leaves Hotel in Sequoyah. He hated staying in towns; he always camped just outside of them except when he had to be in Fort Smith.

He hated being around so many people.

That thought actually helped him smile—a bitterly ironic smile—on his way up the stairs with his saddlebags. He hated being a failed Light-horseman even more, and to rectify that, he would make himself be around people. And not only that, he could force plenty of smiles and be the friendliest man in town.

Never in his seven years as a Lighthorseman had he ever lost a prisoner. Cathleen was his first woman prisoner and his first escaped prisoner.

She was the first prisoner he'd ever gone after with a coat, trying to protect her health.

When he had run to get his saddlebags, in those first awful moments of discovering her gone, he had realized that the thin jean jacket was the only coat that Cat had. So, he grabbed both the slickers hanging on the wall of his back porch and took out after her with it thrown across the pommel of his saddle.

All he could think about was the cold, hard rain and the fact that the weather could give her pneumonia and, without care, she could die. He'd been well into the woods before he asked himself which he was trying to do—take care of her or capture her?

After that, he'd tried to toughen his feelings for her. He would put the slicker on her, all right, but backwards, with the sleeves knotted together. He would lash her to her saddle—hands to the strings and feet to the stirrups.

Because she *had* taken time to get her saddle. She had gathered all her things, sneaked out the

back, and ridden away from his place and he had
not heard or sensed a thing. Fine Lighthorseman
he was.

He hadn't seen or heard her escaping because
he'd been too busy sitting on the porch pretending to be her lover. Wishing that he was her lover.

Talk about insanity!

Her clean escape was nothing but his own just
comeuppance since he'd been sitting there the
whole time thinking that poor, young Willie was
such a fool. Truth was, he, the famous Black Fox
Vann, was nothing but living proof of the saying,
"There's no fool like an old fool."

At first he'd ridden a little way toward Sally's
and Muskrat's, thinking that Cat might have
taken Willie up on his shouted invitation, but then
he'd decided that she hadn't even heard it. Considering the time it had taken her to get to the
barn, saddle her horse and vanish, she had already gone out the window before the silly kid
started yelling directions at her from the porch.

That was when he had decided his only hope
of finding her was to come to Sequoyah. She
might be his first woman prisoner and his first
escapee, however, she was not the first prisoner
he had gone after by listening to hearsay and
gossip.

What galled him so much was that gossip and
hearsay were *all* he had to go on because he had
taken too long to get on her trail. Once he'd gotten

Gray Ghost under control after the incident with the pack of hogs yesterday, he had searched the road and the woods for another hour before he'd headed home for his supplies and his camping gear.

An endless, useless hour. Before he arrived at the hog crossing, he'd thought he saw a fresh hoofprint or two perhaps left by Cat's little dun horse. But, of course, after the road became a hog wallow, there was no hope of following and beyond that spot, he'd found nothing, no matter how hard he'd searched.

So he had given up the chase for the day. Which was the most likely day of finding her, as any lawman would tell you.

Because *anyone*, lawman or not, with a grain of sense knew that he needed to get to her before she reached her lair. That fact had haunted him, now, for twenty-four hours.

Had he turned back before he had to? Never before had mud or rain—no matter how unseasonably cold—stopped him, or even slowed him down. He'd been wet and cold and hungry and hurt many a time on the trail and kept going.

*Did I give up too soon so she could get away? Was that what I really wanted?*

*If she escapes now, I won't have to take a woman in to Judge Parker. I won't have to live the rest of my life knowing I'm the reason she was hanged.*

*Would I do that?*

No, he would not do that. Or if he did, he'd never do it again. He was going to find her now if it was the last thing he ever did.

He had found The Cat the first time, purely by chance after he had looked for her for days and days. Fourteen, to be exact.

He didn't have the patience for that again.

Plus she might not have that kind of time. If she tore her wound open and started it bleeding again . . .

He slammed the door of his mind on that thought as he threw his bags on the bed. Enough! He would not let himself hold one more concern about her. Not one. From now on, he would think of her as he would any other prisoner, and he would find her.

He turned the key in the hotel room door, then the knob, and pushed it open with his shoulder. After depositing his saddlebags on a table near the bed, he strode to the window and looked down at the street. Across, on the corner, with its front facing the woods, stood Tassel Glass's store. From here, Black Fox could see part of the back of it and most of one side.

Of course, when she robbed it, Cat probably didn't go in any of the doors or windows visible from the street. And she might never rob it again.

Or if she did, it might be weeks from now. It would probably take her a long time to heal completely and she'd need to have her usual agility and quickness back again.

*Except that she had enough of both to get away from me in a heartbeat.*

And now she should be scared that her luck was turning, since she'd been both shot and captured. She would want to end her campaign as soon as she could.

Besides the logic of it, his gut instinct told him that she would steal some more from Tassel Glass very soon. What else would she be doing? The Cat had endured a lot of hardship for the sake of revenge and she wasn't stopping now.

She wasn't stopping until she called the man out; she had plainly told Black Fox that herself.

So he would find her. What she wanted was Tassel Glass and if he watched Tassel, eventually he would find The Cat.

Four nights after her escape from Black Fox, deep in the darkest hours of the early morning, Cat rode Little Dun into the edge of the woods growing a long stone's throw from the side of Glass's store. The trees whispered warnings to her, and the moon moving in and out behind the streaking clouds looked to see if she would heed them.

She'd usually felt comfortable out roaming in the night. But tonight, her hands were shaking.

She glanced behind her before she leaned into the stirrup to step down.

Ever since she'd left Black Fox's place she'd had this awful feeling that somebody was following her.

And he was. She knew that well. But he hadn't found her yet and she had work to do.

She threw her leg over and slid to the ground without using the stirrup, so the saddle wouldn't creak. It was a mistake. Even moving as slowly as she could, it jarred her shoulder when she hit the ground and she had to stand for a minute, gritting her teeth against the pain.

Then she took a deep breath, forced her mind to go blank about everything but the job before her, and began to move. The moon vanished for a moment and she ran, not bent double as she usually did to make herself a smaller target because that would make her wound hurt more.

Every time, she went into the store the same way—ducking under the high back porch and through a window into the root cellar with its lingering odors—the sharp smell of whiskey mixing with the earthen smell of the floor and the homey scents of onions and cabbages and turnips. Tassel never had figured this out. He'd made sporadic attempts at blocking the outside doors and wedging the windows shut but he'd never put an obstacle in front of the door in the rear of the store that led to the cellar stairs.

The same was true tonight. She pushed the window open and slipped through, clutching the big canvas bag she'd stolen on her first trip into the store. It had straps long enough to go over her head and across her chest so she could hold it against the opposite hip and fill it with her right hand. It had served her well.

Tonight she wore it the other way, though, to keep the straps off her wound. That would slow her down a little, but not much. She knew what the Masseys needed.

The thought of the thin, desperate woman and her equally skinny little girl made Cat wince. They were doing the best they could farming their few rocky acres of ground but they were about to starve since their breadwinner had died of too much drink. Cat had left food on their porch twice and, that last time, when the child caught her at it, she had promised more.

Then she'd gotten shot and captured and they probably thought she'd lied to them.

She waited for a moment for her eyes to adjust, which didn't take long because she'd ridden over here in the dark. Plus she knew the place well.

The only thing different was that Tassel had moved the pickle barrel inside. The new pickle barrel. She smiled. Just a little more trouble and expense she'd caused him.

Quickly, she moved from the jerky to the beans to the dried fruit and put generous amounts into the small sacks Tassel kept behind the counter. Gingersnaps, cheese, chocolate, and crackers. Raisins and salt. Baking powder and candy. Flour and coffee and the bag was getting nearly too heavy. Her shoulder was aching.

Cat walked quickly along the aisle leading to the back of the store, reaching across her body to hold the weight of the bag up with her right hand. It was awkward and she couldn't do this and run back to Dunny, but it relieved her shoulder for now. She hurried. She had to hurry back to her hideout before her strength left her and before the moon went down.

Right now it was sliding in and out of the clouds, so she'd have some light to travel by. It was also peeking in at the front windows and lighting up a beautiful doll sitting beside a horse carved from wood. She grabbed the doll as she walked by and laid it in the top of her bag. Neither she nor her little brothers had ever possessed a store-bought toy. Or even played with one.

The thought of the little Massey girl, whom she'd once heard her mother call Rachel, gave Cat the strength to get back to her horse. Imagining the smile that would come to that pinched little face moved Cat's legs and feet through the door and down the steps.

There, tucked underneath the stairs, was the barrel of illegal whiskey Tassel had placed there to fill the jars or whatever containers his customers brought in when they didn't have enough money to buy a whole bottle. She took a deep breath, went to the barrel, and, holding onto her bag with one hand so it wouldn't pull her over, bent and used her other hand to open the bung. It began to run a thin but steady stream.

She smiled to herself. That was for her mother and the Masseys. Tassel would lose a lot of money before he noticed.

Then she crossed the dim room to the old tool box beneath the window.

That was where the weight of the bag nearly did her in, but she set her mind on Rachel and forced her injured shoulder to help lift it up and out to lie beneath the porch. Sweating from the pain, she climbed out after it and closed the window behind her.

Compared to those two things, the run back to her horse was easy and she made it without a stumble, keeping to the shadows as best she could. She hung the bag on her saddle horn and climbed up behind it.

Then she grabbed the horn with both hands and just sat there, telling herself she was pausing to listen, but knowing that it was to settle her heart and slow her breath. It was dangerous not to get moving, but the night seemed friendlier now and the sounds of the birds and the rare, muffled noises that came from the livery stable across the way or some other place farther down the one street of the town reassured her that no one was around.

Besides, Dunny would know and would warn her.

It was a good night's work and soon she could really rest.

Her mind needed settling, too, almost as much as her heart. Time was running out for her. Black Fox was after her now and, no doubt, even more determined than he'd been before he'd caught her. She'd been shot for the first time in all her many forays, which had to be a sign.

But worse, she was wanted for killing a federal deputy, and eventually the Parker court would send in its lawmen to help Black Fox.

Not eventually. Soon.

The next time she came to town, she had to do what she had promised on her mother's grave. She had to kill Tassel Glass and then get out of the country.

Black Fox was eating breakfast at a corner table in the café, alone—contrary to his best intentions to be sociable—when Turtle Fields, who owned the livery stable came in. The burly man stopped at the sight of him.

"Well, Lighthorseman," he said, in his customary loud and overbearing tone, "you got something to do on the first morning after you come to town."

Everyone in the place turned to look and listen.

Black Fox ignored them and indicated the other chair at his table. He didn't want Turtle's company but he didn't want to carry on a conversation in front of the whole town, either.

Turtle ignored the gesture and turned his broad face to see who else was there. Clearly, this news was for everyone.

"Tassel Glass opened his store this morning to find beans and flour and meal on the floor, lids off the bins, and many other things missing."

Excited voices moved through the room punctuated with gasps and sudden exclamations.

"The Cat!"

"That boy is everywhere at once."

"He nearly got in bad trouble the other day."

"I was afeared he was shot."

"Old Tassel's fit to be tied," Turtle continued boastfully. Then he paused dramatically before he said, "And, boys, that wasn't all that was on the floor."

Everybody fell silent to listen.

"In the root cellar . . ."

A chorus of three or four men's voices interrupted the tale.

"Turtle!"

"Want a seat over here?"

"Hey, Polly! Bring a cup of coffee here for Turtle."

Black Fox saw more than one man glance at him from the corner of his eye, then significantly at Turtle. Poor Turtle. None of the Fields were known for their brains.

He was as relieved as they were when Turtle clamped his mouth shut and went to sit down. Right now was no time to arrest Tassel Glass for bootlegging and take him to Tahlequah to jail.

But his gut twisted into a burning knot. Why not do just that? He had been right that Cat would come back to do mischief to Tassel and she had—but, embarrassingly enough—without him even knowing it, much less catching her.

He'd chosen to sleep last night and stay up watching tonight, and he'd chosen wrong. He had thought she'd want to recover a little longer before she moved again, and he'd thought wrong.

But if he investigated, found Glass's whiskey, and took him to Tahlequah, he would lose his bait. No telling where Cat would go then. She certainly wouldn't come to the jail to try to get her revenge.

He had let the fact that she was a woman undo him completely. He had allowed his inappropriate feelings for her to cloud his judgment.

While he thought about his mistakes, he set his jaw and stared out the window at the busy town. If he didn't find her soon and get her to Fort

Smith, he was finished—in his own mind, if not in anyone else's. If he didn't find her, he could never call himself a Lighthorseman again.

Cathleen caught a glimpse of someone in the corner of her eye that pushed her heart up into her throat. She clutched her bag closer and whirled to look, reaching for the handgun in the holster on her hip.

A long breath sighed out of her. A tree. It was a *tree* and she'd thought it was a person.

A person named Black Fox.

This pale, before-dawn light was deceptive. It was enough to see by, yet it wasn't. She had to work now, though, because she needed to be headed back to her hideout by broad daylight.

Darting the rest of the way across the Masseys' yard, moving as fast as she could with the burden, she faced the truth. She was imagining things, and she was about to lose her nerve. Getting shot had nearly ruined her.

No, it was Black Fox that had nearly ruined her. Saving her life, taking care of her, washing her hair, kissing her senseless. She could feel his touch and she could even taste him in her memory. Yes, Black Fox had spoiled her by dulling the edge on her anger—and that would kill her just as expediently as Glass or Becker would.

Truth be named, she was losing her mind.

She set the bag on the edge of the porch and quickly began taking the smaller parcels out of it. Cat hoped neither Rachel nor her mother was awake. She didn't want to see them or think about what they'd do from now on, if Glass killed her in the shootout or Black Fox captured her again.

This was the third time she had brought them food and both the other times she'd watched them from the woods. She'd listened to their mother-daughter talk. She'd smiled at their companionship.

She had saved them from starving, she really believed that, and now they would be on their own again.

When she'd emptied the bag, she laid the doll carefully on top of everything else and stood looking at it for just a moment. It was the most beautiful doll she had ever seen.

She reached out and touched its smiling face with one finger, then picked up the skirt of its pink dress and fluffed it free of its folds.

"What's her name?" said a little voice.

Cat whirled. Rachel stood behind her, in a ragged nightgown, one small hand clutching a scrap of quilt to her cheek and the other at her mouth. She sucked her thumb once more, quickly, and removed it so she could talk.

"Is she your baby?"

Cat froze for a moment, then she remembered to lower her voice and try to sound like a boy.

"Naw, only girls play with dolls," she said.

"*You're* a girl," Rachel said.

"Am not," Cat said, even more gruffly.

"Are, too."

An overwhelming urge came over Cat, the desire to reach out and hug the wan little girl and comfort her. Or was it to comfort herself?

She snatched up her empty bag and started backing away.

"Nope," she growled. "That doll belongs to you."

Sparks of joy kindled in Rachel's eyes and a slow smile began on her lips. It grew and transformed her face.

For one long heartbeat, Cat let herself look at it and feel the warm satisfaction that began to spread through her.

"Oh, thank you, Cat," Rachel cried, tucking the quilt scrap under her arm to reach for the doll. "I'll name her after you."

Cathleen turned and ran for her horse.

# Chapter 8

⌒◯◯⌒

During the next few days, Black Fox thought he might have a harder time overhearing any gossip about Cathleen, now that his presence in town had been noted by the whiskey drinkers, but not so. They might not want him to arrest the bootleggers, but no one held any animosity about The Cat's anti-whiskey efforts.

Mostly, it was because they liked seeing the bootleggers made fools of—selfish, overcharging bastards that they were—by a mere boy on a fast horse. The Cat was the underdog in what had become a game and everybody, it seemed, was rooting for the kid. Besides, there were enough bootleggers in the lucrative business that there was no way he could pour out all the whiskey in the Nation—or even one district of it—at the same time, therefore, the populace in general didn't have to worry about that.

So Black Fox made himself stay in Sequoyah for the news, smiling, being sociable, and catching sleep when he could during the day for the purpose of spending the nights lurking in the woods near Glass's store. Most of all, he was fighting the urge to start chasing Cathleen through the woods. Every time new word of her came in, he had to force himself to do nothing but listen. He'd caught her the first time purely by accident, yes, but only in one way. He had also been thinking that she would come back to hit her favorite target again. A Lighthorseman had to learn from the past and control his emotions accordingly for the sake of the law.

Every day but two in that week, there was a report. The Cat had been seen—only a glimpse, but it was a kid on a small yellow horse—one late afternoon in the woods near Hudson Becker's girlfriend's place. That night, somebody had shot into the wagonload of whiskey sitting at the edge of the yard and thrown a match. The fire had been seen for miles.

Two days later, all the way up in the Flint District, John Bushyhead, a small-time whiskey dealer, had been waylaid, robbed, and killed.

That news had made Black Fox sick to his stomach and had given him strength at the same time. Woman or not, Cathleen was a killer and she had to be stopped. Never mind that some on each side of the law would say that her victims needed killing—some because they were lawbreakers and Donald Turner because he was a lawman.

Always there were a dozen bad men wanting to kill a lawman but instinct told him that The Cat wasn't like that. Maybe that one killing, Donald Turner's, hadn't been Cathleen's handiwork . . .

He slammed that thought to a halt in a heartbeat. Her mark had been there. Her mark was on all these other crimes.

And on the good deeds. According to the gossips, there had also been three instances of either food or blankets or wild game left at the cabins of poor people during the week, gifts tagged by the sign of The Cat.

Plus two other known whiskey dealers had been robbed between Sequoyah and Stilwell. Ranging from Stilwell back toward Sequoyah, The Cat's mark was there every time.

It looked as if she was working her way back south to hit Glass again. And, since this was much more activity from her than was normal in such a few days, Black Fox's guess was that she would call Glass out when she reached Sequoyah. She had been doing all the damage she could ahead of time, just in case she didn't live through the gunfight with Glass.

Cathleen was a smart girl. She knew she no longer had much time left. She knew that the Lighthorse would never let a murderer go, and that Judge Parker's court would never stop hunting for the killer of a deputy federal marshal. She knew that one or the other of them eventually would find her, so if she wanted to get her revenge done, she should do it now.

A cold fist squeezed Black Fox's gut. She was liable to kill herself instead, just by pushing her diminished strength to the limit. The girl had lost a lot of blood from that wound. She was riding miles every day and enduring the physical and emotional strain of each of her exploits, plus running and hiding.

It would be a miracle if she didn't collapse.

A sudden image of her—unconscious in his arms, her face pale as death and her booted feet dangling off the side of his saddle—assaulted him. He shook his head and made himself look at reality around him as he walked down the street of Sequoyah. He would go to the livery stable and see who had ridden into town since breakfast and then he'd go to his room and sleep so he could stay awake all night in the woods.

However, as he approached, he saw that the livery's long bench was filled with the usual loafers sitting there whittling, spitting tobacco juice, and talking. Suddenly, he could not face them and the boring conversation that would ensue.

He was tired. He'd been up half the night scouting the woods around the general store and tonight he would do the same. Besides, he was doubly tired of people, unaccustomed as he was to being around them. So he crossed the street and walked swiftly toward the hotel.

When he entered the lobby, however, he found more trouble than a boring conversation with the old men. He found Cousin Willie.

Again, Willie was dressed in his best. One glance inside the livery and Black Fox would have, no doubt, seen the fancy paint horse and been forewarned. Too bad he hadn't done that and slept out in the woods somewhere.

Without a word of greeting, Willie walked to him and started climbing the stairs beside him.

"You come to town to find the preacher?" Black Fox asked sarcastically. "Cathleen's not here."

Willie shot him a slanted, sideways glance. It was an accusatory look. A knowing look.

"Where is she?" he asked, keeping his voice low so as not to be overheard by the button drummer coming down the stairs.

His tone was arrogant, though, and that irritated Black Fox even more.

"She left me," he said, and climbed the stairs two at a time.

"Oh?" Willie said, doubtfully.

Irritation turned to anger in Black Fox.

"Where's your pa, anyhow? Is Muskrat farming or not? How come he's letting you do nothing but run all over the country when it's time to get the crops in the ground?"

"It's my Wandering Year," Willie said confidently.

"Well then you need to wander farther off from here," Black Fox snapped. "You're not seeing new country or learning a damn thing if all you do is come to town."

While he unlocked the door, he turned to look at Willie.

"Oh, I forgot you've been to my place, too," he said sarcastically, "to tell me how to live my life."

Willie followed him into the room without being invited. Black Fox left the door open, hoping the boy would take the hint, but knowing in his heart that it was way too late for that. Willie was behaving as if he had a purpose.

He did. Willie took it upon himself to close the door.

"You don't want the whole town to hear this," he said, by way of apology.

Black Fox didn't take the bait and ask what it was he was about to hear. He walked to the window and waited, looking out.

Damn it all, anyhow. He'd never known Willie to act like this. Love made fools of them all, but why couldn't Willie just go off and be a fool by himself with some other girl and leave Black Fox out of it?

"I know who The Cat is," Willie said.

Black Fox tried not to show his surprise as he turned to look at him. Or his dismay. Surely not.

"Well, then, we could use you in the Lighthorse," he said. "*How* do you know?"

Willie looked him in the eye and didn't give an inch.

"Hoofprints," he said. "Down at PawPaw that day, The Cat's yellow dun horse turned in a little on the right front."

"And . . ."

"And Cathleen's yellow dun turns in a little on the right front," Willie said, "according to the prints her mare left in your barnyard."

Black Fox stared at him.

"Lots of horses turn in on the right."

"Maybe. But these both have a little nick out of the middle of the left front, too."

Black Fox clamped his lips shut and tried to intimidate Willie with a glare. But the boy was like a snapping turtle and always had been—once latched onto something, he would not give up.

"It makes a lot of sense," Willie said. "Even her names. Cathleen. The Cat. I heard her mama call her 'Cat' one time in town."

Black Fox made a dismissive gesture.

"Next you'll be telling me that Cathleen is a shapeshifter. Don't you know that The Cat is a boy?"

But Willie only smiled and Black Fox knew he was fighting a losing battle.

"She hides her hair under her hat and dresses like a boy," Willie explained, in the tone of a teacher dealing with a somewhat slow student. "That day at PawPaw I glimpsed them green eyes blazing, just for that instant when she flew past me. I shoulda known her then."

"You still don't know her," Black Fox said, making one last, futile try.

Willie ignored that. "I'm not telling you anything new," he said. "But what galls me is that you *captured* her and then you took her to your bed."

The outrage in his voice showed in his eyes, too. That, and disappointment.

"I never thought you, of all men, would do that," Willie said.

"She was *wounded*," Black Fox snapped. "She'd have bled to death if I hadn't found her. You think I'd have just dragged her in and laid her on the floor?"

"*Where* was her wound? I never saw it."

"No," Black Fox said nastily, "you didn't. She held the sheet up to her chin the way any woman would do when strange men come bursting into the room in the middle of the night."

"*You* could've slept on the floor," Willie said.

That fanned Black Fox's temper into a blaze.

"And take the risk of letting her get away? I

don't have to answer to you, Willie," he said, furious with himself that he had just done so.

He was letting this boy control him. He was a kid, just a kid, lovesick on merely the looks of a girl he didn't know.

Willie had always been a shy boy and he'd never courted any girl. Willie didn't know what he was doing and Black Fox had to be patient with him.

Not to mention that he had to ensure that Willie didn't talk about this discovery to anyone else.

Black Fox took a deep breath and tried for a calmer, kinder tone of voice.

"Cousin, the girl has no connection to you. Go get your horse and go home."

Willie's eyes narrowed. He didn't move an inch.

"You arrested her for killing that deputy marshal at PawPaw, didn't you? And she got away from you, didn't she? Well, you *ain't* finding her again and taking her to Fort Smith."

Black Fox stood still as stone and held his temper.

"I'll do what I have to do," he said. "Why is it that I have to keep telling you to get out of my business and go home?"

Willie clenched his fists.

"Because I love her," he said.

"You wouldn't know love if it slapped you in the face," Black Fox said. "And you don't know

Cathleen, either. You're too young—that's what your problem is."

Willie only looked at him with the beyond-stubborn expression that Black Fox knew too well.

"I'm not going home," the boy said.

"Then go wherever you want, but get out of here."

"I'm a man of honor," Willie said, "so I came to warn you. I won't let you take her to Parker's court. You know they'll hang her."

The words were a cold knife through Black Fox's heart.

"No," he said, "what I know is that they'll find out whether she's guilty or not." Then, as much for his own benefit as for Willie's, he added, "If she killed Donald Turner, she deserves to hang."

"She didn't," Willie said stoutly.

Unreasoning hope bloomed again in Black Fox, as if Willie's believing that could make it so. He was losing his mind.

"I aim to find her before you do," Willie said, "so stay out of my way."

"You'll be interfering with the law," Black Fox said.

Willie held Black Fox's eye just long enough to let him know he'd heard. Then he turned, opened the door, and threw a last warning over his shoulder as he went out.

"I'd hate to have to shoot you, Black Fox."

"I'd hate that, too," Black Fox said dryly.

Willie closed the door behind him.

Black Fox stared at the blank panel of wood. So. Reality had come to him in the form of his cousin. Willie might keep his own counsel, but other people were bound to come to the same conclusion soon. Many of them would hide The Cat without question.

There was very little time left to find her.

Cat stood, feet apart to give her a solid stance, gun in both hands, and shot at the empty airtights she'd arranged along the rock ledge until all her rounds were gone. Two out of six of the tin cans remained, winking at her in the sunlight.

She looked at them for a long moment, then holstered her handgun. Good enough. Tassel Glass was a whole lot bigger and easier to hit than an airtight.

Besides, the time for practice was gone. She'd not have many more sunny afternoons before Parker's men were here in the Nation beating the bushes for her, if Black Fox didn't find her first.

Black Fox Vann. He was nothing like she'd thought he'd be. Nothing like his reputation.

Well, yes, he was, but there was another side to him, too. Staring silently off into the distance, she let the sweet warm memory of his hands painting that feather—and of his big strong hands in her hair—come over her. Those weren't the hands a bold, relentless lawman should have.

Their strength, their gentleness, that deft, sure touch as he worked in the soap and massaged her head. She would recall every moment of that hair-washing until the day she died.

Which might not be too long from now if she didn't get moving out of his territory. He was, no doubt, searching for her, bound to be even more driven now that her escape had wounded his pride. His hands would never again be so gentle on her, especially not when he tied her hands behind her back.

Quickly, she went to the ledge, picked up the targets she hadn't blown off the bluff into the valley below, and took them back into the cave. No sense arousing the curiosity of any hunter or traveler who might happen by.

She hoped no one would notice, much less enter, this place that had been one of her best hideouts since the beginning of her campaign against the bootleggers. She might need it again sometime, so she would leave a few supplies stored in a hidden cache. She would take the rest with her and hope it was enough to get her out of the Nation when her work was done, assuming her life and her freedom both survived it.

Efficiently, she set to work, disciplining her mind not to think past the job itself. For the thousandth time, she imagined calling Glass out for the gunfight and what that encounter would be like. Once he went for his gun, once he fell dead in the street, she'd leap onto Little Dun and head west.

She would be much safer on the other side of the MK&T railroad tracks that ran from north to south across the Cherokee Nation to connect Missouri, Kansas, and Texas—safer from the law, at least. It was called the "dead line" because west of it, on nearly every trail, criminals posted cards warning certain deputies that they were dead men if they ever crossed the tracks.

From the outlaws, who were said to be thick on the ground out there, she would simply have to protect herself. She'd be safer as a boy, therefore she would put her hair up again just as soon as she hit the trail west. But first, Tassel Glass had to know it was Cathleen O'Sullivan who was sending him to judgment.

She made sure to include canned tomatoes and peaches in her pack, just in case water was scarce farther west. Not knowing the country and the location of the water holes would be scary, but then, nothing important was ever accomplished without some risk.

After working beside her stepfather, Roger, for so long, she could always get a job as a farmhand and make enough money to take the train. She could go to Texas, by horseback or by train. Lawbreakers disappeared into Texas all the time. If she took the train, though, she'd have to buy passage for Little Dun, too.

She could make enough money for that. And once in Texas, she could start a whole new life and work toward a home of her own. It would never have a man in it, though. Men were mostly either drunkards like Roger or ruthless and evil like Tassel Glass.

Except for Black Fox. Black Fox was different from any other man she'd known. Any other man would've taken advantage and bedded her when she had been clinging to him and kissing him with all her heart and soul.

Now she wished he had. She would never know what it was like to make love with a man and she would never even *want* to with any other man but Black Fox, whether he was her enemy or not.

Cat pulled her thoughts up short and went to saddle the small dun horse. She spoke aloud to keep from feeling so lonesome.

"Let's not think about Black Fox," she said. "And let's not think too far ahead."

Little Dun answered with a playful toss of her head and a stomp of the foot. Cathleen checked her packs one more time, stepped up onto her horse, pulled her hat down, and rode toward Sequoyah through the beautiful, green-and-blue spring afternoon. She wanted to fix every minute of this day in her mind.

The woods were bursting with every shade of green—trees and bushes leafing out all over the place and the wild azaleas in pink and white bloom. The meadows lay lush and thick, and the valleys between the hills gleamed dark as evergreens beneath the waving silver tips of the tall grasses. The wind was just enough to bring the mingling smells of pine and cedar down from the mountain.

The sky shone blue enough to hurt a person's eyes if they looked at it too long. It had been that color ever since the big storm.

Cathleen took a great, long breath of the sweet-smelling air and turned a little in the saddle, watching two huge, fluffy clouds float by. Where would she be this time tomorrow?

This hilly, beautiful country was the only home she could really remember. She'd lived off the land and in these woods for so long she knew them the way she'd once known her family's farm. How would it feel to be on a strange land in Texas or way out west? How would the sky look out there? Would there be trees and hills and fast-running creeks that chattered over rocky beds the way Lost Boy Creek was doing below her right now?

Little Dun slowed and started down the steep incline that led to the water. Cathleen smiled as she watched the mare stiffen her front legs and place her small hooves carefully for purchase in the shifting gravel. Dunny was more surefooted than any mount she'd ever seen and she was thankful for such a horse beneath her. On any other mount, she probably wouldn't have survived this long.

The mare carried her into the water. They were in the middle of the creek, picking their way over the rough jumble of stones at its bottom, when she looked up. Her heart stopped.

On the opposite bank sat a man on a horse. She froze with her eyes on him while her mind raced in several directions—telling her that Dunny couldn't run on the monstrously rocky creekbed, noting that the mounted man blocked the path that led up out of the water, warning her that he had a better shot at her than she did at him. He was sitting in silhouette to her while she rode full face to him.

Then she recognized him. The man was really more of a great big boy. It was Willie, Black Fox's cousin, who had burst into the bedroom that night at his house.

The shy, backward boy who had helped her with her wagon wheel.

"I've been looking for you," he said. "Where are you going, Cathleen?"

Gradually, the ice left her veins and she began to breathe again. In fact, her blood started to heat.

He was Black Fox's cousin. Black Fox was looking for her. She was caught if she didn't get rid of him now.

"What business is it of yours, Willie?" she asked, as Little Dun stepped out of the water.

She scowled her fiercest look, meant to drive him away, and sent Little Dun leaping up the steep bank.

"Step out of my path," she said.

"I'm staying in it," he said, much more stoutly than she expected.

"I'll run you down," she warned.

Which was a ridiculous threat. Willie's horse stood two hands taller than hers and five hundred pounds or more heavier.

At the last minute, he backed him enough to make room for her to come out on top of the bank. She let Little Dun stop there and rest from the climb so she'd have enough air to run when Cat decided to make a break.

"Did Black Fox send you to look for me?" she said in a belligerent tone.

"No. I'm *your* partner," he said sincerely. "I'm here to take you away from him."

The words struck her so strangely. No one had been on her side or offered her help in a long, long time.

But they also scared her a great deal. Being a prisoner was being a prisoner, no matter who the captor was.

"I ride alone," she said. "Nobody takes me any-where, Willie."

She laid her hand on her gun.

He stared at it, then raised his eyes to hers.

"I would never shoot you, Cat," he said.

"Well, I wish I could say the same, Willie," she said, "but I don't aim to be taken a step where I don't want to go."

"I know you're The Cat," he said. "You flew right past me when you robbed Old McGill at PawPaw. I saw your horse's track that day and again at Black Fox's place, but I don't reckon you're a killer."

Surprise flashed through her as she listened and watched him. Had other people come to the same conclusion?

"I'm not gonna let Black Fox arrest you again," he said. "You need to stay with me. Where are you headed?"

Evidently he wasn't going to go away, no matter what she said. He was a kind boy, though—he had volunteered to help her that day long ago when he certainly didn't have to. And, right now, with this cockeyed idea of his about being her partner, he sounded completely genuine.

She believed him, but she didn't have time to fool with him now. She had to get rid of him—but in some way that wouldn't hurt his feelings.

Cathleen took a deep breath and sat up straight

in her saddle, taking a better grip on the reins, tucking her heels against Dunny's sides. Underneath her, the mare gathered herself up to run.

"Never mind where I'm headed and don't try to follow me, Willie," she said. "I'm warning you."

Willie just looked at her.

"You're the one needs warnin'," he drawled. "Black Fox is in Sequoyah, just in case *that's* your destination. More'n' that, I seen tracks of two shod horses between here and there."

Cathleen's stomach clenched and her legs went loose in the stirrup leathers. What a piece of rotten luck—she could hardly believe it.

"So Parker's already sent out deputies to find who killed Turner," she blurted.

At least her overall instincts were still good, even if Willie had surprised her. Her time *was* running out, so it was good she was doing this today.

"Looks like it," Willie said. "And Black Fox will tell them it was you."

Then he gave her his shy smile again.

"That's a lot of law after you," he said. "You'd best let me help you, Cathleen."

Just the way he cut his eyes at her made her understand. He was sweet on her, the poor boy!

She thought about that for a minute.

He truly had come to warn her. He would help her if she let him. Maybe she could use his loyalty to her without telling him everything she'd planned and get rid of him at the same time.

"All right," she said. "Tell me where you saw the deputies' tracks."

"At Bushyhead Creek," he said. "They crossed it heading south."

"So I'll be behind them."

"Depending on where you're going."

"Right you are," she said deliberately, watching his face and smiling at him.

He squinted his eyes and frowned worriedly.

"*Are* you going to Sequoyah? I told you Black Fox is there."

"I have some business there before I leave the Nation," she said. "Do you think you could draw Black Fox out of town for me?"

Willie considered that. "You couldn't just make a run for the Dead Line now and let me help you get away?"

She set her jaw and looked him straight in the eye to let him know that she could not be swayed.

"No," she said. "But what I have to do won't take long. I just don't want Black Fox to capture me again before I get it done."

Her mind raced. She didn't want to flirt with Willie and give him false encouragement, but it would be wonderful to have his help with Black Fox. And this chore would get him, as well as Black Fox, out of Sequoyah, too, which would keep him from trying to be a hero when she called Tassel out. He might get shot on her account, which she never would get over.

"Willie," she said directly and deliberately, "I really need you to do this."

His eyes lit up as his gaze searched hers.

"It's done," he said. "Don't worry about it."

"Thank you," she said. "I'm much obliged to you."

He touched the brim of his hat like a quick, little salute.

"Don't worry," he said again, then he added, "I know you can take Tassel Glass."

Cold shock raced through her veins, although his blind faith also warmed her considerably.

"How do you . . . I mean, *why* do you think my business is with Tassel Glass?"

"I seen you practicing a little while ago," he said, and laid the rein against his horse's neck. "I know how fast you are."

He smiled at her once more and then kissed to the big paint horse. They whirled around and vanished into the timber.

Cathleen sat still for a moment, trembling in her saddle. Dear God. Willie had been watching her and she didn't even know it. She'd been too deep in thought about the future and the past to be vigilant in the present.

That kind of carelessness could get her killed.

Or she could get *herself* killed in just a little while. *Carefully* get herself killed by calling Tassel Glass out to face her.

# Chapter 9

❧

**B**lack Fox lay on the bed with his boots on, crossed feet resting on the railing of the wrought iron footboard, waiting for his inner voice to tell him what to do. Young Gray Ghost stood waiting, too, tied to the hitching rail in front of the hotel, saddlebags packed and ready to ride.

But Black Fox hadn't yet gotten that gut feeling to tell him which way to go when dusk fell: north into the woods to search for Cathleen or south and east just one long stone's throw to watch Glass's store—again—for her arrival. He'd been in Sequoyah long enough and time was running out. Maybe trying to use Glass for bait wasn't going to work.

Maybe Cathleen had made another plan for revenge. Or maybe Cathleen was lying in the woods somewhere, sick or hurt, alone.

His stomach clenched. There were black bears and mountain lions all through these hills, animals normally afraid of people, but any wounded person was prey and therefore a completely different proposition.

Her last exploit that he had heard anything about had been three days ago. Anything could've happened since then.

Willie could've run across her trail, for one thing, out there in the woods, or he might even know where one of her hideouts was—he could've accidentally run across it at any time in the last year. If he had to take Cathleen from Willie, it might be a bloody fight between kinsmen. That boy was stubborn to the point of bullheadedness.

He closed his eyes and tried to still his mind enough to listen and stop borrowing trouble. The breeze blew in fresh and cool through the open window. A long, deep breath of it helped to take him toward his center and his balance.

But only a little way.

His gut instincts hardly ever failed him but today he couldn't really feel any kind of direction, no matter how hard he tried.

Come to think of it, he hadn't felt his feet firmly planted on the face of the earth mother or his spirit completely at peace for what seemed to be endless days and nights. Not since the moment he'd opened Cathleen's shirt and seen that she was a woman.

That realization made him open his eyes and stare at the ceiling. Now the sight of her fine, high breasts filled his memory and he'd never be able to settle.

Wagon wheels creaked along out on the street, horses nickered, men's shouts carried on the wind to each other and to their animals. Black Fox tried to close out the noises, then he let them in. He might as well try to distract himself.

Farther away, there was a commotion of some kind, then came a man's louder yell with words he didn't quite catch. Then, a sudden silence fell and the wind brought a woman's voice.

Dear God, it was Cathleen's.

"Tassel Glass! I'm calling you out. This is Cathleen O'Sullivan."

Black Fox lunged off the bed and ran to the window.

Was he imagining things? Had he lost his mind entirely? How could she be so foolish?

But hadn't he known all along she would be? Hadn't he been sitting right here waiting for her to do this very thing?

What he *hadn't* expected was the deep, cold horror that rose up in his veins with the reality of it.

People were gathering at the corner of the street and staring toward the store.

"Hear me, you craven coward of a woman-killer," Cathleen called, determination vibrating in her husky voice. "Tassel Glass! Come out here, armed, or fall in your blood on the floor of your store."

She *couldn't* go in there—Glass and his men would cut her down the instant she stepped through the door.

Black Fox whirled and rushed out, grabbing his hat as he ran. He threw himself down the stairs, five at a time. At the bottom, three men were crowding the doors, trying to see into the street.

"Clear the way," he shouted. "Lighthorse."

Even so, he was on them before they could move, pushing his way through, plunging across the sidewalk to his horse. He jerked the reins loose and leapt into the saddle without touching a stirrup, already heading the big horse toward the store before his seat brushed leather.

Cathleen wouldn't—and couldn't—turn back now. And he couldn't interfere with an honorable challenge. The most he could hope for was to keep her from getting killed.

Maybe Glass wasn't there.

No such luck. Before he reached the corner, a gasp went up and people began falling back to get vantage points out of the line of fire.

Black Fox crossed the street cater-cornered and rode into the woods, glancing fast to the left. He caught a glimpse of Tassel Glass stalking out onto the front porch of the store, letting the screen door slam shut behind him, his huge bulk moving toward Cathleen's small form. She stood firm in the middle of the path leading to the steps.

She had her hair down and her hat off, he saw in that instant. Clearly, she wanted there to be no mistake about who was going to lay the big man low.

"Cathleen, honey, I got no notion what you're talking about." Glass's voice, deep and oily as ever, rose louder with each word so everyone could hear. "No notion at all."

"Lying about it now will only add to the sum of your sins," Cathleen said clearly. "Be careful, Tassel, for this is your Judgment Day."

Her voice didn't waver. Black Fox had known from the first time they met that she had grit, but he hadn't known how much.

Working his way through the sparse trees so he'd have a clear path to her, Black Fox noticed her little dun horse half hidden by a rhododendron bush. He went straight to the little mare, took the reins, and looped them in a quick slipknot through a ring on his saddle. He had to be ready, not only to get Cathleen out of this confrontation alive, but also to get her out of town.

He eased both horses into place behind a thin grove of maple saplings where he could see the whole front of the store. No one would notice him, anyway, since all eyes were on Cathleen and Glass.

"Now, now, Cathleen, you've gotta settle down," Glass said. "You can see that you've done shot me up to where I can't fight worth a damn."

He pointed to the sling that held his right arm across his chest. Black Fox remembered that Glass had been shot on the right in that fight with her and Becker's gang but he couldn't remember whether Glass was left-handed or not—if he had ever known it.

"My mother wasn't strong enough to fight *you*, either, but you killed her anyway."

Her strong voice didn't break when she said that, but some note in it made Black Fox think how young she was and how much she missed her mother. And now here she was, facing down a gun.

He caught a movement in the corner of his eye and looked up. His jaw tightened. Cathleen was facing more than one gun.

A man was crawling over the hip of the roof on Glass's store, staying under the limbs of the huge overhanging oak tree for cover, headed for the porch. He moved awkwardly and sideways because he carried a gun in one hand.

No doubt Tassel had a gun just like it hidden in his sling. The man on the roof was sent to shoot Cathleen before she could get off a shot, just at that last second of her draw so it would look like Glass had killed her honestly.

Black Fox took his foot from the stirrup and slipped his rifle from the scabbard beneath his leg. This rescue might be far more of a trick than he'd thought.

That realization steadied him, stilled the fear for the beautiful girl that had been running through his veins like a winter river. It sent a white-hot iron determination charging through his blood like a fever.

He felt almost exhilarated. He had done harder things than this many times. He could save her.

"I don't know one cottonpicking thing about how your mama died," Glass said loudly, "I had nothin' to do with it."

"I am a witness," she said. "I saw you with my own eyes."

A knowing pity stabbed at Black Fox's heart. Cathleen had been older than he was when he saw his own parents killed by the Intruders, but that didn't make it any easier. It didn't matter that she and her family were Intruders, too. Such a horror should come to no child, ever, anywhere.

"You mistook another man for me, Little Girl," Glass argued, clearly trying to buy time for the man on the roof to get into position.

Also, when he said it, he glanced toward the watching townspeople as if to say that this was just a foolish woman child and he hated to have to shoot her. He was trying to show them that he had no choice and when she lay dead at his feet, he would cry what a shame that she'd been so mistakenly stubborn in blaming him for something he didn't do.

"Never," Cathleen said. "I would know you on a dark night in a driving storm. Ever since you trapped me in the back room of your store and put your filthy hands all over me, I'd know you just by the stink you carry."

Black Fox's breath came short. There was *another* horror Glass had visited upon her. His fist clenched. It would give him so much satisfaction to smash Glass's face that he couldn't begin to imagine it.

But he didn't have time to think about revenge. Glass wouldn't stand there for many more insults from Cathleen, a mere girl and a nobody at that.

Somewhere in the crowd, a man laughed and Tassel wouldn't be able to take that, either.

"I didn't see it but my heart knows that you killed Roger, too," Cathleen said. "I overheard you that day when you offered to mark our whole account paid, plus give him all the whiskey he wanted—my poor stepfather, who wanted all the whiskey in the world—if he would let you bed me."

"Your stepfather was a drunk," Glass snapped. "He died of drink."

"He died of a bullet to the *back*," Cat retorted. "I

was the one who found his body—facedown in the corncrib."

For the first time, Black Fox realized just how hard her life had been, and unlike him, she had no Aunt Sally and Uncle Muskrat to turn to.

"I'm through trying to reason with you," Glass snapped. "Anybody could've shot the man. Any long rider or drifter in the Nation could have come onto his farm and shot him."

Black Fox trained his rifle on the man on the roof. All this palavering was about to end. The shooter was still in the shadow of the tree limbs, but he was very close to the porch roof now and getting settled lying on his belly, getting ready for Cathleen to draw. As Black Fox watched, he brought his knuckles down on the tin roof—a signal to Tassel, no doubt, that he could quit talking now.

But the drumming of hooves drowned him out. When the man took his eyes off Cathleen, Black Fox risked a glance toward the sound, too.

Dear God in heaven, it was a big, fancy paint horse and the rider was Willie, still wearing his Sunday shirt. Black Fox nearly choked as his breath turned to a knot in his throat.

A strange slash of jealousy cut through him. There was Willie, trying to be a hero when he didn't have a logical thought in his head. Willie, trying to be a hero and save Cathleen when he was still wet behind the ears.

Damn it. He, Black Fox, should've put a stop to this whole situation before it ever went this far. Before Willie could've arrived to put in his two cents worth of craziness. After all, he could hardly protect *two* foolish kids at once, and if Willie got himself killed, it would kill Aunt Sally, too.

The big paint horse tore into the store yard from the east and slid to a stop a few yards from the showdown. Willie threw himself off the gelding and strode toward Cathleen.

Glass went pale with fury.

"What d'you think you're doing, boy?" he demanded.

"I'm here to back Cathleen," Willie said.

Cathleen half turned to glare at him. She, too, was clearly furious.

"Get out of here, Willie," she said. "This is my play."

"I know that," he said. "But you need somebody . . ."

He never finished the sentence. A gun barked, flashing flame from overhead. Black Fox fired a second too late to stop it but he shot the man off the roof.

Glass turned and ran, Cathleen fired a shot at him, Willie went for his handgun and started shooting, somebody shot from the woods and that was all Black Fox knew because he was moving too fast, then, to see anything but Cathleen.

He bent over the gray horse's neck and rode

into the melee reaching for her as soon as he got his rifle stuffed back into its scabbard. This was his chance to get her out of town and it was the only one he'd get.

"Wil-lie-e!"

The one word was a long scream rising above all the rest of the noise—hoofbeats, more shots, shouts, and confusion—and it was coming from a girl in a blue calico dress racing on foot directly across the gray horse's path. She came so close Black Fox narrowly missed hitting her.

He wanted to look and try to see whether Willie was hurt but, for this one precious moment, Cathleen was standing still. People were becoming thicker, his young horse was trying to shy from all the noise, and he had to get to her fast.

Pounding up behind her, leaning far out of the saddle into his right stirrup, he swept her up in one arm and held her across his thigh as he forged through the gathering crowd until he found his seat again. Then he dragged her, kicking and screaming, up into the saddle in front of him and headed out of town at a gallop.

She waved the gun under his nose and he smelled the powder she'd just burned.

"Put me down," she yelled, above the noise of the horses. "You let me go right now, Black Fox Vann!"

She pointed the muzzle at his chest.

He grabbed her gun away from her and, juggling it and the reins in one hand, managed to lift her with his forearm, take her left leg with his free hand and turn her to sit face front, astraddle of the horse. Thank goodness, he had managed to take her out of trouble unhurt. If she'd done that to anybody else, she'd be dead right now.

They rode through the little town at a high lope, racing for distance before anyone could come after them, keeping both horses moving on and on down the road until they had trees and brush and plenty of distance between them and Sequoyah. Finally letting the horses slow, Black Fox listened for sound of pursuit and heard none.

Still, he stayed just as he was. Her thigh felt slim and succulent in his hand. So warm and sweet he couldn't bring himself to move at all. Cathleen didn't move, either.

The shape of her against him felt even better than he had remembered. She fit him as if she were meant to be exactly where she was at this instant.

Her skin smelled of her special chamomile soap and her hair smelled like a faraway, peaceful meadow full of clover—underneath its fresh scent of gunpowder, which filled his senses with the sharp memory of that other time, the time when she'd lain across his bed while he washed her hair. And kissed her.

Her bottom was sitting right against him, the side of her high, rounded breast rested against the inside of his arm. His loins stirred. He could not let her go.

For a minute longer, headed into the falling dusk, she let herself be molded to him. Firm, warm flesh and delicate bones resting against his, fragrant hair tickling his nose, the curve of a flower-tinted cheek to tantalize his eye.

Suddenly she seemed to wake to the fact that they were traveling much slower. She stiffened and began to struggle again.

"That wasn't fair, what you did," she said, jerking at his wrist to pull his hand off her thigh. "I've waited more than a year to call Glass out."

"Be still," he growled. "You'd better just be glad it's me that's got you."

"Oh, sure," she said sarcastically, leaning away so she could turn and glare at him with those huge green eyes of hers. "Since *you're* the only one who's trying to hang me."

The truth of it hit him like a slap in the face. It made him sick to his stomach. What, on the face of Mother Earth, was the matter with him that he could forget?

He hadn't saved her. He had arrested her. Again.

He wasn't her lover, as he had pretended to Willie. He was her captor.

His life was dedicated to upholding the rule of law. She was an outlaw.

A *woman* outlaw who was playing hell with his

mind as well as his body. He had better get a handle on this situation and get this girl to Fort Smith before he completely forgot who he was.

The trembling that had seized Cathleen and turned her insides to jelly at the first glimpse of Tassel Glass was still with her. It wouldn't stop, not even now that Black Fox held her in his arms.

But yet . . . no, this was different. The scare she'd had wouldn't quite leave her, true, but this new weakness in her limbs came because of Black Fox's muscled arms around her waist making her feel as if she wore no clothes.

He clamped her against him as if he meant to never let her go and she couldn't sit up straight and away from him. She was trying, but not even the thought of hanging could make her do it.

She didn't have enough room between him and the saddle horn, for one thing.

For another, she didn't have the energy. Now that it was over, she could feel that confronting Tassel Glass had taken all the starch from her bones.

She had called him out but she hadn't finished the job. Because of Black Fox, she would never know whether she would've had the power to hold her gun steady enough to kill him.

The thought sent anger shooting through her, rousing her blood again. But she couldn't even lift her head. She let it sink against Black Fox's big chest, managing to turn to speak so he'd be sure to hear.

"Damn it, Black Fox," she said. "Now I'll have it all to do over again."

He knew instantly what she was talking about.

"No," he said, "I'll do it. I promise you that I'll bring him to justice."

"Which is no promise at all," she said bitterly. "There's no such thing."

"There is," he said. "It's not perfect, but it's there."

"Hah."

He didn't argue with her. He seemed to sense the sudden deep weariness that had taken her just now—maybe he could feel it through her clothes, just as she could feel the strength of the muscles in his arm.

Her whole body sagged against him and she had no way to stop it. His arms felt right and warm to her; she felt safe with him holding her inside the circle they made.

What in the world was the matter with her? With Black Fox Vann she was anything but safe.

Yet, stupidly, she wanted to feel his big, hard hand on her thigh again. She wanted to feel it stroking over her skin, with its calluses and its marvelous, restrained power that she well remembered from the time he washed her hair.

Damn it all, she wanted him to kiss her. Her bones had turned to jelly and she was scared and she wanted to forget everything and be carried off into that hot, sweet world of his mouth.

"The law is the only way," he said, speaking low and in no hurry at all, as if talking to himself and thinking about what he was saying as he went along. "Anything else and we'd have nothing but turmoil. Just like today—you didn't have a chance of taking Glass. And if he'd killed you, it'd have made people even more afraid of standing up to him."

That put the fire back into her. She sat up straight and looked at him.

"Don't say that. You *can't* say that. Don't tell me I can't do it, because I have to, and I will."

"Then you'd better wear two guns and look up at the roof once in a while," he drawled.

He brought the horses down to a trot and headed them off into the woods, following a faint trail.

"I will," she said, with a stoutness she didn't quite feel.

The trembling got worse again.

"But first," he said, with a new, hard edge coming into his voice, "you'll have to get away from me, Cathleen."

She wouldn't let him know how shaky she was on the inside.

"I'll get it done," she said, imitating that sharpness of his tone.

"You'll play hell if you do," he said, stung as if

she were being disloyal somehow. As if he hadn't been the one to bring up the subject.

"Why not?" she retorted. "After all, some say I run with the devil."

He chuckled.

"You're not quite that tough, I'm thinking."

"Ask Hudson Becker. He called me a little son of Satan."

Black Fox actually laughed. It was a beautiful, low sound that wrapped them together all of a sudden.

Somehow it drew her back closer to him instead of her sitting up so straight holding onto the saddle horn.

"It takes one to know one," he said. "Hudson Becker himself is the devil's spawn."

"I didn't stop to tell him that," she said, "but I have to agree with you."

All of a sudden, he fell quiet.

After a little way, he spoke again. Harshly this time.

"What were you doing palavering with that lowdown piece of pond scum, anyhow?"

It just hit her wrong—that possessive, protective inflection in his voice when, not five minutes ago, he'd been telling her she couldn't get away from him. That she was his prisoner.

It also hit her wrong that she liked this business of being in his arms. Of sitting in his lap. She liked it far too much. Her body was trying to betray her.

She had to be thinking of escaping—just one more time—not of what he smelled of, which was cedar and pine and horse and leather. And sweat. A man's good sweat that carried the scent of his skin. The scent of Black Fox.

When she took a deep breath and drew in a long draught of that fragrance, it set up a new kind of quivering inside her. Something that was a whole different thing entirely.

Something that she didn't recognize but she knew, anyway, was an elemental part of living that was as old as time. A part of living that had to do only with a man and a woman.

And, in a way that she could not have said, she knew that Black Fox was feeling it, too.

*That* was what she had to be scared of, not some old bag of trash like Tassel Glass.

"Oh," she said airily, "Hudson and I visit from time to time. We outlaws have to hang together, you know."

Black Fox snorted rudely and neck-reined his horse off the trail.

"Apt choice of words," he said.

The image those words raised in his mind infuriated him. The fact that his arms instinctively tightened around her infuriated him even more.

*Damn it. Why did you have to shoot those two men? Did you shoot them, Cathleen?*

"You can stop now and let me get on my own horse," she said.

"Not a chance," he snapped. "You outlaws have to take your punishment. Once I get you to Fort Smith, I'll come back for your buddy Hudson to keep you company."

That made her mad.

"Don't plan too far ahead," she said. "You haven't got *me* there yet."

Then she snapped her mouth closed as if she'd said too much and didn't say another word until he rode out of the woods and into the long, sweet valley tucked away between the hills his people called the Quannessee, after a Cherokee town that had once been important and much beloved back in the Old Nation in the east. This was a valley with only one way in and one way out.

He rode to the place where he had camped the last time he was riding this way and found the circle of rocks he'd used for his fire still there on the bank of the creek.

"Whoa," he said softly, and stopped the horses beside it.

He tried not to think about the empty feeling in his arms when he lifted Cathleen down to the ground.

"You can rest now," he said. "It's a steep-sided valley, so don't try to run. You'll only wear yourself out."

The words were a waste of breath. She was clearly too tired to try anything.

He tried not to think about where they were going or why as he spread her bedroll for her and, while she was gone into the bushes to wash up, built the fire and made the coffee and heated the biscuits and ham he'd brought from the hotel kitchen.

The efforts were a waste of energy. He didn't feel like eating and, as for Cathleen, she came back, stretched out to wait for the food and fell into a hard sleep.

When he had taken care of the horses and banked the fire and spread his bedroll beside hers, he tied her ankle to his. Tired out or not, she had fooled him before and he probably wouldn't be so lucky as to catch her a third time.

As soon as his head hit his saddle, she reached for him. She took his arm and hugged it to her, curled her little body around it, and threw one fine, slender leg over his.

# Chapter 10

C at woke with the sun shining on her face. That was a rare thing, because she never slept past sunrise. She never had—except a week ago when she was at Black Fox's house and so weak from loss of blood. On the family farm, every scrap of daylight had to be used for working and surviving. Then when she went on the run, every daylight minute had to be used for scouting and surviving.

For that first, delicious moment when her mind was coming back up from unconsciousness, she luxuriated in the warmth of the day. It went all the way through her skin and bones into her heart and brought the satisfaction of being well rested to every muscle in her body. Inexplicably, she felt lazy and safe and she even took her own sweet time to open her eyes.

Even after she did, though, it was the strangest thing. She lay right there and looked at Black Fox Vann grooming Little Dun and the coziness stayed with her.

Until she recalled the reason why he was there. Why *she* was *here*, sleeping in his camp instead of in one of her own secure, hidden places. Dear Lord, she was a prisoner on her way to being hanged!

She threw her arm over her eyes and fought the panic. Her comfort vanished and her brain started frantically working.

Worse, she had tried and failed to kill Tassel Glass. Black Fox had caught her at exactly the wrong time and place just as surely as he'd caught her at the right time and place the first time. It had to be right, since he'd saved her from bleeding to death.

But now she was a prisoner again and what was she going to do? Hot despair washed through her. She tried to fight it off. She would not give up, not after the rough living she'd done for the past year. That would not, *could* not, all go for naught.

She bolted upright, shading her eyes and squinting at Black Fox through the bright light. He appeared to be combing Dunny's tail. Still combing Dunny's *black* tail?

"Hey," she yelled, scrambling out of the bedroll, "what are you doing to my horse?"

He barely glanced up as she ran toward him in her sock feet. She stepped on a rock, hopped a little way, and then plunged on. Black Fox dipped his rag into the jar—it looked like stove blacking—and rubbed some more into the pale yellow tail.

"You're making her tail *black*?" she cried despairingly. "*Why?*"

Right then she noticed the dun's mane, now almost all ink-dark against the shining gold of her neck.

Black Fox rubbed the blackening into poor Dunny's last few strands of hair that were still flaxen-colored.

"Disguising her," he said.

"What are you *talking* about?"

"At a distance, she'll easily be taken for a buckskin," Black Fox said. "You'll be a girl. Maybe at the sight of you, people won't immediately think about the boy called The Cat on the fast little yellow dun horse."

Some giant hand just reached in and scooped out Cathleen's insides. It was like she was losing her horse and herself and her whole reason for being, all faster than she could wipe the sleep from her eyes.

"You're afraid we're so well thought of that one of our admirers might try to rescue us from you?"

"That's it," he said, and went right on with his work.

She narrowed her eyes.

"You're the one who'll be needing rescue," she said, from between clenched teeth. "You've got a lot of gall to take such liberties with my horse."

"It's my job to get you to jail as fast as I can," he said.

"Wouldn't it be faster to hit the trail at sunup instead of burning daylight *trying* to disguise my horse?" she said sarcastically. "Everybody in Sequoyah already knows I'm a girl and as soon as you rode up dragging my horse behind you and snatched me into custody, anybody who didn't already know it, like Willie did, figured out that I'm The Cat."

He made no reply but to keep on with his work.

"They know," she insisted, "because The Cat has picked on Tassel Glass from the beginning and now everybody knows why."

Black Fox shrugged. "Most of them don't travel much," he said. "We may be able to stay ahead of the word as it travels."

Fury and fear stirred in her empty stomach. And loneliness. This morning, Black Fox seemed like a rank stranger.

"*I'll* tell somebody as soon as I get the chance," she said. "It's *my* job not to go to jail at all."

The threat didn't so much as make him look up.

"Well, for now, you'd better eat your breakfast," he said. "Here pretty quick, we're going to ride."

Ride they did, and fast, for the rest of the morning, traveling right out in the open on the road that led to Muldrow and PawPaw. Then it would carry them across the border, out of the Cherokee Nation, out of the Indian Territories, and take them into Fort Smith.

Black Fox spent his energies keeping his horse close enough to Little Dun to prevent any possible break for freedom and his emotions as far from Cathleen as he possibly could. He had to stop thinking about her, therefore, he had to stop those infernal conversations with her.

He had come to that conclusion sometime just before daylight, after he'd thought about her all night long, especially while she clung to him in her sleep. He stuck to it, speaking with her only as much as was necessary.

Until she provoked him, as only she could do.

"If you don't want to look at me or talk to me now that I'm on my way to jail, that's fine," she said tartly. "But you don't have to kill the horses. Slow down."

Anger stung him. She was right. He *had* been pushing them too hard.

And he *was* trying to pull back so it wouldn't be

so difficult to leave her behind bars. Did she know that? Or did she think he hated her because she was an outlaw?

He didn't want her to think that but he didn't want to talk about it, either.

He let the Ghost drop back into a slow trot. The dun horse followed suit.

"Dunny's famous across the whole countryside as a fast one," he said. "I don't know what you're fussing about."

"Yeah," she said sarcastically, "but now that she's carrying all this stove-blacking in her hair, she tires out sooner."

"Trying to delay in order to stay around this part of the country as long as possible isn't going to help you, Cat," he said. "No matter who steps in or what happens, I've got to take you to Fort Smith."

"To have me hanged for no reason," she said bitterly. "I did *not* kill Donald Turner."

"Of course you didn't," he snapped, in a sarcastic tone. "And I'm sure you say the same about John Bushyhead."

Her head jerked around and she stared at him in an innocent-seeming manner.

"Who is he?"

"A bootlegger up in the Flint District," he said. "Don't try to tell me you didn't know that."

"I do the best I can," she said dryly, "but I

haven't made the acquaintance of every whiskey dealer in the Nation."

She sounded honest. He had a practiced ear. He'd questioned many a culprit and usually he could tell when a person was lying.

"Bushyhead was shot a couple of days ago," Black Fox said, searching her eyes for the truth, "in an ambush signed by the mark of The Cat."

"I was not there," she said, her tone so sincere that the old hope tried to come to life in him again.

"From what I heard," he said, "his was an identical murder to Turner's."

"Good," she said. "That'll prove I didn't do it."

"Some people would argue that it proves you *did* do it," he said wryly, "since your mark was there both times."

She held his gaze as they rode slowly along, staring straight into his eyes with her steady green ones. Those eyes talked to him without words. They willed him to look into her heart and believe her.

"If my horse is famous, my mark is famous," she said. "Everyone knows it and anybody can use it."

"In the last few days, that mark was also found on the porch posts of two other bootleggers between Stilwell and Sequoyah," he said. "Both were missing large sums of money."

"Leander Rabbit and Tophat Martin," she said, nodding assent. "I robbed them both."

"Word also reached Sequoyah town that several families up in the Flint District these last three or four days woke up to blankets and money and food on their doorsteps," he said. "Under the paw print of The Cat drawn with charred wood."

Cathleen didn't break the look between them. She nodded.

"I made those marks," she said, blushing a little as if being caught doing the good deeds embarrassed her.

Then she shrugged.

"If only I'd thought of it, I could've used stove blacking," she said.

But she didn't smile and neither did he.

"I can't prove I'm innocent of those killings, Black Fox," she said.

The sound of his name in her sweetly husky voice thrilled him like a caress on his skin. He was losing his mind. This girl was an outlaw and a killer.

But he certainly could understand why, considering the things she'd said to Tassel Glass.

"Unless you give me a chance to find out who *did* do them," she said.

Then she looked at him so hopefully he could hardly stand to meet her gaze.

"You wouldn't know how to begin," he said.

He couldn't let himself think about that; it was foolish. Her mark had been there both times.

She hated whiskey dealers. She had reason to shoot lawmen. Maybe Donald Turner had been trying to arrest her.

He had to change the subject, had to let these horses blow and then set them loping again so she couldn't talk to him.

But there was one thing he had to know.

"It's my guess that Willie rode into Sequoyah just to back you yesterday," he said. "How did he know where you were and what you were doing?"

He was happy to hear the professional tone in his voice. It held no trace of the strange jealousy he'd felt when Willie appeared.

"He hunted me down in the woods to warn me you were waiting for me in town. He figured out for himself that I was on my way to call Tassel out." She looked at him straight. "I asked him to go on ahead and get you out of the way, but something must've delayed him."

Black Fox felt a twisting in his gut.

"Great," he muttered, "my own kin, conspiring against me."

"That's because he's sweet on *me*," she said, as if trying to comfort him.

His head twisted, too, and made him feel nearly dizzy. The whole world was upside down and sideways.

"And you're sweet on him?" he blurted.

Black Fox didn't even know where the question came from, much less how it popped out of his mouth.

"I feel obliged to him now," she said. "He got shot for my sake." She glanced at him defiantly. "Willie might show up to help me again."

"He's a lovesick kid," Black Fox snapped. "He could've got himself killed and you, too."

"What he got was a flesh wound," she said. "The man on the roof shot him in the arm—or else Tassel did. Whichever, it didn't look serious."

Black Fox grunted.

"I wondered," he said. "I didn't have time to look at him."

"Who was that girl who was running to see about him?" she asked.

"How the hell should I know?" Black Fox said, anger getting into his voice in spite of all. "Maybe he's sweet on *her*, too."

Cathleen flashed him a surprised look and he held it defiantly.

"So you never thought you might have a rival?" he asked.

He felt petty and childish as the question fell from his tongue but he couldn't seem to bite it back.

"No," she said, with a chuckle in her voice, "but I hope it's true—for Willie's sake."

"No need to laugh," he said stiffly. "You're the one who brought the subject up. I don't know what difference it makes, anyhow."

He didn't know what he meant or why he was even talking. He was losing his mind.

She held his gaze. Was that a twinkle in her eyes? Was she actually laughing at him?

Had he just made a fool of himself? He certainly felt like one.

The sound of approaching hoofbeats pounding toward them from behind made him turn in the saddle to look. Around the last bend in the road came two horsemen, riding fast, already guiding their mounts to the right to pass by.

Something about the big bay horse looked familiar. He knew that rider. Then he saw that he knew them both.

About the time he realized that, they recognized him, too, and started slowing.

"These won't be the ones to rescue you, Cathleen," he said quickly. "They're deputies from Fort Smith."

He looked away at his fellow lawmen again, his heart beating faster. Why, in the name of all good sense, had he said that?

Because he wanted to protect her from any other lawman knowing that she was an outlaw. It was that simple.

But *why* was he warning her? It shouldn't matter to him if she told them she was The Cat. Telling them that wouldn't cause her to end up in Judge Parker's court any faster than she would anyhow.

Yet his heart was pounding like a war drum as they all stopped in the middle of the road. Both deputies looked at Cathleen with a great deal of interest.

The wild beating of Black Fox's heart slowed with dread. Had they come from Sequoyah? Had they heard about The Cat's identity? Would they see that her "buckskin" horse had a dyed mane and tail?

He should tell them who she was, but even as he had the thought, he knew he wouldn't. He'd wait until later to figure out *why* he wouldn't.

He turned to The Cat as if this were a social occasion and someone else had suddenly inhabited his body.

"Miss O'Sullivan," he said. "Deputy Fielding and Deputy Burke."

Both men tipped their hats and repeated her name politely.

"Gentlemen," she said, in a regally dignified tone.

Black Fox stared at her.

Her back straight and drawn up to her full height—which wasn't much more than five feet—her shoulders thrown back, and her chin up, as usual, she was sitting her horse looking at the deputies like a queen receiving her subjects. Her hat was hanging down her back on its stampede strings so that her curly mass of hair caught the sunlight and sent it back into the air, dazzling red and gold.

But it was her manner that dazzled Black Fox. Suddenly, she was like an actress in a play; she was like a stranger.

Which she was. He did not know this child/woman at all, did he? Yet a minute ago he'd been inquiring about her suitors. He was the one who needed to be locked up—for his own protection.

Both the deputies had trouble taking their eyes off her but they finally focused on Black Fox, clearly wondering why the two of them, the girl and the loner, were traveling together. He pretended not to see the questions in their eyes. He didn't owe them any explanation.

"How long have you men been in the Nation?" he asked. "I hadn't heard you were here."

"Couple of days in this part," Fielding said. "Trailin' The Cat."

Burke shifted in his saddle in a gesture that was both arrogant and confident. "And we'll have him in custody by sundown tonight," he said.

"Oh?" Black Fox said, feeling a great relief at hearing the word, "him."

"Damn straight," Burke said, "if we don't burn too much daylight sittin' here jawin' with you."

"The kid has got to be stopped or there won't be

a bootlegger left in this country," Fielding said dryly. "Then all you Lighthorse will be out of a job."

Burke grinned at the joke.

"Yep, he's thinnin' 'em out," he said. "Shot another one last night."

A strange, sharp lurch of excitement took Black Fox's stomach down into his boots and back up to his throat.

"You're sure it was The Cat?" he asked.

"His cat's paw sign was big there on the porch floor," Fielding said. "Shot old Foster right through the window. Right through the left shoulder, too, but he missed his heart."

"Hmm," Black Fox said thoughtfully, "must be losing his aim."

"I guess because he was in a tearing hurry to get to the next thing," Burke said. "A couple of hours later, he robbed a wagon driver right back there at the Little Creek crossing."

"You know it was him?"

"Yep. His mark was drawn on the sideboard of the wagon clear as you please."

Black Fox frowned but his pulse was leaping with hope.

"Did the wagon driver see him?" he asked.

"No, he was gathering wood to make camp for the night," Burke said. "The Cat made off with his moneybag and two cases of whiskey. Looks like the boy may be hooking up with some partners—we found tracks of four horses leaving the crossing."

"How'd you get word of all this since last night?"

"The wagon driver found us," Fielding said. "And word of the shooting spread fast."

"Anyhow," Burke said, reining his horse around to get going again, "we're on his trail. We can't linger now." He shot Black Fox a look back over his shoulder. "You Lighthorse have tried long enough," he said sarcastically, "so we're gonna show y'all how to catch a Cat." He laughed. "How to catch a Cat and skin it," he said, and took off at a lope.

The man was an arrogant ass.

Black Fox smiled as he watched them go.

It would serve them right, Burke especially, to spend several more days riding around and around in the woods on a wild goose chase.

But that wasn't what was making him happy. He tried to hold the feeling back, but he couldn't.

Because he had hope again, too. Maybe Cathleen really *wasn't* guilty of murder. Maybe she'd been telling him the truth all along.

He watched the two deputies riding away—at a long, fast trot that meant business—until they disappeared behind a grove of blackjack trees that grew in a bend in the road. He couldn't turn and look at Cathleen until this wild uplift of excitement in him had subsided.

It *must* subside. A lawman made decisions based on facts, not feelings. He had to think.

*Still*, he didn't know anything for sure. She could have been lying to him all along. He didn't know her—he'd been right about that—and even if someone else was using her sign now, that didn't mean that person was the one who had shot Donald Turner in the back.

He couldn't let himself believe in her innocence unless it *proved* to be true. He was a Lighthorse, the most respected one of them all. The one who had rid the Nation of more bad men than any other. That was who he was. A lawman had to have *facts* and proof.

"Well?" Cathleen demanded. "Do you believe me at last? There's somebody else running around this country using my sign! So you know I haven't killed anybody."

She was still sitting straight in the saddle, alert now with eagerness instead of dignity, her rein hand lifted and ready to signal the dun to go again. Her face glowed, alive with a high excitement.

Black Fox could hardly bear to look at the light in her eyes. What if it wasn't true?

He had to keep his guard up, he had to hold his own hope under control, he had to keep his head now, of all times.

"I *want* to believe it," he said.

Disappointment wiped the smile from her face.

"But you don't," she said sarcastically, fighting

to keep her shoulders from slumping. "God help me, Black Fox, that's exactly what you said the first night you caught me."

Her eyes blazed more but now it was anger that fired them.

Anger and panicky frustration.

"You heard those men," she cried, leaning toward him and holding his gaze with the sheer passion in her will. "And they are *lawmen*, aren't they? Members of Judge Parker's court, where you tell me *justice* is served. So you know it's true that somebody else is out there pretending to be me."

"If all their information is correct, I know that somebody was using your mark last night," he said. "But last night has nothing to do with Donald Turner."

She stared at him in disbelief for a second, then wheeled her horse around and took off. He set his heels to the gray and both horses raced down the road at a gallop, the dun's natural speed making up for the longer stride of the gray, Cathleen a half length ahead. Until they reached the creek, where he caught her.

Black Fox reached out and grabbed the dun's bridle.

"Don't try running away from me again," he said, his eyes narrowed in anger. "Ever."

She tossed her head defiantly.

"I'll run if I want to. You have no right to hold me now that you know I'm innocent."

"Never mind whether you shot Donald Turner," he said. "You've admitted to enough robbery and stealing to warrant a long stint in jail."

"*Why*? Surely you aren't going to take me to Fort Smith for *stealing!* You know Tassel Glass deserves every grief I've ever given him . . ." Her voice tried to break on the last word but she wouldn't let it. ". . . because you know that they are *nothing* compared to the grief he has given me."

Her face had gone pale and her eyes stared out of it, dark and huge. She was desperate now— everything about her demeanor told him that— and it was tearing him to pieces.

All he wanted was to lean from his horse and pull her into his arms, hold her close and comfort her.

But he couldn't accept her word for her innocence. He was a lawman. He needed to prove it. He *would* prove it, if it was so.

He forced his mind away from what Tassel Glass had done to her family and all the reasons she'd become an outlaw in the first place. He was not going to fall into sentimental sympathy for her because that would cloud his judgment.

What he should have done was turn her over to Burke and Fielding, who would've headed straight to Fort Smith with her. Then he would've been free to try to prove her innocence of murder without losing his mind.

But letting her go with *anyone* else—any*where*—was as unthinkable as considering the fact that he might be unable to prove she didn't kill Donald Turner. He didn't want to find out what he would do if that was how it all turned out.

What he ought to do right this minute was turn her loose, but that was the last thing he wanted to do.

"Cathleen," he said, speaking as calmly as he could with such crazy emotions surging through him. "Your word is not enough. I'm a lawman. The law demands proof and right now the only proof it has is that your sign was on the tree above Donald Turner's body."

Her eyes flashed as they locked on his.

"Then I will have to find out and prove who did kill him," she said flatly. "You say justice does exist—*I* demand proof of *that*. Prove it. Set me free to look for the real killer."

He looked into the green blaze of her gaze and let it burn through to his heart.

"I can't set you free," he said. "But I'll help you."

She stared at him in shock. Tears sprang to her eyes but she didn't let them fall.

"Does that mean *you* believe I didn't do it?" she asked.

She spoke with such fervor, such hope, that he couldn't lie to her. His answer meant a great deal to her, for some reason he didn't quite understand, since he'd already said he would help her.

*The only reason she wants you to believe her, Vann, is to keep her pretty neck out of the hangman's noose. You are not that important to her in any other way.*

Maybe. But whatever the reason, her hand on the rein shook slightly and she held him with a look that wouldn't let him go. He had to be honest with her.

"Yes," he said. "I believe you, Cathleen."

It was the truth. It was the cold, hard truth living in his gut at that moment.

He only hoped, for his sake as well as hers, that it was more than wishful thinking.

He only prayed, for his sake and hers, that it was his trusty instinct talking to him and not his desire for her.

Because he did desire her and he had since that first sight of her as a woman—even if he had never admitted it in his deepest self until that minute. He desired her more than any woman he'd ever seen or known.

He kissed to his horse and started them moving, letting his mind wrap around that thought. Desire was one thing but acting on it was another.

This woman, by her own admission, was a virgin. She was also an outlaw who was his captive.

She was too vulnerable on both counts for a man of honor to touch her.

# Chapter 11

She reached out and touched him, laid her small hand on his arm. The shape of it burned into his muscles through his sleeve.

"Thanks, Black Fox," she said, and even though he quickened the gray's trot, she held her horse right beside his until he turned his head and looked at her.

"It means a lot to me."

Her face was luminous. She blinked away the tears.

Damn. Talk about raising the stakes.

"I haven't got it done yet," he said.

*And what if you can't do it, Vann? She won't be*

*looking at you the same way then. She'll still be on her way to hanging, then.*

"You will," she said, and her voice held all the faith in the world.

When she took her hand away, he could still feel it.

A rush of feeling came up in him, so deep and complicated he couldn't name all its parts. He tried to ignore it and concentrate on the task ahead.

It wouldn't be easy. But wasn't he known for getting his man? He'd tracked her for two weeks, hadn't he, when he thought she killed the deputy marshal?

But two weeks in the woods with her at his side, working with him, talking to him, looking at him—now that would be more than he could stand and keep his resolve not to touch her. That would make him crazy.

What would make him even crazier was if he had done nothing right now but to prolong her agony and give her false hope. His gut told him that she hadn't shot anyone in the back and that she had a good heart.

He would hate himself forever if he couldn't prove her innocent now. *Why* had he ever even suggested it? Everybody, lawman or not, knew that it was impossible to prove someone innocent.

They'd better find the guilty one and find him fast.

"Reckon we should turn around and go back to Foster's place and the Little Creek crossing to look at the trail for ourselves?" Cathleen asked.

His gut clenched. Maybe. That was just the first of many decisions he'd better get right. Time to stop thinking and start going by his instincts—if he could hear them past his awareness of her.

"Burke's an irritating son-of-a-gun," he said, "and not the best tracker in the world, but he can generally tell which way his quarry's headed."

"I wish we had asked exactly what makes him and Fielding think that my impostor and his friends are headed this way. They didn't give us any details."

"Most likely they found a few tracks and some signs scattered here and there at the crossing and in the woods where the ground is moist enough to hold them."

Cathleen considered that and nodded.

"The tracks were leading away from the crossing to the south. When they hit the road, they had to pick a direction, and they probably just took a chance that the thieves kept on going south."

Black Fox thought about it a little more.

"Sequoyah's back north and—depending on who the false Cat is—maybe more people who know them. If they want to spend the money now, they'll not want to explain where they got it."

"Right," she said. "To the south, there's Sallisaw and Muldrow and the railroad and maybe more people who *don't* know them. They could also take a train and leave the Nation."

"Or," he said, "they could be anywhere east or south or north or west of here. They could've separated and scattered by now and disappeared into the hills."

Cathleen nodded agreement.

"If they're old hands at being outlaws they could have hideouts already," she said. "More than one, so well hidden that nobody can find them. Like I do."

*Like I do.*

The careless remark cut at his heart. Didn't she know those days were over for her? Hadn't she realized yet that she didn't have anything at all anymore, much less hideouts and the freedom to use them—unless they could prove that someone else had shot Donald Turner in the back?

Damn!

Yet, somehow, just talking it over with her like this gave him a hopeful feeling. It was a new thing for him to have someone to partner with.

An ironic grin touched his lips with that thought. He was partnered up, all right—with an outlaw.

"Yes," he said, talking to himself as much as to her, "and if Burke and Fielding couldn't pick up the trail after the fake Cat got to the road, then they're doing the only thing they can do now: guess and hope they're guessing right."

He caught her gaze and held it with his sharp, calculating one. She read his mind.

"They may not be quite so sure of their prey as they acted," she said.

A warm satisfaction shifted through him.

"My thought exactly," he said.

She nodded and smiled, then turned again to watching the ground ahead.

"I wish it wasn't so dry," she said.

"Wouldn't help us any to have mud instead," he said wryly, "since we don't know what we're looking for."

She gave a wry laugh.

"No, we don't, do we? And here I am, watching for the right tracks as earnestly as if I'd seen them myself. We'll have to catch him drawing my cat's-paw sign to know him."

Black Fox looked at her.

When her eyes looked so bright green like that, she was even more appealing. He wanted to touch her. Just to cup her face in his hand and, with his thumb, to trace the corners of her lips when they were upturned like that in fun.

She was gallant. Not many women, or men either, would be this undaunted in such a situation.

"Right," he said.

"Oh, I know!" she said mischievously, like a

child playacting, "I'll ride up in front of him while he's drawing my sign and distract him and then you can slip up behind him and jerk him off his feet and up onto your horse."

Those words conjured an image of Cathleen in danger that struck Black Fox with a chill.

Not only had he perhaps given her false hope, he might have drawn her into a bigger danger. What had he been thinking? She could get killed looking for a killer.

But what choice was there? He had to keep her with him, keep an eye on her. There was no other way to do this.

"Wherever we are, try not to attract attention," he said. "And remember that there are four of them. At least. Maybe more. You watch yourself and stay close to me."

*Stay close to me.*

Cathleen's whole body warmed to those words, including her heart. Her battered, stiff-frozen heart. Her lonely heart.

She'd better watch herself, all right. She knew that—after all, hadn't she survived alone in the woods for a year?

It was Black Fox that was the real danger. It would never do to start counting on him too much.

It would never do to get attached to him, either, just because he believed her now when she said she wasn't a murderer. Not just because he was her companion now who said, *"Stay close to me."*

The wonderful, warm, insane *comfort* that she was taking from being with him now, riding beside him and having him believe in her and help prove her innocence could easily turn to more and deeper feelings, since she already knew and longed for his touch. She *ached* for it, for no more than just the thrill of his hands in her hair or on her skin.

That way lay huge danger. For not only did he attract her physically but he had a big heart and he believed in her and he was going to help her. All of that could make her love him.

Didn't everybody she loved vanish like smoke? The same would be true of Black Fox.

When they had caught the impostor and the job was done, he would either turn her loose or, since he was such a lawman, believing in justice, he would try to take her to jail because of the goods and money she had stolen. Probably, he would turn her loose.

Surely he would, wouldn't he?

Black Fox Vann was known far and wide as a tough but fair-minded man and he knew all her good reasons for tormenting Tassel Glass. She hoped he'd turn her loose.

Maybe he would.

And then, it wouldn't matter if she loved him or not or she admired him or not, or if he believed she was a murderer or not.

Because she intended to be the one to vanish. She would call Tassel Glass out and kill him honorably and then she would vanish. Even if a fair gunfight would keep her from being arrested again, she would have to disappear because Tassel Glass had bad men working for him who would want to avenge him.

Always, bad men wanted to make a reputation for themselves. But she wasn't going to think about that now.

And neither was she going to think about how strong and hard Black Fox's arms had felt around her, how they'd held her in a circle so safe no one could break it. Or about how his heart had been beating deep in his chest, beating sure and steady against her ear as he carried her on his lap to his house that time.

Absolutely, she was not going to think about how his hands had felt on her skin and in her hair and how his mouth had felt—and tasted—when he kissed her.

She wasn't going to think about anything except finding out and proving who killed Donald Turner. That had to be done quickly and then she had to get on with her real work.

Only when Tassel Glass was dead and she was in Texas or way out west could she think about a life in the future.

Only then.

* * *

Sallisaw was a railroad town and big enough that, unless Burke and Fielding had caught their man or picked up a sure trail leading away from it, that's where they would probably be. Black Fox stayed on the road as it approached the outskirts of town.

"Don't you think we should hide in the woods now?" Cathleen asked. "Just in case somebody *did* come in from Sequoyah who knows that The Cat is a girl with red hair. Those two federal marshals might not understand about you and me trying to prove my innocence."

He glanced up. Now would be the test.

"You're right," he said. "It'd be best for me to go into town alone. You won't try to run, will you?"

She eyed him solemnly.

"I'm not stupid," she said. "I know my only chance of proving my innocence is if you help me."

"You could decide not to even try to prove it and just leave the country instead."

He held her gaze as they rode side by side.

"*You* could take the train, too," he said. "The other Cat and his gang aren't the only ones with that choice."

"I'm not leaving the Nation until I finish what I've started with Glass," she said flatly.

The hooves of the horses plop-plopped on the dry ground. As Black Fox laid his rein against

Ghost's neck, they walked in step off the road. They had reached the grassy plain on the edge of town and were well in sight of the main street, so he guided the horses off into a grove of cotton-woods that grew in a bend of the winding creek called Long Turtle.

All the while, Black Fox was looking into her eyes. Trying to see into her soul.

She let him.

She had nothing to hide, at least as far as an at-tempt at escape was concerned. He believed that. All his instincts told him that she was telling him the truth.

"I believe *that*," he said. "But what's to keep you from heading back to Sequoyah to do it now?"

"Finding my impersonator," she said. "No telling who he might rob or shoot next. He's liable to stir the whole Nation up in arms, trying to lynch me—and now they know who I am."

Relieved that she understood her situation, Black Fox smiled.

She smiled back, obviously happy that he trusted her.

They looked into each other's eyes and for a moment he couldn't resist teasing her.

"I don't know," he said, "it's a shame to waste your horse's disguise . . ."

"Ha!" she said scornfully. "My poor horse looks like a yellow dun somebody tried to make into a buckskin. Like the victim of a demented boot-black running amok."

He grinned.

"I had to hurry," he said. "I was afraid you'd wake up and take the boot polish to my face instead."

"Which I may do yet," she said. "Buy me a can of it when you go into town."

"First I have to talk to the marshals if they're here," he said. "Might as well find out if they've caught our man."

"If not, get the details of what they found at the Little Creek Crossing—and at Foster's," she said.

"Yes, *ma'am*," he said, and stopped the horses in a grassy spot in sight of the creekbank. "Any other orders?"

"Candy," she said. "I'd rather have candy than boot polish, to tell you the truth."

They both dismounted. Black Fox took his canteen off his saddle and went to get Cat's.

"I'll get you fresh water," he said, "then you stay out of sight while I'm gone."

"I will," she said.

She was standing so close to him that he could smell the scent of her hair—and the fresh-rain fragrance of her skin. His fingers trembled a little as he untied her saddle strings.

For an instant, he thought she wanted him to touch her. She was looking at him, and she didn't move away when his arm brushed her shoulder.

Then she did. She turned and walked to her horse's head and looked through the screen of trees at the tumbling creek.

"You could throw a rock from here and hit the back of a building on the edge of town," he said. "So you'll have to keep a lookout for somebody cutting through here or coming to the creek."

"I will," she said again.

He walked past her at an angle to get to the creek. He had an insane urge to take her in his arms.

Heedless of getting his boots wet, he went out to the fresh, fast-running water and filled both canteens, then he brought hers back to her. She looked up into his face. Their fingers touched when she took it.

He stood there without moving, thinking about the way she had looked at him out on his front porch, over his painted feather. He had wanted to kiss her then. Now, suddenly, he wanted that again.

Even aside from the desire, he felt reluctant to leave her.

He was losing his mind.

"I've been a wild outlaw for a long time, remember?" she told him, and her eyes told him she knew what he was thinking. "I can take care of myself, Black Fox."

"See that you do," he said gruffly.

"I'll meet you right back here," she said.

He walked past her to his horse, tied on the canteen, and mounted up.

"I'll be back directly," he said.

"All right," she said.

Then there was nothing he could do but leave her.

Yet he was in town, riding down the middle of the main street, listening to the noise and watching the traffic of a Saturday afternoon before his mind left her, too. He was in deep trouble. After only parts of two days and one night of riding together, he felt strange without her beside him.

He tried to ignore the feeling. Immediately, he set his thoughts firmly on the task ahead and didn't let them waver again. It was Saturday, the town was full, and he had business to conduct. He had better pay attention.

He was a Lighthorseman and Sallisaw was a rough town. There could be any number of men here today who would like to see him shot off his horse and lying dead in the street.

Cathleen would really be in trouble if that happened.

He rode down the street scanning both sides of it from beneath his hat brim. Lots of farmers and ranchers were in town, lots of wagons pulled to the side of the street, loading and unloading. Dust blew everywhere from the traffic still moving on the street.

It was early yet, but a few men were going in and out of the two saloons, which, handily, were right across the street from each other. Several more men were standing on the street corners, loafing.

Horses were tied at the hitching rails of almost every establishment, and the lot behind the livery stable held a dozen more. The wagon yard on the other side of it contained a half dozen wagons camped for the night.

Black Fox rode all the way to the end of the one main street, turned around and came back, hunting seriously now that he'd looked over the general situation. There. Burke and Fielding had tied their horses in front of the Tin Whistle, the saloon on the north side of the street.

Neither was much of a drinker, as far as he knew, but sometimes the watering holes were a fine place to come across characters who might have some connection to a lawman's trail gone cold. He rode up to the Whistle, tied his horse beside theirs and went in through the swinging doors that had been tied open to let in the feeble breeze. A fair amount of dust came with it, but no one seemed to mind.

Sure enough, the two lawmen were sitting at a table in the corner, side by side, facing the door. Burke lifted his glass in greeting and Fielding beckoned Black Fox over.

"Never know who they'll let in here next,"
Fielding said, as Black Fox took a chair and
dragged it around so that he, too, could see the
door.

Black Fox leaned across to catch Burke's eye.

"Looks like you're resting, Burke," he said,
needling him a little. "You already have The Cat
out there somewhere chained to the prison
wagon?"

Burke scowled. "Not yet," he said, staring out
the door, "never could pick up the tracks again."

"And no gangs of four bad men hanging
around town drinking to a job well done?" Black
Fox asked.

Burke gave him a dirty look and wouldn't say
another word. He kept looking around the room
as if The Cat would leap up from behind the bar
any minute and he needed to be ready.

"Not yet," Fielding answered for him. "Best
bad man we've heard about since we got here is
Hudson Becker, and he's alone for oncet. Evidently, he's been here in Sallisaw for three days."

"What's he up to?" Black Fox wondered aloud.

"Hirin' a wagon built, looks like," Fielding
said. "That's what the smithy and the wagon
maker both told us."

"You talk to Becker himself?"

"Ain't seen him yet."

"Maybe he's gonna haul his own whiskey shipments all the way from Fort Smith," Black Fox

said idly. "Maybe take a bigger piece of old Tassel's pie."

"Yeah," Burke said nastily. "You Lighthorse better start puttin' a stop to some of this liquor traffic or every Indian in this Nation'll be a falling-down drunk."

Black Fox fought down the quick anger that seared him so he could give Burke a long, lazy look.

"Soon as you white-boy deputy marshals catch Turner's killer you'll have a chance to help us," he drawled. "Reckon that's what we're waitin' for."

Fielding laughed. And, to his credit, Burke gave a sheepish little grin.

"Right now, *I'm* here to help *y'all*," Black Fox said. "Give me a little more information about those tracks you saw at Little Creek."

For the next ten minutes he asked them every question he could think of and found out that the stolen moneybag had been made of white canvas and had contained sixty dollars in gold and American paper money. The tracks had been of unshod horses, three of them weighing maybe eight hundred pounds or so and one tall thousand-pounder with a long stride who had a nick out of the inside of the left rear hoof. One of the smaller horses was a pacer. The rider of the tall horse rode with his weight to the right. The stolen whiskey's brand was Monongahela.

Word was, some of the same tracks had been found at Bootlegger Foster's house.

When Black Fox was satisfied that he knew as much about that shooting and the Little Creek Crossing robbery as they did, he stood up to go.

"We just can't figure The Cat taking on three partners after all this time alone," Fielding said. "But it ought to make him easier to catch."

"Yep," Black Fox agreed. "It ought to do that, all right."

He went out and walked up and down the street a couple of times, but he didn't see Hudson Becker anywhere. Lingering in a shadowy spot where he could see both the wagoner's and the smithy's yielded nothing.

Finally, he ducked into the general store and bought as many food supplies as he judged he could carry in what space was left in his saddlebags. He still had a feeling that the impostor Cat was going to come to Sallisaw or that he would find a clue here but there was no telling where this chase would take them and he had another mouth to feed now. Sometimes, when he was traveling alone, he went long stretches without food but that wouldn't be good for Cathleen, especially since she was still recovering from her wound.

That made him remember, and, as the merchant added up his purchases, Black Fox took a handful of stick candy out of the glass jar on the counter and had him add it to the sum he owed. He only hoped no one had come through the cottonwood grove since he'd been gone.

When he'd paid, he carried his packages to his horse, stowed them away, unhitched Ghost, and stepped up into the stirrup. As he turned the gray's head away from the rail, he glanced up.

A flash of brightness glittered in a window on the second floor of the hotel. A figure shifted quickly into and then out of the opening behind the lace curtain—a woman who was quickly gone.

His stomach clenched. He'd thought he'd seen Cathleen.

It scared him to death. What was the *matter* with him? He had damn sure better get hold of himself.

The horse moved up the street on his own as Black Fox kept his eyes fixed on the window but the woman or whoever had been there was gone. The curtain never moved.

He was imagining things, he was getting light-headed, he needed to eat. He'd only thought he'd seen her because he'd bought the candy with her in mind.

Heading slowly down and then back up the street, he made himself go over the information he'd learned and look for Hudson Becker instead of thinking about Cathleen. Becker was said to be a talkative sort and he might get some kind of a lead out of him. One time, in the process of hauling Becker to jail, another Lighthorse, Means Whitepath, had got him talking and learned of a killing back in the mountains that otherwise never would have been discovered by the law.

Black Fox had almost given up, had almost reached the hat maker's shop, which was the last one at the end of the street, on his way back out to the cottonwood grove, when he spotted the short, stocky form of Hudson Becker walking across the street toward him. Two cowboys rode around him and went on. Black Fox rode up in front of him and stopped.

"Becker," he said. "I'm Black Fox Vann."

"Well, if it ain't the Lighthorse," Becker said. "I know your face, Vann."

Then he squinted up at him suspiciously and asked, "When did you ride into town?"

"Not an hour ago," Black Fox said, "but I already heard you were here getting a new wagon built."

Becker shrugged—as best he could with his arms full of packages. Black Fox looked them over.

"What are you doing?" he asked. "Sneaking into town here with sacks full of whiskey? You're liable to get shot horning in on the saloonkeepers' territory, Hudson."

The bootlegger grinned wolfishly.

"This ain't whiskey," he said. "I'll open up these pokes and show you if you don't believe me. I'm gittin' out of bootlegging."

"No," Black Fox said, "surely not. Don't lie to me, Becker."

"I *ain't*. I'm through peddling liquor."

Black Fox relaxed in the saddle and rested his arm on the horn as if settling in for a long talk.

"What in the world would bring that about?" he asked. "I thought the reason you were having a new wagon built was to haul it by the barrel."

Hudson Becker put on a solemn look.

"You ain't heard? I'm surprised, you being the best of the Lighthorse and all."

"Heard what?"

"We're getting some bad competition, me and Tassel are," he said. "I'm gonna step back and let them have it."

"With all due respect, Hudson, that's hard for me to believe. If my recall is good, I believe you went to jail for bootlegging three different times and served your sentences, only to go right back to it again."

"That's past," Becker said. "Now, I quit. The Cat's done took up bootlegging and I cain't set around and wait for a boy to steal my customers and plow me under."

"No!" Black Fox said.

"I'm tellin' you the truth," Becker said righteously. "You may not know it, but I heard he robbed Pate Moynahan at the Little Creek Crossing last night. Took everything he had."

"See, The Cat hates bootleggers," Black Fox argued. "Hasn't he waylaid and robbed nearly every whiskey dealer in the Nation at one time or another?"

Hudson nodded and narrowed his eyes.

"And don't that make sense when you really look at it, Mr. Lighthorse? Think about it. That boy has done harm to ever one of us."

He took a step closer.

"I'll tell you something that you lawmen ain't figgered out yet. The Cat don't hate whiskey. The Cat hates the rest of us whiskey *sellers*. He wants us *gone*."

Black Fox gave him a skeptical look.

"You don't say."

"I do say," Becker said insistently. "You just look at it straight. The Cat is trying to wipe the rest of us plumb out and have all the liquor trade to hisself."

Black Fox looked at him doubtfully.

"So what? I don't know why you'd let a mere boy back you down like that," he said.

" 'Cause everybody thinks he's a merciful angel to the poor folks," Becker explained, in a tone that said Black Fox should already know that. "They call him a damn Robin Hood."

Black Fox shook his head doubtfully.

"I am tellin' you this for your own good," Becker insisted. "I know nobody can catch that boy but you ought to at least know who's doing the mischief around here."

"So it's not you, huh, Becker?"

"Nope. You Lighthorse don't have to think about me no more."

"What are you going to do for a living?" Black Fox asked.

Becker smiled.

"Farm," he said. "From now on, Mr. Vann, you can count on it. I'm not the man you're lookin' for. I'm on the farm."

"So *that's* why you're getting a new wagon," Black Fox said.

"Yep. Gonna haul watermelons and pumpkins, stuff like that. And that's *all*."

Black Fox lifted his eyebrow and gave him a long look.

"Well, good luck with your farming, Hudson."

He lifted his hand in farewell and rode on at a jog trot even though he wanted to ride straight to Cathleen at a high lope. He could hardly wait to tell her every word that Hudson Becker had said, and see if her reaction might be the same as his.

But when he rode into the stand of cotton-woods he found only the dun mare, all alone, tied to a tree. He searched the little grove, his heart beating faster by the second, only to find nothing and no one.

Cathleen was gone.

# **Chapter 12**

❧

**C**athleen's heart beat so hard and fast it nearly smothered her. She ran the rest of the way across the grassy meadow that rimmed the north side of the town, then sank to her knees at the edge of it to rest a little bit. She stayed there, hidden, for a minute or two, drawing in deep breaths of air and willing strength into her limbs.

When she parted the tall turkey-foot grass and looked in both directions on the road, no one was in sight. The woman in the buggy who had stared at her so steadily was gone, swallowed up by the town, and so was the man on horseback who she'd thought might be the sheriff. Thank goodness.

She stood up and started walking along the

edge of the road toward the cottonwood trees where Little Dun waited. That should attract less attention than running through the grass.

And it should be easier. Thank goodness, her bag wasn't heavy. Fear streaked through her as she acknowledged just how weak she was. Much weaker than she'd have ever guessed, so it was a good thing that she'd partnered up with Black Fox.

Except that now she'd have to explain to him every decision she made and everything she did. The very idea of that galled her thoroughly—she was used to her freedom. Besides that, she had always resented authority, maybe because she'd known very little. Mama had been too sick and overworked and Roger too interested in drinking to give her very much oversight and she'd had pretty much free rein in everything she did.

Black Fox was going to be so mad at her.

But that was all right. She couldn't just give up control of her life completely and turn everything over to him. She had to keep her hand in, didn't she?

Shifting the bag to a more comfortable position on her shoulder, she hurried as fast as she could until she reached the trees. The best she could hope for was that he hadn't come back yet and she could be there with Little Dun, waiting for him when he returned.

Well, he might as well be mad. She could *not*

have simply sat here and waited for him, even if she'd tried. She would've been not only mad but crazy, too, from just sitting around here wondering what was happening in town.

Maybe what she had found would soften his anger.

"Cathleen!"

Scared, she whirled at the sound of his voice, which was right behind her.

Black Fox's big hands enveloped her shoulders. The heat of them came through her clothes as if she were naked.

"You're alone?" he asked. His grip tightened and he pulled her closer, his eyes hot with demand.

"Y-yes. Who would be with me?"

"I thought somebody took you. The dun is here," he said.

Stunned by his touch, by his nearness, by the hoarse sound in his voice that wasn't all anger, Cat stared up at him. She kept trying to read his face.

"I . . . thought she might . . . attract attention," she said.

"Ah, Cat . . ." he said, and he crushed her to him.

She clung to him like a child rescued from an unseen danger.

He thrust both hands into her hair and, for a long moment, held her head against his chest and his hard-beating heart, then he tilted it back and bent to take her mouth with his. Instantly the storm inside him raged through her whole body.

Then the shock of it melted into a bright, shimmering thrill and shivering streams of radiance came to life in her blood. She kissed him back hungrily—surely and confidently now that he'd taught her how to kiss a man—and she stood on tiptoe to press her body to his and be still closer to him.

His strong arm around her back held her nearly off the ground and his other hand cradled the side of her face as if he were holding a treasure. He tasted of trees, elm and cedar, and of Black Fox. The same Black Fox who had kissed her before.

The taste of him always reminded her of the sweet bite of wild honey.

His mouth was still hot as the sun.

And it was fast becoming her world. The sharp, desperate need for more of him came quickly alive, deep in her womanhood, and went shivering through her like the relentless, cold touch of a fever.

He seemed to know that, because he pulled her closer as if to protect her, to warm her.

She tried to lift her arms to put them around his neck but the weight of her now-forgotten bag hindered her. He slipped it from her shoulder and let it drop while he settled her still closer against him and drew the very heart out of her with his kiss.

Cat melded her body to his as if there were not a bone in it and slid her hands over the wide, muscular expanse of his shoulders. It was a wonderful, delightful journey that infused an insatiable desire into her blood through her palms—desire and an overwhelming urge to caress the back of his neck.

That touch made him groan and hold her even closer, caused him to twine his tongue with hers and explore the taste of her as if he were a starving man. Never would she have thought that her fingertips held such power!

Then he tore his mouth from hers and pulled back to look down at her but he didn't turn her loose. His fingers burned their shapes into her upper arms.

"Don't ever do that again," he said abruptly.

"Don't do what?" she asked.

Her lips tingled so, they felt so bruised and sweet and good for nothing but kissing him again. She was amazed they would even move to form words and let her talk.

He held her gaze with his darkly burning eyes—and her fate in his hands. The thought came unbidden, in a whirl of others, a feeling, really: he could kiss her and look at her like this and touch her and encircle her close and safe in his arms and say, "Cathleen" in that low, rough way he had and he would hold her fate, all right. She would do anything.

This couldn't be. She had to be free.

"What is it you're ordering me not to do, Black Fox?" she demanded. "Kiss you back? You grab me and kiss me senseless and I'm not supposed to kiss you back, is that it?"

He dropped his hands to his sides. She wanted them on her again, wanted them holding her, even though she'd been on the verge of jerking away. She needed the heat and the strength of his palms and his fingers and his skin flowing from him into her.

She didn't *want* him to set her free.

"I was . . . overcome," he said hoarsely, his eyes still on hers.

But, this time, he didn't say he was sorry he had kissed her. He *wasn't* sorry, and he could see that she wasn't, either. His eyes told her that. It must be written all over her face, plain to see, that every nerve in her body was still thrumming with what that kiss had done to her and that she was longing, *aching*, to reach for him with everything she had.

He must be feeling that very same way.

A great gladness came over her. Because the kiss was nothing to be sorry for; it was something good, something to be happy for, and to remember. Just as their first kiss had been.

She would cherish the memories, that's what she would do.

"What I'm saying is don't leave when you say

you'll stay someplace," he said, holding her gaze as if to make her promise.

Her natural stubbornness rose in her and she opened her mouth, but he spoke again before she could.

"We have to be able to trust each other," he said.

Those words touched her more deeply than she wanted. She had been expecting him to say that she should stay out of the investigation, that he'd be the only one to go into danger, or that he'd do all the work.

No, really, she'd been expecting him to say that she had to follow his orders at all times or else go to jail.

Tears sprang to her eyes for no reason whatsoever.

She turned on her heel, picked up her bag, and walked to a fallen log to sit down.

"I never promised to stay here, if you recall," she said. "I said I'd meet you here."

He crossed the little open space and straddled the other end of the log to sit down facing her.

"I guess you did," he said solemnly, "but I'm not one to split hairs."

"I'm not either, usually," she said. "It was just that I thought if you knew what I was planning, you'd tell me not to do it."

"So where'd you go?"

"Into town."

He stared at her for a minute, as if he couldn't quite believe his ears.

"You knew you could be recognized—if we rode down here from Sequoyah, anyone else could have, too," he said, and the wondering tone he took made her feel even more guilty for the worry she'd caused him.

Yes, he'd been worried and it had been relief that made him kiss her like that. Which meant that he had been *very* worried about her. But she wasn't going to think about that and she wasn't going to accept any guilt.

She had been living alone for months and if she could do anything, she could accept life and see the truth of it. He was a famous lawman and he was worried sick about losing his prisoner. He had caught The Cat and that would put a big feather in his already famous cap.

If she got away from him now, it would knock a big hole in his great reputation as soon as Burke and Fielding heard the story of her calling Glass out at his store and put that together with the girl they'd met riding beside Black Fox. She had never been one to fool herself and she wasn't going to start now.

He might have kissed her out of relief, but it was relief for his lawman's renown, not her safety, not her as a person. She must believe that.

*That* was what she must remember when she

looked at his full, sensual mouth and longed to taste it again.

His very next words confirmed her thought.

"You took a chance on Burke and Fielding seeing you," he said, beginning to lecture. "By now they could've heard about you calling Glass out of the store."

"Yes," she said tightly, "and then they'd have been looking for you to find out why you didn't tell them who I was, wouldn't they?"

He shrugged, as if he didn't care about that.

"That would've shot a big hole in your precious reputation," she said nastily, taunting him.

She hated that tone in her voice. She hated that she couldn't just accept things the way they were and go on. This wasn't even normal behavior for her.

But she couldn't seem to stop herself.

"Everyone would be talking about you running all over the country with a woman captive but not acknowledging the fact," she said. "They'd be wondering what you'd been doing with me."

He brushed that away as if it were a pesky fly and looked down at her bag.

"What have you brought from town?"

"This," she said, bending over to open it.

She brought out a bottle of whiskey. Black Fox stared at it.

"Where did that come from? What did you do, rob the saloon?"

"No. Hudson Becker's hotel room."

Shaken as she was by the way he was looking at her, she still had to laugh at the expression that came over his face.

"You don't have to look so astonished," she said. "You do know I'm a burglar by trade, don't you?"

He didn't bother to answer.

"What the hell," he said. "So I did see you."

It was her turn to be astonished.

"You *saw* me?"

He glared at her with a face like a storm cloud about to break.

"Through the window," he said. "Your hair caught the sunlight."

"I can't *believe* you could see me," she cried. "I wasn't in there five minutes."

"What were you doing in there at all?" he said sharply. "How'd you even know Becker was in town? Explain yourself, Cat."

He crossed his arms and waited, pinning her gaze with his as if he thought she was lying.

She crossed hers and glared back.

"You sound suspicious as if I'm in league with Becker or something. What's the matter with you?"

"What's the matter with *you*? The man could've caught you in his room and killed you. Or worse."

That made her feel a little better. Which was stupid.

*Wake up, Cat, you're thinking like a silly girl. Black Fox's feelings mean nothing. The important thing is finding out who killed Donald Turner.*

"I was going down the alley on my way to the livery stable," she said, "intending to see if I recognized any of the horses stabled there."

"What a plan," he said sarcastically. "Well worth risking your life for."

She bristled and glared at him.

He set his lips in a straight line and listened.

"If I'd recognized any horse, it might've given us someone to follow," she said, "assuming that my impostor was someone from up around Sequoyah, and that Burke and Fielding were right about the direction he took from Little Creek."

"So?"

"You sound like you think I'm the dumbest person in the world," she said. "Stop it. I've survived, haven't I?"

*Why do you even care what he thinks? Stop this, Cathleen.*

He glowered, his eyes blazing.

"Spit it out," he said, "it's *your* hide we're trying to save here, remember?"

"Exactly," she said, sarcastically, "which is why I was in Sallisaw looking around, thinking that I might come across someone drawing the mark of the cat on the wall of a building."

"And *did* you?" he said, mimicking her tone.

"I was near the hotel, walking fast with my hat pulled down, when Hudson Becker, of all people, kicked the back door open. He was coming out with his arms full of packages."

"Right," Black Fox said judgmentally, as if this were some kind of test and she'd answered one question correctly.

She stared at him harder.

"He didn't see me because he was looking back, calling to someone to get his bill ready, that he'd be back in a few minutes to pay."

For once, he stayed silent, so she went on.

"The clerk said, 'Yes, sir, Mr. Becker, that's Room Nine, isn't that right?' So it was easy as could be."

Black Fox was still looking at her as if she'd lost her mind.

"And you sneaked into his room just because it was his? Because this was one person in Sallisaw you recognized from Sequoyah?"

"Partly," she said, "but also because I thought it was strange for a ruffian like Hudson Becker to be staying in a hotel instead of camping out."

He nodded as if he'd already thought that, too. Well, good. Maybe he'd find out she wasn't so dumb, after all.

"Also, it was not like Becker to be alone," she said. "I've never seen him without a half dozen hangers-on. And, judging by the stuff he was carrying, he'd obviously been spending some money."

Black Fox studied her hard, his black eyes telling her nothing but trying to see straight into her mind. No, he was looking right through her, thinking about what she'd said.

His dark eyes narrowed as he looked at her prize again.

"Do you think this bottle came from the wagon master at Little Creek Crossing?" she asked.

"Yes," he said slowly, "I do."

"Because . . ." she said.

"Burke and Fielding said the whiskey on the wagon was all Monongahela. But it's just a gut feeling I have because it could have come from anywhere."

"Does the saloon have any of this brand?" she asked.

"I don't know. They'd sell it by the bottle, but they'd want a pretty penny for it and I'm doubting Becker would pay a premium price when he could get something else cheaper."

Cathleen nodded. "He doesn't strike me as a man of really fine taste," she said.

Black Fox smiled. "Me neither," he said. "Besides that, I talked to Becker in the street and he brought up the subject of the robbery at Little Creek Crossing."

"Well," she said, "that in itself doesn't mean anything. Those two deputies themselves have brought the news of the robbery and Foster's shooting to Sallisaw."

"Right," he said, and the affirmation warmed her blood out of all proportion to its worth.

*What he thinks of you doesn't matter, Cathleen. Only as it speeds things up in finding Turner's killer. That's the only importance Black Fox's opinion has to you.*

"But thanks to you," he said, "we know that this brand of whiskey, at least, was in his possession."

Her treacherous heart bloomed with happiness in her chest at the praise.

"Why were you talking to Becker, anyhow?" she said.

"He wanted to visit with me," Black Fox said. "To spread the word that *you* are going into boot-legging and he's getting out of it."

Her jaw must've dropped a mile, because he laughed.

"Becker complains that he can't compete with you," he said, "because everyone who thinks you're Robin Hood will buy liquor from you, and he and Glass will have no customers left."

It took a minute for all that to soak in, partly because it was so unexpected and crazy and partly because she was watching the way Black Fox's face changed when he laughed. And the light that came into the depths of his dark, dark eyes when he did.

*Stop watching him and his looks, Cat. Stop feeling entirely. Try to think, darn it.*

"So," she said, her excitement rising as she thought it through, "Hudson is trying to get all the lawmen after me for murdering Foster. Is he my impostor, do you think? He and his men robbed the wagon master? And shot Foster and killed him?"

"Could be," he said, "but townspeople told Burke and Fielding that Becker's been in Sallisaw for three days."

"He could've ridden from here to Foster's and Little Creek Crossing and then back again," she said. "It'd take most of the night, but it could be done."

"That's what I'm thinking."

Black Fox held her gaze with a long, straight look.

"And Tassel Glass didn't do it—even though he actually has more reason, since you're openly trying to kill him—because he knew you were with me last night."

Cathleen grinned mischievously.

"Maybe he took that chance to implicate you, too," she said, teasing him. "Maybe our friend Tassel thinks he can get us both hanged."

They laughed.

"It might be both of them at different times," Black Fox said. "Maybe now Hudson's taking a page from Tassel's book. Tassel had a lot more reason to kill Donald Turner and leave your mark there than Hudson did because Turner was carrying a warrant for Glass's arrest."

"The Fort Smith deputies were after him for bootlegging? When did they start policing the Nation for that?"

"Not for bootlegging. For shooting an Arkansas whiskey supplier. White man."

"And Tassel was furious with me yesterday for calling him out," Cat said. "Do you think, by any chance, they could be working *together*?"

"Stranger things have happened, but I doubt it. Maybe they're both just seizing on The Cat as a scapegoat to keep the law from looking too closely at them."

"Maybe. But why in the world would Becker tell you that I'm a bootlegger when I've poured out whiskey and done everything I could think of to put them all out of business?"

"That's just it," Black Fox said. "He says you want them gone so you can have all the customers to yourself."

Cathleen raised her eyebrows.

"Well, there's a certain logic in that," she said. "Who knows? Hudson may be smarter than we give him credit for."

"He may be."

They thought about it for a little while longer.

Suddenly, almost at the same moment, both of them got to their feet.

"Smart or stupid, he's all we've got," Cathleen said, and Black Fox finished her thought, "and he's leaving town."

They headed for their horses like old partners who didn't need to say another word.

*Good. You can do this, Cat. Remember it's only partners that y'all are. And only until you prove who killed Donald Turner. After that, you still have work to do.*

Hudson Becker led them back north and up the road they came in on. He traveled at a good pace, but he did slow at unpredictable times and Black Fox and Cathleen almost ran up on him twice.

"I should've left that bottle of whiskey," Cat said regretfully. "He's suspicious that somebody's following him now that it's missing from his room."

"Maybe, but he probably thinks the desk clerk or the maid took that," Black Fox said. "He's not used to going it alone, as you said. He might be expecting some of his men."

An hour or so later, when they caught a glimpse of Becker again, he had two companions.

"It must be nice to always be right," Cathleen

said, teasing him. "No wonder you guessed I'd come to Sequoyah so you could catch me."

He flashed her a slanting glance and a grin that lit his whole face.

"Aren't you glad I did?" he asked lightly.

She raised one eyebrow and returned his look.

"I'm reserving judgment until we see how all this turns out," she said.

"Better think about it," he said. "Remember that shooter on top of Glass's store."

"Willie would've saved me," she said lightly. "He was drawing his gun when you rode in there and messed up his plans."

"And yours, too, I'm thinking," Black Fox said wryly.

"We need to see about Willie," she said. "I feel bad that he got shot for me."

"He's sitting propped up against a stack of pillows somewhere with either my Aunt Sally or that girl in the calico dress waiting on him hand and foot."

"I hope it's the girl," Cat said. "That's another thing I feel bad about—not loving him back."

"Forget it. He just likes thinking he's in love," Black Fox said.

"Well, thanks a lot," she said. "I thought it was my beauty that he couldn't resist."

"Nope. He can't resist trying to be a hero and you seem to need one."

"*What?*"

Astonished, she jerked around in the saddle to stare at him.

"I do *not* need a hero," she said. "How do you think I've survived the outlaw life? Taking care of myself!"

He shook his head.

"Willie helped you with your wagon, I found you shot and bleeding to death, and we both helped you out of that ruckus you caused with Tassel yesterday."

"Not so! You two caused that 'ruckus' to go wrong. If it hadn't been for y'all interfering, Tassel would be dead by now and I'd be done."

"You'd be done *for*," he said. "You had bitten off more than you could chew that time, Miss Cat. You might as well own up to it."

"I'll do no such thing," she cried. "If this isn't just like a man! Women do the work and the men try to take the credit."

He held her gaze for the longest time, shaking his head a little, smiling to himself about things he didn't tell her.

"Don't you be laughing at me," she said, shaking her finger in warning.

But suddenly, she wasn't mad anymore.

He wasn't making fun of her, she could tell. Actually, there was something sort of admiring about the way he looked at her.

And there was a tender light in his dark eyes.

She smiled back at him. It was a moment she

would never forget, if she lived to be a hundred. It seemed to come upon them so naturally there was no way to explain it.

She wouldn't get used to times like this. She wouldn't let herself.

# Chapter 13

⟨⟩

**B**ecker and his men didn't stop until nearly dusk, when they reached the roadside establishment called Possum's. A longtime fixture at the ford of Red Dog Creek on the Sallisaw/Sequoyah Road, the long porch of the place had followed the bend of the creek in a rough crescent shape as the proprietor, Possum Harnage, periodically made a ramshackle addition to one end or the other.

This evening, business was good. A freight wagon stood in the campground a few yards on up the road where customers sometimes went to drink from the bottles of moonshine Possum made or to eat the food his helper had cooked.

Several horses stood outside in the dooryard along the rail where Becker and his men tied theirs.

Black Fox and Cathleen held their mounts back in the brush, out of sight, as they watched their quarry get down and go inside.

"They went into the tavern," she said. "I could go into the store and maybe hear what they say."

The thought of her in the same room—no matter how big it was—with Becker and his cronies made his skin crawl.

*Well, then, Vann, how will you feel when you turn her over to the court at Fort Smith?*

He wasn't going to let himself think like that. His interest in her was purely professional.

"You're my prisoner," he said. "You go where I say."

She whipped her head around to burn him with her hot, green eyes.

"I'm not guilty of murder and you know it now," she said. "You have no right to control me."

"You're guilty of stealing," he shot back, "and escape from an officer of the law."

"You know I won't run off," she said incredulously. "Have you forgotten I didn't when you left me earlier today? What's the matter with you?"

*I can't bear the thought of you in danger, that's what.*

"Remember Becker and his men know you by sight," he said.

She swept her gaze scornfully away from him—as if that were the most pathetic excuse in the world—and fixed it firmly on the open door of Possum's.

"I've got to get in there," she said, half under her breath.

She bit her lower lip and narrowed her eyes in deep thought. Not a trace of fear showed in her face.

"I recall several windows along the back," she said. "And Possum's too tight to light it all. I'll wait until it gets a little bit darker."

Black Fox's stomach clenched.

"I know you well enough to know that there'll be no stopping you short of tying you to a tree," he said. "So get ready."

She hit him with her wide-eyed gaze.

"I know you well enough to know you're fair," she said. "And it's only fair that I get every chance to prove these are the men who've been using my mark."

"What proof will it be in court if you say one of them jumped up and proposed a drink to the fact they shot Donald Turner in the back? Since you're the one whose mark was found at the scene of his murder?"

She clenched her jaw in anger.

"You know I'm not a liar," she said, through her teeth. "You know that, Black Fox."

"It'll be the three of them, plus maybe Possum and whoever else is in there, against one."

"Answer me," she said, her anger rising so that she laid her hand on the gun she wore, "tell me I'm a liar if you think I am."

Her spunk just never ceased to amaze him. It tickled him.

Any other woman would be batting her eyes at him and begging *him* to go in there to look for proof. Any other woman he'd ever known would be begging to get down and rest after all the hard miles they'd ridden that day. Any other woman would not be challenging his opinion of her.

But this was The Cat.

Of course, any other woman wouldn't be in this fix. This girl had been out of her mind for a long time. Too long, living alone with grief and rage.

She wasn't sad now, though, and she wasn't scared. Her eyes were snapping with challenge and the rage was directed against him. She had sand, all right, and he really believed she would dare anything.

Somehow, it just made him want to smile but he tried not to because he knew it would just make her madder.

"You're fast," he said thoughtfully. "I don't doubt that, since you judged yourself ready to take Glass on. But I'm faster, Cathleen. Don't try me."

That mollified her some.

"I *do* have good judgment," she said, relaxing a little. "I'm glad you know that. And I don't want to kill you, Black Fox."

At the way she said his name, a small burst of gladness raced through him. He didn't quite know why.

"I thank you for that," he said solemnly. "But did you ever think it might be the other way around?"

Her eyes shone bright in the growing dusk.

"You wouldn't kill a woman," she said flatly, "if you hate so much to take one to jail."

"And you think I'm a good enough shot only to wing you?"

"I know you are," she said, in that same, sure tone.

She sounded as if she knew him well. And she looked at him almost fondly, as if she were glad about that.

"Don't worry," she said. "I don't mean for them to see me and they won't. I've had a lot of practice at being a burglar, you know."

His throat tightened.

"That's a dangerous business, sneaking around men who are known to be killers and thieves," he said. "Let's . . ."

The sound of hoofbeats on the road interrupted

him. Two riders were coming from the north, one on a loud, black-and-white paint and the other on a dark chestnut Tennessee Walker.

"I recognize both those horses from the ones carrying Becker's gang the day you got shot," Black Fox said, watching them come. "Those two renegades are here because he is."

"Maybe it's a pow-wow," Cathleen said. "If they're planning some new jobs for The Cat, we'll find them out! This is our chance to find out if Becker's our man."

"Maybe they're just here to sell something they've stolen," he said.

She thought about it.

"But they wouldn't *all* need to be here for that," she said. "I think they're going to steal something or shoot somebody else tonight and leave my sign."

They looked at one another, each pondering what further argument to make. Then she gave him a smile that nearly blinded him.

"I have to protect my reputation, Black Fox," she said. "You understand, don't you?"

He couldn't endure that kind of heat from her eyes without reaching for her. He couldn't watch her beautiful lips and not kiss them.

So he turned and scanned the road in both directions until he felt sufficiently strong to look at her and risk the force of another smile.

"Flirting will get you nowhere," he said.

The words came out in a much lighter tone than he had intended.

"Aw, come on," she said.

She smiled again and he decided he might have misjudged his own strength.

"You've never seen a demonstration of my burglaring skills."

"Yes, I have," he said wryly. "You forget I saw you light out of Tassel Glass's store like the devil himself was after you."

She looked shocked.

"But I was in broad daylight then," she cried. "I went in there openly, which was my mistake. It nearly got me killed, too."

"Yes, it did. But what you have to realize is that it's even more dangerous to get caught sneaking around and eavesdropping on a bunch of thieves and murderers."

"I won't get caught," she said passionately.

The determination in the set of her pretty chin was unmistakable.

"I *will* have to tie you to a tree," he said. "There's no way around it."

She knew exactly what to say. She knew exactly how to look at him, her eyes wide and innocent. And filled with sureness of his understanding.

"It's my *life* at stake, Black Fox," she said quietly. "You are a man of honor and if we don't find who killed that marshal, you'll take me in and I know it."

Searching his eyes for confirmation, she smiled sadly.

"No matter how much you hate to have to do it, you will," she said. "And I wouldn't respect you as much as I do if you didn't."

He wanted to deny it. If *words*, simply words, would keep her safe, he would say them.

But he couldn't. She was right and she knew it.

"I have a right to try to save my own life," she said. "And you know it'll come down to a hanging if you take me in. Somebody else using my sign once or twice wouldn't create enough doubt in the minds of Judge Parker or a jury."

The light went out of him as if she'd snuffed a candle. His throat felt so tight he didn't think he could speak.

But he nodded.

"Then you'll not give me any trouble about going in there to Possum's?"

"No," he said, and found that that was all he could say right then.

*He* was the one who was out of his mind—both for the way he was feeling and for letting her go in there.

"I can do it," she said reassuringly, as if she could see the fear he was trying to hide.

He looked away. The riders were stopping at Possum's and getting down.

Finally, he got control of himself again.

"At Glass's store I counted seven men with Becker," he said. "That may have changed by now, but maybe not. The other three might show up here in a little while."

"Traveling in twos and threes so as not to draw attention," Cathleen mused, "way off down here so far from where they usually roam. I call this an important meeting."

She turned and poured that clear, green gaze on him.

"Don't you agree, Black Fox?"

"We could give it a little while and see if the last three come, too. Let it get full dark," he said, and cleared his throat when his voice came out raspy. "You can't stay too long once you get in there and if they're not talking business because they're waiting for the others, it'll be wasted effort."

Slowly, reluctantly, she nodded agreement.

"Come on," he said, "there's a little cove down here in the bend of the creek. We can leave the horses there."

She turned her horse to go with his.

"You can stay and hold them," she said.

He whipped his head around to look at her.

"No. I'm standing lookout for you."

She frowned.

"If eight of them found you, they'd kill you, Black Fox."

They looked at each other while the horses walked toward the chattering creek.

"Even five of them," she said thoughtfully, "might be enough."

He felt a quick flash of amusement. And maybe something more. Something else, some kind of pleasure akin to pride or happiness.

"You think I could handle four of 'em?" he asked.

She nodded wisely.

"I really think five," she said seriously, although her eyes were smiling into his, "but you might need just the least bit of warning."

The horses walked on.

He smiled at her and realized that he could not rest if he let her go into Possum's alone.

"Then I'd be the perfect one to sneak up and listen in on their palaver," he said. "How about if we turn it around and you're the lookout?"

Her eyes darkened.

"Don't start that," she said. "You promised not to give me any trouble."

"Cathleen, if they slipped up on *you* without warning . . ."

She interrupted, "They won't. I know what I'm doing."

His jaw tightened.

"Don't look like that," she said. "You'll be right outside and it'll make me stronger to know it. I'm not accustomed to *any* help."

"Yeah," he said.

"And I'm not accustomed to anybody caring whether I come back alive," she said quietly. "Thanks, Black Fox."

The grateful innocence of her tone grabbed him by the throat and tied a knot in his breath.

He looked ahead to the sweet cove hidden by the weeping willow trees.

"All right, then," he said.

But nothing was all right and he wondered if it ever would be again.

Cathleen threw one leg over the windowsill, felt around for a place to set her foot, and waited for her eyes to become accustomed to the deeper darkness. Outside, there were stars and a three-quarter moon. In this room at the back of the building, it was pitch black except for a slanted line of light at a door in the opposite corner.

The best she could tell, it was a storeroom of some kind. She wanted to take a last look back to try for a glimpse of Black Fox but she wouldn't let herself. So she stayed there, bent almost double to get through the small opening, staring inside while she tried to slow her breathing.

Faint voices sounded somewhere deeper inside. She felt what seemed to be the dirt floor under her boot and slipped on inside. It took forever to feel her way among the scattered boxes and barrels to the faint line of light.

From there, she couldn't distinguish a word from the low buzz of conversation she judged to be coming from the tavern room. Her legs trembled a little but she made herself look, and then step, into the hallway. The light, as well as the sound, was coming from the tavern.

She took a deep, bracing breath and slipped along the shadowy hallway toward the light and the voices. Her limbs trembled a bit and her lungs wouldn't let go of the air she'd taken in.

*This is no time to lose your grip, Cathleen. Go, go.*

And so she did, watching the shadows, lifting her feet carefully, wishing she'd left her boots off and outside every time they scraped a bump on the floor or hit the wall. She hadn't mentioned it to Black Fox, but she wasn't accustomed to thieving in inhabited places. It was a whole different proposition.

Or maybe the reason she was shaky and obsessed with danger was because so much was riding on what she might hear.

*Yeah. It's your life at stake, Cat.*

Finally, after an age of creeping through the roughly built addition to the main structure, she stood plastered in the corner at the doorless opening to the tavern. It was one step up from where she was and it had a wooden plank floor.

She was on the front side of the long building now, keeping out of the spilling light that fell the other way. However, in spite of being in the shadows she was fully visible to anyone coming from the direction she had come. For the first time, she noticed that there was also an opening at the end of the hallway, a crooked rectangle filled only with the night.

Pray God no one came in that way.

Her teeth tried to chatter but she set her jaw against them. It couldn't be helped; there was nothing more than shadows to hide her and she couldn't hear from any farther away.

After listening for a minute, though, her heart sank. Somebody called, "Possum, pour me another one."

A different voice told a card player, "Show your hand."

Her heart sank. There were several occasional voices, even a hum of conversation, but Becker and his men weren't distinguishable. She had risked all this danger for nothing.

Weak with desperation, she sank back against the wall.

"I'm havin' the sideboards of the wagon reinforced," someone said.

Through the wall. She was hearing this voice through the *outside* wall, which was made of poorly covered pine slats.

"So when we set the ambush, some of us will be hidin' in the wagon bed?"

Wagon. Becker was having a wagon built.

The first voice answered. "Yeah. And the rest'll be scattered in the woods along the edge of the road."

She knew that voice, almost. No, she *did* know it! It was Becker's rough way of talking, only in a quiet tone, not in a yell the way it had been at the cave that night she'd been shot.

Instinctively, Cat turned her head and pressed her ear hard against the rough wall.

"What about a couple of men on the bluff?" another man asked.

"Yeah," Becker said. "One on the ledge on the east side and the west one on the lookout rock to give us the heads up."

"Seven of us can do it," another voice said. "They likely won't be more than a driver and two outriders with the shipment."

"Right," Becker said. "And Glass and a couple of his men to accept it and take it on into Sequoyah."

There was a buzz of conversation that was too low for Cat to catch many words, then Becker spoke again.

"Whaddya think, boys?" he said.

"I think Tassel Glass is gonna burn this Nation down huntin' fer The Cat," someone answered.

"That's *only* if he's not there for th' ambush," Becker said. "If he is, he better not get out of the gap alive or *I'll* be huntin' *y'all*."

"We'll git 'im, Boss."

"Yeah. He ain't takin' over all the damn Cherokee whiskey trade and gittin' away with it."

"He'll wish he never started no blood feud."

Dear Lord. Becker and his men were on the *front porch*. She could've heard them better if she'd stayed outside in the yard and never risked coming into Possum's building at all!

Somebody scraped a chair against the floor just inside the tavern end of the huge room that included the store and the pawnshop that were some of Possum's many enterprises. Cat shrank back into her corner as far as she could, but whoever got up apparently went the other way.

Fear surged through her anyhow. If she was caught, everybody in the place would gather around, including Becker. They were talking blood feud here, and she would bet anything, even her precious Little Dun, that when Glass's killing happened it would be signed with the mark of The Cat.

Becker would have to have her dead or keep her with him to prevent her having an alibi. The law and Glass's men would all be after her once the deed was done.

A chill burst into her blood and flowed deep into her bones.

She wasn't used to this—being a pawn in someone else's game. What she was used to, what she

wanted, was to be invisible again and unknown.
Unnoticed.

Free and alone.

Except for Black Fox. Sudden longing for him
tugged at her heart, tried to pull her away from
the wall and out of this place.

Stubbornly, she fought it and stayed where she
was. The only person she could depend on was
herself and this was her chance to find out even
more about Becker's plans.

"How much whiskey do you expect it to be,
Boss?"

Becker answered, she could hear the rumble of
his voice but his words were too low to make out.

"Hey, what the *hell*?"

Those words were crystal clear and they were
*not* outside the building.

Cat whirled around to see a man standing in
the open doorway at the end of the long hall, staggering a little and reaching to the wall for support.
His other hand fumbled at his side and came up
with a handgun.

She could see him outlined against the moonlit
night as he made slow progress toward her, waving his weapon.

"Somebody there?" he called, looking straight
at her, hiding in the shadows. "Martin, that you?"

For the space of two heartbeats, she froze.

*Run, run, run! Get out of here or it's all over! He'll*

*shoot. With a drunk's crazy luck, he might hit what he's aiming for.*

Still she couldn't move. She would have to run right toward him.

If only Black Fox . . .

*You can't let him be right about this. You told him you could come in here and not get caught. He'll never let you out of his sight again.*

Her little voice of truth was browbeating her.

But somewhere, in another part of her, was an even stronger feeling.

*Get to Black Fox and everything will be all right. All you have to do is get to Black Fox.*

She bolted almost before she knew her feet would move. As she ran, she watched for the door of the storeroom in the dark and held her hands out in front of her so she wouldn't miss it.

It was farther than she'd thought and the drunk wasn't more than an arm's length from her when she found the line of light again—this time from the moon and starlight coming in the window. He fired and the blast of the gun roared in her ears.

She plunged through the doorway, rushed into the room and bumped into a stack of boxes. When she drew back, she knocked into a barrel.

"Wait just a minute, you thievin' son of a bitch!" the drunk yelled.

Then he was in the room with her, slamming her against the door.

"Who are you?" he called. "Hey, Marty? Wait a *minute!*"

Cathleen made it to the window. She barked her shin and rammed a splinter into the heel of her hand, but she threw her leg over the windowsill and bent her body over it to fall out into the night, shoving with her other foot as if to push herself as far away from the building as she could. With a thud, she landed on her side in the dirt, already damp with dew.

Before she could even absorb the shock, she was scratching and scrambling for purchase and, finally, after what seemed ages, hit her feet running. She didn't dare call out for Black Fox, but surely he would see her.

"Marty!" the drunk roared, from the open window behind her. "Wait. You owe me five dollars, you little skunk!"

He must've had two guns. He started shooting and the reports seemed to go on forever, but it may have been only the five rounds that would have been left in the six-shooter.

Once, she heard the zing of the bullet, and once again, something hit a rock or a tree somewhere behind her and ricocheted. He could be a hundred percent accurate, drunk or sober, she didn't know.

She wanted to look back, for her own protection, to see if he had roused the whole population of Possum's tavern and store but she didn't dare slow enough for that. And she didn't dare take her eyes off the way before her. She could see fairly well in the moonlit places but in the shadows it was black as pitch.

She ran full out in spite of that, pursued by far more than the gunshots of a staggering drunk who'd mistaken her for somebody else. Now that she knew what it was to take a bullet, she had a sudden conviction that she wouldn't be able to survive that again.

That was stupid. She wasn't afraid of pain. She knew she could take it.

But the night was closing in around her and it didn't feel friendly, as it usually did. It felt like a strange, faraway place she didn't know. A foreign place where she was alone.

All she knew for sure was that the trees were the only real cover she could find. She had to concentrate on getting to them, even if they were filled with an even deeper blackness.

When she reached the pines, she stayed at the edge of them and started a big circle around Possum's place to head for the cove where she and Black Fox had left the horses. That way, if Becker or anybody else from Possum's came out to chase her, she could run into the woods and hide.

She stopped once, just for one deep breath, and looked back, searching fast for a glimpse of Black Fox more than for pursuers, but she saw nothing.

Her heart was beating hard enough to smother her and she tried to slow it with her mind but she couldn't.

Where was he standing watch for her? Why wasn't he here on this side of the building where she'd gone in the window?

He would meet her at the horses, though. Surely he would head back there.

She cast one more longing look at the moonlit grassy space behind the store, willing every shadow to be him. He wasn't here. She had no sign of him. She had to get back to the cove.

"Marty, you're a high-ridge rider and a no-good thief," the drunk man yelled. "I aim to get that five dollars back and I'm takin' it out of your worthless hide."

Forcing her feet to move and her head to turn to watch where she was going, she began to run again. For distraction from the fear that was tearing at her lungs, she forced her mind to work.

He sounded so clear he must be hanging half out the window she'd jumped through. Judging from his condition, who would've thought he could navigate through that dark, cluttered room?

Maybe nobody would pay any attention to him because he was drunk.

What an irony that she had taken all that risk and snuck into Possum's place when she didn't have to! She could've heard much, much more of what Becker and his men were saying if she'd have hidden under the porch or in the bushes that grew alongside it.

But distractions could only hold her for so long. She didn't even care about any of that.

Where had Black Fox been all this time? Where was he now?

Had Possum or some of his lawbreaking customers come across Black Fox somehow? He could be lying helpless right this minute, hit over the head. Or worse.

It could be that she should be retracing her steps and going back to find him.

Her legs went weak with the longing to see him and know he was all right. But really, she just wanted to hear him say that *she* was all right.

She tried to put all her energy on running and watching where she was going but the new fear was sapping her in spite of her best efforts. *Fear* was what was pursuing her. It was as if all the risks she had taken so lightly in the last months had come back to haunt her now.

Had getting shot done this to her?

Taking in a great gulp of air, she veered around a mulberry bush to go behind Possum's log smokehouse and ran into the moonlight again. She felt it on her back, marking her, making her vulnerable, and she half-expected the slam of a bullet between her shoulders.

A horrible realization chilled her: What it came down to was that she was losing her nerve.

Even though she had escaped detection again, she was more scared than when she'd first gone in at that window.

Because, somehow, she had come to depend on Black Fox. She had become accustomed to having him ride with her. She couldn't believe she had let that happen, but it had.

If she could only find Black Fox, everything would be all right.

# Chapter 14

**H**alfway to the cove, when Cat had made it as far as the east end of Possum's place, something reached out and snatched her by the hair. She fought free with the pure, terror-stricken panic beating in her blood like a clarion call. She was too scared to scream, too shocked to think. Instinctively she whirled in a circle and tore herself loose. Sharp pain from the bramble bush's scratches on her hands and hysterical relief from knowing it wasn't a person who had hold of her both went stinging through her from her skin to her bones.

She jammed the heel of her hand to her mouth and ran on, sucking away the pain, flaring her nostrils to get the air she needed to go even faster. All she had to do was get to Black Fox.

It was too late, she was too far gone to think, when she burst into the cove. She startled the horses. They shied and snorted and pulled back on their tie ropes to roll their eyes at her but when she slowed—her enervated legs were collapsing under her—they knew her and settled again.

For an instant, for one, impossible-to-breathe, impossible-to-accept instant, she couldn't see him. She couldn't find him and she whirled around, straining her eyes to search the whole of the grassy circle bound by trees on the one half and the creek on the other.

Then, like a miracle, when she turned back from the cold sparkle of the faraway stars on the water, Black Fox was there.

Thank God in heaven, Black Fox was there.

He stepped out into the shifting moonlight.

The world was spinning; Black Fox stood in the middle of it, solid as an oak tree, and he was all she had to cling to. With a yearning cry and the last of her strength, she threw herself at him.

He caught her in his arms and she wrapped herself around him, burrowing her head into his chest.

"I couldn't find you," she said, in a tiny voice. "Where were you, Black Fox?"

"Watching your back," he said. "Since I couldn't catch you."

That made her look up but she didn't loosen her hold on him.

"I didn't see you."

"I didn't aim to be seen."

"Did anybody follow me?"

"No. Your drunk came on out to the front porch, hunting for help, as soon as he ran out of ammunition but they all told him to sit down and sober up."

She smiled and her eyes caught the starlight.

"Thank the Good Lord," she said.

Then she dropped her head and burrowed into him again.

"I knew you wouldn't leave me," she muttered, in a barely discernible whisper.

A hot happiness went through him with the words. She trusted him. She depended on him.

She melded herself to him as if she planned never to separate again. Well, he wasn't going to push her away.

She'd been scared half to death, poor kid.

*Kid.*

The word rang false in his head. This was no child he held in his arms. From the minute he had opened her blouse that first night he'd caught up with her, from the instant he'd known that this was no boy, he had tried to tell himself that she was a girl.

She wasn't. Cathleen O'Sullivan was a grown woman. A brave woman, with strength and grit.

Tonight, and yesterday, and many, many times before then, she had dared to take risks that many a man would not have the courage to take.

No matter her age in years, she was a woman, a very unusual woman. A woman he could fall in love with if he wasn't very, very careful.

But right now, he wasn't holding her because he wanted her, he was holding her only because she was so scared. She had just escaped from a dangerous situation and she was needing comfort. He clasped her tighter against him and tucked her head underneath his chin. He buried his face against the cloth covering her hair and held her there.

Black Fox thought, for a long moment, that it was only Cat trembling. He really believed that the poor girl was shaking so hard that he could feel the quake of her panic in his own bones. She needed to lie down. She needed to breathe deeply and take in the fact that she was safe.

However, when he grabbed up the saddle blankets and carried her across to the grassy, brush-hidden spot by the creek, he found that his own legs had gone weak from the fear he had been trying not to admit. It had hit him in the gut when he heard the first shots and it still held him in its grip.

His imagination kept bringing back the sight of her lying in that pool of her own blood the first time he'd seen her. It would've torn him up bad to find her like that again.

Finally, to his great relief, he made it to the pretty spot by the creek and managed to kneel and lay her down without dropping her and without his knees buckling. He'd never been so glad of anything in his life.

Until she clung to him so fiercely that he had no choice but to go down with her.

It brought him an inordinate pleasure that she wouldn't let him go. Vaguely, he wondered at why he needed that—after all, he was a lawman and given to protecting people all the time.

But that was the Nation as a whole, not one person. At that moment, the realization that she depended on him to save her from her fear was somehow more moving to him than any satisfaction he'd ever taken from his job. It was even stronger than his sensual attraction to her.

Until she thrust her fingers into his hair and lifted her face to find his mouth with hers.

Her kiss was urgent and trembly as she was, but relentless, too—desperate for comfort and seeking warmth. He couldn't have resisted it for more than the one heartbeat if his life had depended on it.

It melted him deep into the dew-damp grass and he gathered her closer. And closer. He did it in spite of the fact that her lips seared through him with the truth: he was already too far gone in his need for her.

Their kisses quickly grew wet and wild and so passionate that his blood ran hot.

He must stop this. He must break this kiss that would lead them both to perdition. She had started it and he had to stop it.

But his treacherous arms only pulled her closer and his tongue laved hers, then explored her mouth as eagerly as if he'd never tasted sweet before. Sweet *or* spicy.

She was both. And she pressed against him as surely as if she knew she'd been created just to fit into his arms. Her small, soft shape fit into his big, hard one to send such a sensuous arousal all through his body that he let himself go ahead and fall into the kiss with a passion that made his head dizzy and his pulse wild.

Her tongue answered his in a true, purposeful challenge and desire swept through him faster than the creek could run. Faster than his blood could carry it.

Stronger than his heart could beat.

Deeper than he could control and keep this whole encounter to only a kiss.

He had better put a stop to it now. She didn't know what she was doing. She'd just been scared out of her wits, she was clinging to him out of fear, and one thing had led to another. That was all.

Except that he knew it wasn't. They both remembered exactly how to kiss the other.

She shifted her mouth and let her arms fall loose and warm around his neck with such trust that he felt the weakness take him again. He ought to stop this now. His heart was drifting closer and closer to that terrible danger of caring too much for her. Wasn't he already desperate to protect her, when he should be only concerned with her outlawry and with justice?

But his arms wouldn't move, they wouldn't let her go.

And his lips couldn't leave the full, luscious feast that hers offered him. He ravished her mouth with slow, sensuous strokes, and every thought he'd had faded away.

She moaned and let herself sink against him, melted into him while her mouth turned to hot honey. Lifting one arm with a slow, lazy gesture, she traced her fingertips along the side of his neck. They trailed fire.

He was the one shivering now.

His hands knew exactly what they wanted and they moved with a slow, steady purpose that wouldn't be denied: he had to caress her before he let her go. He pushed off the dark bandana she had tied over her head and brushed her hair back from her face. His hand lingered, lost in the springy, silky curls that twined around his fingers to hold him there.

Without breaking the kiss, he angled his mouth to ravish hers more deeply. She hesitated only for an instant, then responded with her tongue, her lips, her teeth with a passion that set his nostrils flaring. The light, tantalizing woman-scent of her filled his whole body.

He ran his hand down her side, memorizing the shape of her.

Her nipples hardened against his chest where her soft flesh already tortured him. Without breaking the kiss, he pulled back enough to slip his hand inside her shirt and cup her breast.

Yes. She was a perfect handful as he'd known she would be, an exactly right fit for the palm of his hand.

She went still as he held her. She gasped as he caressed her hard nipple with his thumb.

Cat tore her mouth free.

For one, flying second he thought she would put a stop to this and save them.

His hand went still on her breast. But he couldn't make it leave her.

"Don't stop," she said.

Then, shameless and unafraid, she lay back on her elbows, smiling at him.

His blood roared in his ears. The moonlight poured cream onto her skin and the stars threw fire into her hair while her eyes went huge and luminous, dark with the night shadows and the wonder of it all. .

Desire slammed into him like a freight train. Desperately, he reached for power over himself. Power over her.

Power to separate them.

He was Black Fox Vann and if he made love with Cathleen O'Sullivan, he would never be the same again.

He was a Lighthorseman and that was his life and he couldn't make love with an outlaw and let her take it all away.

Hadn't he felt he would die if he couldn't kiss her again?

*So then, Vann, how can you make love with her and then take her to jail?*

But that wasn't even the most hell of it. She was young and she was trembling more since she had felt the touch of his hand on her and she was a fine person and . . .

"No," he said huskily, "you don't know what you're doing, Cathleen."

Her eyes widened with hurt.

"Well, I'm trying to learn, Black Fox."

He smiled, then scowled to try to hide it.

"You've never . . . you're a virgin."

"Yes," she said, her full lips pouting, "but I thought I was doing all right so far."

Could that be a tear shining? Had he made her cry?

"I'm sorry, Cathleen, but I would hate myself if . . ."

She encircled his wrist with her fingers that couldn't quite reach around it and held his hand where it was.

"We don't either one know how long we'll be alive," she said, narrowing her eyes in that way she had when she was being truly stubborn, "and I don't know how long I'll be out of jail."

She sat up, then, reached to touch his face with her other hand, and looked at him in a way she'd never done before.

"Listen to me, Black Fox. Right this minute, I'm alive and I'm free . . . sort of. I'm not going to waste that. I want as much of life as I can get."

It cut his heart to ribbons but it made him smile, too. He did not know why, but he couldn't help but smile at her.

"You don't even know what you're talking about," he said, surprised that he was unable to make his voice more than a hoarse rasp.

"Then why don't you just go right on ahead and show me?" she whispered.

She reached around to his back and pulled the tail of his shirt out of his jeans.

"You were making a good start on my education," she said, and finally let go of his wrist to slide both her hands up under his shirt.

She ran her small palms slowly, slowly, up his spine and over the muscles of his shoulders.

The freight train turned around, roared back and hit him again.

He grabbed her, folded her into his arms and held her closer than ever as he rolled over onto his back to lift her out of the wet grass. Sinking into it himself, oblivious to the damp, heedless of everything but the feather weight of her body lying along his length and the high, firm magic of her breasts calling to him again.

"I see you brought the saddle blankets," she whispered into his ear just before she nipped at it. "What did you have in mind?"

He followed the shape of her with his hands, pulled the tail of her shirt out of her jeans in turn, and stroked the satin skin at the small of her back.

"Making you a dry bed to sleep on," he said.

"I'm not aiming on sleeping," she said.

"Well, then," he said, and kissed the tip of her nose, "in that case, we don't want the night to go to waste."

"No, we don't," she said, in that decisive way that always tickled him. "I reckon you better go on with my lesson."

She was right. They could both be dead by morning. And sometimes life surprised a person in a good way. Maybe it would turn out that he wouldn't have to take her to jail, after all.

Those were his last thoughts that were even halfway logical or sensible. Cathleen was kissing him again, along the line of his jaw this time, then down the side of his neck.

"I reckon you don't need any lessons," he murmured. "It all comes natural to you."

He slid his hands underneath her jeans and caressed her small, naked hips. She whimpered deep in her throat and dug her nails into his shoulders. When she pulled back his shirt and kissed the hollow of his neck, then trailed her tongue up it, he began to undress her in earnest.

Somehow, they got naked and onto the blankets, so tangled up in each other, legs and arms so intertwined, that Black Fox couldn't tell them apart. He didn't want to. All he wanted was to keep his mouth on hers and her hands on him.

Shivers and sparks of desire danced all over his skin. She was shockingly, instinctively, sensual and she moved beneath him as if they'd been together many times. He held back as long as he could. He suckled both her breasts and left a trail of kisses from between them all the way up her throat to her sweet, lush mouth.

But when his hand found the pool of hot, wet invitation between her thighs, he knelt and entered her, carefully, slowly, then clasped her to him and taught her to move in the ancient rhythm of a man and a woman while the creek chattered over the rocks beside them and the night birds called. Until the sweet earth moved beneath them and they left it to fly into the night sky to ride the bursting stars.

Until Cathleen tore her lips from his so she could cry out his name.

Cat woke, blinked at the dawning sun, and immediately squeezed her eyes shut again. She curled up into a ball and grabbed for the blanket that Black Fox's ruthless hand was peeling off her.

"Get away from here," she mumbled, "that's mine."

"I've tried everything else but a bucket of cold water," he said brusquely. "We've got to get going, Cathleen."

She held on as hard as she could but then she had to add her other hand and finally she had to open her eyes, sit up and prop her feet against his to get enough purchase to hang on.

"It's too early in the morning for games," she said.

She shook her hair back and turned her face up so she could look up at him.

His dark gaze met hers and held it.

They both went utterly still. The heat in his eyes made her weak.

It made her remember everything they had done last night.

And it made her wonder. It was desire, yes, but there was something else mixed with it—a large part was his usual stubborn determination, part of it she couldn't read, and part was regret.

"As a matter of habit, I don't usually play games," he said flatly.

She kept on searching his hot dark eyes, trying to gauge exactly what he meant. His sensual mouth was a hard line and his jaw was set.

"I know that," she said quietly. "Neither do I."

Her lips felt nearly too worn and bruised from his kisses for her to be able to talk. Remembering the taste of him, reliving the feel of his mouth on hers, made her long for it again.

"I owe you an apology for last night . . ." he said.

She interrupted, narrowing her eyes at him dangerously. "I wish just once you could kiss me without apologizing for it," she said. "If you'll re-call, Black Fox, I asked for it . . ."

"You didn't know what you were asking for. You're too young . . ."

She broke in again. "And I may never live to be old," she said. "But no matter how long I have, I'll never forget making love with you and I'll never regret one moment of last night. I *know* you didn't intend it as a game."

He startled, then gave a quick, involuntary nod, as if just realizing that that was the truth, which he didn't particularly want to acknowledge.

"I didn't," he said, almost formally. "And I hope it'll prove true that you have no regrets. Now put on your clothes."

He turned his back without another word and went to the horses.

Cat reached for her clothes, threw on her shirt without buttoning it, jammed her legs into her jeans, her feet into her boots and scrambled to stand. She felt as hollow inside as if she'd waked to find him gone.

"I'll saddle my own horse," she said, more sharply than she'd intended. "Leave him. I'll be back in a minute."

The whole time she refreshed herself and washed in the cold water of the creek and finished dressing and tried to bring some order to her hair, her heart felt so heavy it weighted her arms like lead. She needed to feel close to Black Fox—to *be* close to him, physically *and* emotionally—and that realization scared her more than Tassel Glass had ever done.

Sitting there looking up at him in the pale light of the dawn, she had been weak as a child with the longing for more. More of his kisses, of his holding her, of his skin against hers, and, most of all, more of him inside of her and the two of them moving as one. The power of him, the fire of him had awakened every inch of her body and now she'd never be without this wanting for him.

She knew that as surely as she knew what she'd told him was true: she would never regret one instant of last night and she would remember every one of them always. She would always want the feeling of safety she'd had when she buried her face in his chest and held on around his neck as if she'd been running to get to him for all of her life.

That was the only time since she'd been an outlaw that she had been able to give up all the trouble that ruled her. Now she had to go back to thinking about vengeance and the law and danger and being alone.

Nobody had cared a whit about her since her mother had died. Nobody had touched her since then.

Except for Black Fox.

But, with him, she felt the old yearning for comfort and love mixed with something even stronger and more powerful. It was almost more than she could carry around inside her.

Black Fox had set a fire to burning in her—heart, body, and soul—that no other man could ever have done. That was the one other thing that she knew to be true.

They rode right up the middle of the road, headed north, past Possum's place and then away from it at a soft jogging pace. In the campground, the freight wagon still stood, now surrounded by the horses of Becker's gang. They grazed peacefully on their stake ropes while nothing else moved in the long, narrow meadow. Under a big oak tree at the south end of it, several bedrolls lay scattered around a low campfire gleaming orange in the low mist of dawn.

When Cat and Black Fox were well past the place, he broke the silence between them.

"Looks like everybody's got a lot of moonshine to sleep off," he said, and sped up their pace to a long, fast trot. "I thought Becker was knocking them back pretty good for a man in the middle of making a plan."

Cathleen grasped at the topic like a drowning woman, in spite of—or because of—the disappointment slicing through her. She should've already told him what she'd overheard from Becker instead of waiting for him to speak.

Instead of hoping he'd want to talk about last night again.

Hoping that he'd give her one word to show that their lovemaking was something that he, too, would never forget and that he felt something in his heart about it besides worry that she would have regrets.

All she needed to hear, one more time, was that making love with her had not been a game with him. She wanted to know what it had meant to him.

Yet that very hope proved that she was losing her mind and losing it fast. What kind of future could they ever have, even if they managed to prove that Becker killed Deputy Turner and left her mark on the tree? Black Fox Vann was the best of the Cherokee Lighthorse. She was a thieving outlaw, as he had reminded her more than once.

Besides which, she was still going to kill Tassel Glass. Becker wouldn't have to worry about him getting away from the ambush alive.

"You were listening to them on the porch?" she

asked. "When I came running out of there, I looked for you."

She sounded scared all of a sudden, as fear filled her all over again.

Forcing her voice to be steadier, she said again, "I looked for you. I wondered where you were."

He sent her a sharp glance. Up to now, he'd not only been silent but he'd rarely been looking at her.

Which was for the best. Every time she looked at him all she wanted was to lean into her stirrup, reach over and touch him.

For one heartstopping moment he rode his horse closer to hers and shifted in the saddle. She thought he was going to reach for her but he dropped his hand against his long saddle muscles that she could clearly see through the thin jeans covering his thigh.

She wanted to lay her hand beside his and feel those muscles against her palm, to feel his primal power.

Desire flooded through her limbs and made them weak.

She wanted to lie in his arms again and feel him, all of him, skin to skin.

His dark eyes burned into hers.

"I'd hate it if you felt I made a sorry partner right then," he said. "But I saw Becker and his men come out the front door and I thought you'd not know where they were, or if you did, you'd have no way of hearing what they said."

"It was pure luck," she admitted. "I accidentally leaned back against the outside wall and I could hear them talking."

He kept looking at her. Nobody had ever, ever looked at her like that. Not in that utterly sensuous way that heated her blood like a flame.

"I wasn't too scared," she said reassuringly. "I knew you were around there somewhere."

"Good," he said, and he did sound relieved.

But she could still see the shadow of worry in his eyes, too, as he turned away. She didn't want that. She needed him to look at her, to make her feel that he was *with* her.

"I knew everything was all right," she said, and he did meet her gaze again.

Everything wasn't all right now, though. It never would be again unless she could feel his body against hers. She tried not to, but she let her gaze drift down to his mouth and linger there.

Suddenly she couldn't speak. For a minute it seemed that he couldn't, either, and a sense of her own power flooded through her. The hope he'd say something personal came alive again.

"Then you know they're planning to ambush a shipment of whiskey meant for Glass," he said.

The disappointment stabbed her again, too. But at least he kept on looking at her, and although his face told her nothing, she knew—without a doubt—that he wanted to touch her, too.

After all, hadn't their feelings for each other been so powerful that they hadn't even mentioned the fact that Becker existed up until now? Not for hours and hours, not all night long, despite the fact that their real partnership was to prove her innocence. That fact was what she must remember.

Dear Lord, her very *life* was at stake. She had better get her mind on that.

"Yes, I heard them say that," she said, flogging her brain into action, "and I'm thinking they were talking about Limestone Gap."

He gave her an approving nod.

"From that description, it has to be," he said, "and that's where I'm going to set up an ambush."

"To shoot them or arrest them?" she asked.

"That's always the outlaw's decision," he said. "I can't know ahead of time which a man will choose because ninety percent of the time he doesn't know either."

"Do you think Tassel Glass will be there?" she asked.

"My guess is that he will be," Black Fox said. "This shipment has to be a lot of whiskey, maybe more than usually comes into the Nation at one time, or Becker wouldn't be having a wagon built and setting up a daylight confrontation. He's a coward at heart and he knows Glass has more men than he does."

"But Becker will have surprise on his side," she said.

"Right. And surprise is a powerful friend."

"We'll have surprise on our side, too," she said. "But Black Fox, won't we still have to have some help?"

"That's where we're headed now," he said. "I've got to find somebody I can trust to send to Fort Smith for some federal marshals. I hope we can arrest Becker and Glass and both their gangs."

Her heart beat faster. Somehow she had to get Glass first. Rotting in the Fort Smith jail would be far too good an end for him. Besides, he might get out someday.

Her heart began to race, along with her mind. She couldn't do anything before the ambush, though, could she? Black Fox probably wouldn't let her out of his sight but even if he did, she didn't want to ruin the ambush. Becker was the only one who could clear her name for the Turner killing.

She had to be cleared. She wanted everyone in the Nation, especially Black Fox, to know without a doubt that she did not shoot a man in the back. Glass she would kill legally.

"Black Fox, how can we make Becker confess to killing Donald Turner?" she asked.

"It'll help a great deal in your trial if some of Parker's other federal deputies can see your mark on the ambush and Becker's men putting it there," he said. "But you're right. We'll really need a confession to seal the deal."

*Your trial.*

Those words chilled her to the bone. The way he said them made them even worse. His tone assumed that she would have a trial, no matter what.

In that brief instant, he turned into a stranger. A lawman stranger who lumped her right in with the same ilk as Glass and Becker.

She fought down her hurt to stay where he could never see it.

"Who will you trust to go to Fort Smith?" she asked. "And what will we be doing while he's gone?"

"If word gets out to *anyone*, this will never work," he said. "I need Willie to go."

"But he's hurt."

"Maybe it was nothing but a flesh wound."

"We'll have to find out if that girl took him home," she said.

"Yes, and you'll have to stay at the rendezvous I choose while I do that," he said. "We can't take a chance on you being seen around Sequoyah after the way we left there."

"You can trust me, Black Fox," she said, feeling

like the worst of all liars. "I want my name cleared."

*And I also want to spy on Glass.*

She couldn't call him out again, though. Not with no backup at all, since he wouldn't fight fair.

So that meant the ambush had to happen for her to get a shot at him.

But mostly the ambush had to take place to prove that Becker was using her sign.

"I know," he said absently. "I think, counting whichever Lighthorse I can find and whether we have time to bring some in from Fort Smith, six or seven lawmen will be all I can gather. That'll have to do."

"If we find Willie, he'll help," she said, "and counting me and you, that'll be nine or ten."

He gave her such a sharp, slanting glance that she felt she'd been cut with a knife.

"You're not in this, Cathleen," he said. "I'm not taking that risk."

# Chapter 15

Cat's feeling of being abandoned multiplied itself a hundred times. She felt hollow, as if it were a scarecrow sitting in her saddle.

No, her head was what was hollow. She was losing her mind, and wanting to stay close with Black Fox was the cause of it. If only she'd never gone into his arms!

"What kind of risk?" she demanded. "Are you worried that I'll run away or that I'll get shot?"

He shot her an annoyed glance.

"Didn't I just say I'll leave you at the rendezvous while I find out what happened to Willie? Does that sound like I'm afraid you'll run away?"

She blinked back the tears that threatened her—angry, disappointed tears. Stupid tears. She *wanted* him to leave her, didn't she, so she could spy on Glass?

Why couldn't she be independent as she always was and keep her thoughts on getting her revenge as she always did?

"You said we are partners," she blurted, unable to control her tongue any more than her thoughts. "I don't know how you can call yourself a lawman, Black Fox Vann, when you lie and cheat and go back on your word all the time."

"What the hell are you talking about?"

Now he was angry, too.

"I'm talking about the fact that I *am* in on this bootlegger ambush," she said, "if I have to ride out of the woods or a cave or wherever you try to stash me and *shoot* my way into it."

"All right, all right," he said, dismissing her with an irritated sweep of his hand. "You can be a lookout, you can hold the horses, you are in on it."

"*No*," she cried, "I don't want a *girl's* job. Becker and his men are trying to get me hanged. I want . . ."

Black Fox interrupted her tirade and finished the sentence for her. ". . . to know how we can find out the date of this little shindig."

Clearly, he was trying to distract her and it worked. She stared at him, her eyes wide.

"I never once thought about that," she said.

"We don't know what message to send when we find our messenger."

They burst out laughing. All the warmth came back between them and she felt close to him again.

But what difference did that make? What was she doing, going back and forth between loneliness and happiness on the strength of a word from him here and a laugh from him there.

She had to stop this thinking about him and how she felt about him all the time. What she *really* had to stop was making love with him. In addition to destroying her mind, just one night in his arms had also destroyed her usual good control of her feelings.

Usually she could put aside fear and loneliness with an iron hand in order to damage the bootleggers and rob Tassel Glass.

Usually her hatred of Tassel Glass was the dominant emotion in her life. Now it wasn't.

That realization shocked her to her toes. It couldn't be true.

Yet it was.

"*That's* a man's job that you can do," Black Fox said, as they rode along at a faster pace. "What's the best way to find out when Tassel Glass is expecting a big shipment of liquor?"

Cat thought about that.

"Sometimes I've found messages in his desk

from Henry West in Fort Smith. He's usually the one who sells whiskey to Tassel."

"What do they say?"

"Most of them appeared to be answers to notes Tassel had sent to him about where and when to have their men meet."

"Because Tassel would be the one keeping track of us Lighthorse," Black Fox said.

"Yes, he kept track of the Lighthorse and . . ." she said, smiling wickedly, ". . . of The Cat. He thought. Until he realized after I shot up his newly purchased bottles twice on the trail that I was either reading his mail or talking to one of his men."

"Where did they meet?"

She shrugged.

"Different places. Usually not too far from Sequoyah, because Tassel's so greedy he tries to get everything out of West that he can and he always makes him travel most of the way."

"To lessen the chance that Glass will be arrested in the Nation in possession of the whiskey," he said.

"That's right," she said. "But mostly it was his men in danger of that because he usually didn't go pick up the shipment himself."

"He wouldn't want his men arrested either, though," Black Fox said. "He needs them to tend all the irons he has in the fire."

"They never met at the Limestone Gap, to my

knowledge," Cat said. "The place they used most often was the Green Corn Campgrounds on Spunky Creek."

"Limestone Gap is the best place for an ambush on the way back to Sequoyah from there," Black Fox said. "Remember, Becker's like you—he wants Glass to pay for the whiskey before he takes it away from him and he doesn't want any white whiskey merchant involved."

Cat thought about that.

"Right. And who knows? Maybe Becker found out about this whole deal from whoever's selling because he might be his supplier, too."

"Could be."

His eyes twinkled at her as he smiled his beautiful smile that was so rare. It held her gaze fixed on his sensuous mouth.

"Or maybe Becker's like you," he said. "He may've been reading Glass's mail."

She fixed him with her fiercest scowl.

"I'm insulted," she said, trying to sound entirely serious about it. "If you can't quit saying Becker is like me, I'm riding alone."

She lifted her horse into a lope and left him behind.

She would ride ahead of him the rest of the way so she couldn't see his handsome face. When he smiled at her like that it made her heart go right out of her body.

\* \* \*

Black Fox spent the whole way to Sequoyah coming up with a plan, but the minute he really started thinking it through, he knew that he couldn't hide Cathleen as far away from him as the cave, which was the first place that came into his mind as they rode closer to Sequoyah. Anyone could see her; word must have spread that she was The Cat, and Tassel Glass would, no doubt, love to get his hands on her. Anything could happen. He had to keep her close to him but out of sight.

So, when they reached the outskirts of town, he left her in the woods where he had first sat his horse and watched Becker's raid on Glass's store. The first day he ever saw her.

Now, he waited hidden again, this time watching the side shed of the blacksmith's shop where Willie was working, dunking hot horseshoes into cold water. The girl who had run to Willie when the bullet knocked him down was the blacksmith's daughter, according to Black Fox's friend, Jake Mink. Jake didn't talk much and working at the livery stable hadn't loosened his tongue, so he could be trusted not to mention that Black Fox was in town.

He didn't want any questions about what he'd done with The Cat and he didn't want any requests to go after any other lawbreaker. All he wanted was Willie's undivided attention.

Finally, the horse was shod and the customer

rode away, passing by Black Fox's hiding place in the deep shadows of the alley without a sideways glance. He was a white man, of course, since he rode a shod horse, and a stranger to Black Fox. He looked to be respectable, though, and he was dressed like a preacher. Probably a circuit rider missionary who would never be of any concern to the Lighthorse.

Black Fox turned his attention back to his cousin. The blacksmith took off his leather apron, hung it on a post, and walked toward the small house set off in a field behind the shop, leaving Willie alone to sweep up the trimmings. Dusk was falling, most townspeople had gone home for supper and the street was quiet. Black Fox crossed the street, leading Ghost Horse at a walk into the shadows thrown by the blacksmith shop itself.

"Willie," he said quietly, "I need to talk to you."

Willie startled and turned to him.

"Black Fox," he said. "What are you doing here?"

"Looking for you."

"I'm all right." Willie grinned and his teeth gleamed white in the dimness. "The bullet only knocked me down and bled me a little. I sent word to the folks but Mama had to come to town and see for herself I was alive."

"Sounds like Aunt Sally, all right," Black Fox said. "I'm glad you weren't hurt, man."

"I was glad she didn't try to make me go home," Willie said, "but now I wish I'd gone anyway."

"How come?"

"Kinesah is about to drive me plumb crazy, that's how come," Willie said mournfully.

"She's the girl who ran to you when you fell?"

"Yes. Her and her mama acted like I was on my death bed and bandaged me and waited on me hand and foot for a day or two, so *my* mama decided I ought to work for her daddy some to return the favor."

He pulled out a bandana and wiped his brow.

"Kinesah's acting like we're gonna get married," he said, "and I don't know what to do."

"I thought you were looking for a girlfriend," Black Fox said. "You're not hunting a wife?"

"*No*," Willie said vehemently. "I surely am not. And it was *Cathleen* I was sweet on; then you had to go and put her in jail."

Black Fox opened his mouth to correct him, but Willie went right on.

"You ought not to have done that, Black Fox. All she'd done was steal from Tassel Glass, and everybody knows what a cheater he is."

Black Fox shook his head. No way did he have time to argue this with Willie.

"Even if she wasn't in jail, though," Willie said thoughtfully, "I don't want Cathleen for a wife no more than I want Kinesah. Them girls get to tellin' a man what to do and if he won't do every little thing, they bust out cryin'." He mopped his brow again. "I can't take much more of this bossin'."

Black Fox stifled a smile. In fact, he really wanted to laugh, poor Willie was so pitiful.

"You feel good enough to do some riding for me?" he asked.

Willie dropped the broom. "Where to?"

"Fort Smith. But you cannot tell a soul in this Nation—except for the Lighthorse—where you're going or why. Willie, Cathleen's life depends on you keeping your mouth shut."

Willie's eyes went so wide Black Fox could see the whites of them in the gathering dusk.

"I'll do it," he said.

"Along the way, before you leave the Nation, find Rainwater or Adair or any other Lighthorseman. I need them fast."

"What do I say?"

"To the Lighthorse, tell them to get word to as many lawmen as they can."

"All right."

"To Judge Parker, say I need as many federal marshals as he can send to round up two gangs of bootleggers. We can catch them redhanded. There are white-men killers and thieves among them."

"I'm on my way," Willie said.

"When you've delivered the messages, you meet me, too. On your way back, watch for a big wagon load of whiskey coming out of Fort Smith. Rendezvous is Long Man Lake, at the foot of the bluff, *ayanula*. Fast. Tell everyone soon as they can ride there."

"I'm gone," Willie said.

He turned toward the pen full of horses behind the blacksmith shop. Black Fox saw the big paint horse among them.

"He's stout," he said. "But is he fast?"

"Faster than that gray bag of bones you're ridin'," Willie retorted, throwing the words back over his shoulder.

"I can give you supplies from my saddle bags," Black Fox said.

Willie dismissed that with a wave of one hand.

"See you at Long Man Lake," he said.

Black Fox went to the gray, turned the stirrup, stuck the toe of his boot into it, and swung up into the saddle. Night was coming on. He had to get back to Cathleen.

He took the alleys and stayed off the street, except to cross it at the corner as he'd done the day Cat called Glass out. For a moment, when he rode into the trees, he didn't see her but wonder of wonders, she had stayed hidden close to the spot where he'd left her.

"I'm surprised to find you here," he said, with mild sarcasm. "I was expecting to have to rescue you from inside the store where Glass had caught you going through his mail again."

"Hmpf," she said, nudging her Little Dun horse out of the thicket. "I don't believe I needed any rescuing the last time you left me hidden. I got in and out of town on my own hook."

"In Sallisaw, yes," he said dryly, "but the last time you were in Sequoyah town, I believe I carried you out right before you met your maker."

"That's hard to say," she retorted. "I might've mowed them all down."

"And I might've mistaken you for my Aunt Sally," he said sarcastically.

"I did think about searching Tassel's desk," she said, "but I decided the ambush will probably be a week from yesterday."

She pointed her horse in the direction he indicated.

He looked at her incredulously. "Why did you decide that?"

"Lots of times they do their devil's work on Sundays," she said. "I don't know why."

Black Fox thought about it. "Maybe you're right. Becker has his men together but he still has to have time to get his wagon and drive it to the Gap."

"When I was following Glass's men and shooting at the merchandise, I used to think maybe West sent shipments into the Nation on Sunday because he used his wagons and men in Fort Smith during the week," Cat said.

"Could be. Of course, they'd have to have started from Fort Smith early Saturday."

Soon they were heading, single file, through the

woods toward a deer trail he knew that would take them straight southeast to Long Man Lake. Black Fox sent her ahead of him so he could watch their backs.

"Take it slow," he said. "When we cut the trail, I'll tell you."

"I guess I know a deer trail when I see one," she said wryly. "I've only lived in the woods for a year."

"You might not," he said. "It's coming night and you're a white girl."

That made her laugh. He loved that little silvery sound of her laughter.

"Whoever sees it first doesn't have to build the fire tonight," she said.

"What fire?"

She turned in the saddle to look back at him. Her movements were so fluid and full of grace and her seat in the saddle so sure, with her pert little bottom and tiny waist calling to his hands, that he couldn't have looked away if he wanted to. Suddenly, he couldn't wait until they made camp. She would take off her hat and her bright hair would gather the moonlight.

But he wouldn't—he *couldn't*—touch it, he couldn't thrust his fingers into it to feel its silky thickness, or cradle her head and tilt her face up for his kiss. He wouldn't make love to her anymore. He would not. He was getting in way too deep.

He wanted to protect her so badly that a knot came in his throat every time he thought about taking her to jail.

"Listen here, Black Fox, don't be saying 'What fire?' to me. I want a hot supper."

"We all want things we can't get," he said, teasing her.

"But I *can* get that," she said, finally breaking the look shimmering between them to turn around and watch where she was going. "Last night we couldn't make a fire without attracting attention but tonight we'll be far away from other people, won't we?"

"We should be. At least, nobody lives near Long Man Lake."

Neither of them said anything else for a little while. Cat concentrated on ducking under overhanging limbs and finding the best way through the brush, and Black Fox concentrated on watching her.

A stick broke somewhere behind him.

He was so engrossed that, for an instant, it didn't register with him. When it did, he turned in the saddle and looked back but it was already getting too dark to see well. Another noise came, maybe the jingling of a bit and he caught a low scrap of sound that might've been a man's voice.

"Cat," he said, "whoa up here."

She did and he rode up beside her and indicated the back trail. They both listened.

First there was nothing, but then the noises came again and they were unmistakable. Men and horses.

"Could be they don't know we're here," he said quietly, "or it could be somebody followed me from town and Glass is trying to eliminate one lawman before the big shipment comes in."

He set his jaw in anger at himself. Half the town could've followed him and he would never have known it. He'd just realized that he hadn't even been watching his back trail as he left Sequoyah, and that was a lifelong habit. All he'd been thinking about was getting to Cathleen.

And now he had put her in danger.

"Or Tassel may have heard you didn't take me to the Tahlequah jail," she was saying, "and he's had no reports we reached Fort Smith, either. He may think you can lead him to me."

Her eyes were big and beautiful in the dim light. They held no fear. She was trusting him, they said, to know what to do.

He only hoped that he did know.

"Glass would love to kill me in secret," she said confidingly, as if it was something he didn't already know, "because if I'm not in jail, he knows I'll call him out when I get a chance and embarrass him all over again."

Black Fox's stomach contracted and a cold fingertip touched his spine.

Surely she wouldn't mess with Glass again.

Surely, if their ambush of the ambush was successful and they proved Becker had killed Deputy Turner, then she would give up on revenge and simply be glad she was alive and not on trial on a charge of murder.

Maybe Glass would be coming through the Limestone Gap with his men and his whiskey and he would be killed in the shooting. There was bound to be shooting.

If not, it would come down to Cat being able to give him, Black Fox, the slip again. She was under arrest, she was in his custody, and he was going to keep it that way.

"Whoever it is, if they're interested in us, we don't want to take them with us to the lake," he said. "Follow me and stay close."

She did as he said as he led the way, veering more to the south from the easterly direction they'd been going. The others were making enough noise that, if Black Fox could keep the gray and Little Dun mostly on pine needles and soft ground cover, they might move nearly silently and leave few tracks.

They bent over their horses' necks and, heading into the bigger pines, Black Fox started a large circle to go back behind their pursuers and hit the road that had brought him into Sequoyah on that first day he'd seen her. The day he'd found her bleeding and had saved her life.

He could still see her beautiful face, so pale he had feared she was dead. He was going to do everything in his power to keep that from happening again today.

The adrenaline began to kick in and his senses grew stronger. His hearing sorted out the creaking of their saddles from the sounds coming from behind them. At first he heard nothing at all from their pursuers.

Cat was doing the same thing, because when he glanced back at her she gave him the thumbs-up sign. Either the men behind them were staying on the southeasterly way, thinking about that same deer trail, or they weren't interested in him and Cat at all.

They were still a good ways from the north-south road. A long way. At least when they got to it, they'd have some room to run if they had to. He thought about the terrain ahead.

The woods covered most of it, but the pines finally ended where the land sloped down into a grassy meadow. It was probably a mile across it from the cover of the trees to the road. There would be no cover there except the darkness, which was falling fast.

Maybe they wouldn't need it. Maybe what he'd thought were men hunting for them was only men going hunting for meat.

He sped up their pace and kept them moving

faster, as fast as he dared; Cat stayed right with him, and they made good progress. There were no more sounds of anyone following them.

They left the pines and Black Fox searched for an old footpath he remembered that led to Sequoyah from a long-abandoned homestead. The ruins of the house sat on the edge of the woods above the meadow. It would be the quickest way through the blackjack oaks.

He found the path, and started south with Cathleen on the little dun horse hot on the gray's heels, and let out a sigh of relief. They would take the road for three or four miles (after waiting in the dark to see if anyone else came behind them across the meadow), and then they'd head across the river valley to the lake. It would be midnight before they got there and they'd had a long day in the saddle but before he slept, he wanted the isolation of the lake and the protection of Long Man Hill to his back.

They were within a quarter of a mile from the old homestead when the moon rose and the night breeze sprang up. A north breeze carried the call of a bobwhite and the sound of some animal moving through the woods.

The next noise he noticed was like something striking against a rock. Then it was something rolling downhill, it seemed, breaking through the brush.

Black Fox held up his hand and turned to look at Cat in the growing moonlight. She glanced at him once, then turned to look back as they halted their horses.

Immediately, it came to them: the unmistakable low, companionable nicker of a horse. It came from somewhere not too far behind them.

Of course something had rolled downhill. Whoever it was had come out of the pines and knocked a rock off the rough trail.

Whoever it was, Glass's men or no, they were definitely following Black Fox and Cat. They were good at tracking and now, farther away from town, they were much quieter in the woods. They were not greenhorns.

He and Cathleen were still too far from the homestead and the meadow. It went against every nerve and muscle in his body not to make a run for it, but he needed to create a diversion instead. If he were alone, he would take the chance and race for the meadow and then the road, but the shadow of the hill would go only so far and the moonlight would turn into an enemy.

For someone shooting down from the old house's ruins, he and Cathleen would be easy enough to hit.

He looked around. The trail curved to the east just ahead. Before their pursuers saw that bend— which he planned to follow—he wanted them to go west. Five or six yards farther along was an opening in the trees—which appeared to be the beginning of an old trail—for them to take.

Quickly, he dismounted and motioned for Cat to do the same.

"We'll wait here and send them west," he murmured. "Pick up a couple of rocks and follow me."

They managed, but with more noise than they intended, to lead their horses off the trail and get them hidden on the east side of it. Thank goodness, the wind was with them.

Black Fox put his arm around Cathleen's shoulders and his lips against her ear. The scent of her filled his nostrils and made him weak.

He couldn't resist taking in another draught of it, even though it made him shaky inside with a sudden yearning for the taste of her, as well. This was ridiculous in a time of danger.

"Hold their muzzles so they won't greet the other ones," he whispered and handed her his reins.

She traded him the fist-sized rock she had picked up and wrapped her arms around the horses' faces. They were tired and happy to stand. Little Dun nudged her affectionately.

Nearby, Black Fox found a fallen log thick enough to be about knee-high and stepped up onto it, rock in hand. They waited. Little Dun nudged Cat affectionately. Young Gray Ghost cocked one hind foot to rest.

Muffled sounds began coming closer, turning into squeaking saddles and thudding hoofbeats. One man quietly cleared his throat. Black Fox waited until he could see that there were two of them and they could see the old trailhead or whatever the opening was on the west side of the trail.

He drew back his arm and threw the rock up into the trees in that direction. As quickly as he could, he threw another one after it.

"Thataway," one man called to the other.

They kissed to their horses as they turned them west, picking up their pace to a long trot, fighting overhanging tree branches as they went.

Black Fox reached into his pocket for one more rock. He threw it even farther than the others, he judged, but he never heard it hit because of the commotion it caused. Something—probably a deer, judging the size of the animal by the noise it made as it went crashing through the timber—ran in a panic to the west, away from him and Cat.

The men who had been pursuing them took after it with a vengeance.

# Chapter 16

The moon was high and glinting off the water when they finally rode up on the shore of the lake. Black Fox looked at Cathleen, who was so tired from the long day of riding that she occasionally slumped in her saddle from weariness. Remorse stabbed him.

"I should've taken that old couple up on the offer to bed down in their barn," he said, stepping down from his horse. "I shouldn't have pushed so hard, Cat. I'm sorry."

"I'm not tired," she said, straightening up quickly. "Besides, this place is safer. We didn't know if we could trust them or not."

"They're fullbloods, old-fashioned in their ways, so they would always protect their guests," he said. "But I didn't want to have to be polite and spend half of tomorrow visiting with them. Rainwater or Adair could be here by the middle of the morning."

"I'm just glad they gave us hot food," she said. "If I can have a decent meal once in a while, I can ride for days."

"You're such a pampered lady," he said, teasing her.

He went to her horse and reached up for her.

"Come on. Let me help you down. I'll take care of the horses."

She dropped her reins, leaned toward him, and he took her into his arms.

Then he couldn't move again.

She fit so perfectly against him. He could feel her heart beating against his chest.

"I'm going to set you right over there at the foot of the bluff," he said, but he didn't take a step, "and you can drink the rest of the coffee the Cornsilks gave me while I make camp."

Cat pushed back his hat and looked up into his eyes. Her hand brushed his cheek like a feather's touch.

"No," she said. "When the day comes I can't take care of my horse before myself, I'll be too old to ride."

She stopped abruptly and bit her lip. The same thought sprang into both their heads and hung in the air between them.

Until she voiced it.

"If I live that long," she said.

His heart cracked open. What the hell was he doing? Why didn't he just turn her loose, right now, and let her go? Within hours it would be too late because other lawmen would be riding in from all directions.

"Put me down, Black Fox," she said.

He did.

He'd been a fool to stand there holding her. Hadn't he promised himself not to make love with her again? Just lifting her off her horse had caused all the wild desire to surge through him again.

She turned her back on him and began to unsaddle the little dun.

"Let's stake them over there by the bluff where the grass is thickest," she said.

Then she talked to the horse instead of to him.

"You're a good, good horse, Little Dunny," she said, "the best anybody could ride."

She put the saddle down, took off the blanket, turned it over to the dry side, and used one corner to rub the sweat off the dun's back.

"Don't you ever let anybody tell you different, either," she said, crooning to her as if she were a baby.

Talking to her as if she were saying good-bye.

Such a mixture of anger and regret grabbed Black Fox by the gut that he could hardly stand it. Damn it. He was only doing his job.

Suddenly he realized he was just standing there with his arms hanging helpless. He walked back to his own horse and started undoing the latigo.

"We're going to prove Becker killed Donald Turner," he blurted.

"Nobody knows what will happen," she retorted. "All we know is that everything's about to change."

She finished untacking her horse and put the halter on her. Then she stayed there and he turned around to see what she was doing. She was toeing off her boots and taking off her socks, and rolling up the legs of her jeans.

Then, without a word or a glance at him, she picked up the lead rope and led her mare across the rocky ground and out into the edge of the lake to drink. He stood there with his saddle in his hands and watched her. He couldn't have taken his eyes off her if his life had depended on it.

The moonlight bathed her in a pale light that took the rest of the color out of her faded clothes and made it look as if she were dressed in white. Only her hair still had color. And fire.

She looked off into the distance at the shape of

the dark hills against the sky. Both her hands were twined into her horse's mane.

It was stiff now with the boot blacking he had put in it. He shouldn't have colored it—it hadn't really done any good, anyhow. If only he could keep them together until it grew out again, enough to feel silky in Cathleen's fingers.

The girl and the mare, her long neck slanted down to the water, stood as still as the midnight moon. They drew him with a magic he couldn't fathom.

Finally, he forced himself to turn away and find a place for the bedrolls and saddles. Then, on an impulse too strong to resist, he took off his own boots and socks, haltered his own horse and led him out into the water.

Cat turned and looked at him when she heard the splashing.

"Cold, isn't it?" she asked.

"Now see what you've started," he said, "we'll have to sit up all night thawing out our feet and holding our horses' hooves to the fire."

She laughed that silvery laugh of hers.

"Can't build a fire," she said playfully. "Don't want to draw attention. We'll have company soon enough."

"I hate that," he blurted. "This is too pretty a spot to share."

"It is," she said, and went back to looking at the hills.

Her mare lifted her head from the water and stared off in the same direction, water dripping from her muzzle.

But now an awareness vibrated between him and Cat. She wanted to turn to him again; he could feel it as surely as if she had spoken.

He wanted to reach for her.

Without a word, she turned and led her horse back to shore. He watched the graceful way she moved, feeling the bottom with her bare feet, reaching up to caress the mare, who blew in her hair and nuzzled her neck.

He let his horse finish drinking before he followed.

They worked together, holding the long ropes while the horses rolled to scratch their sweaty backs, then staking them in the grass. They didn't talk and they didn't acknowledge the tension that was trembling in the air as surely as if they were reaching for each other.

He could *not* reach for her. He would not let himself. It would be best for both of them to leave it.

If he had not been so foolish as to make love with her that once, then he wouldn't be in this agony. If he made it two times, the pain and longing would only be doubled.

He went to the best spot beneath the overhang of the bluff and started rolling out his bed, then bent over to put his saddle at the head. Cathleen did the same with hers.

Then she straightened up and looked at him.

He looked back at her. Their eyes held for a long, solemn minute.

Then she cocked her head to one side and smiled at him, her big eyes gleaming in the moonlight.

"I dare you," she said.

Then she turned and ran like a deer. He unbuckled his holster and laid his gun on his bed but still he was right behind her when she raced into the lake.

He caught her as she reached a spot deep enough to swim but she slipped free of his hand and threw herself prone on the water. She swam fast but Black Fox stayed right beside her.

Laughing, she grabbed him around the neck and dunked his head. He did the same to her, then pulled her into his arms, shaking with the cold.

He kissed her quick and hard on the mouth, then he reversed their direction and started kicking hard, pulling with one arm to propel them back toward shore. Both of them were gasping and shaking, freezing from the air hitting their cold skins.

He could only get out one word at a time.

"You . . . are . . . crazy," he said.

"You're . . . as wet . . . and . . . cold as . . . I am," she said.

"I'm . . . rescuing . . . you," he said.

"Ha!"

She began swimming, too, and they raced back to their camp.

The minute they were on their feet, he scooped her up and carried her, clinging to him with all her might, her face tilted up to his, her wet hair a heavy weight to hold it that way. She was still gasping for breath but her eyes sparkled with pure mischief.

He bent his head and thrust his tongue between her parted lips, kissed her open mouth until the fire inside him started to drive away the cold outside. When he reached their beds, he started to set her down onto her feet.

She clung to him instead, kissing him back until his head spun, pressing her breasts against his chest through their wet clothes until he was wild with wanting to get rid of even the two thin fabrics covering their skins. He knelt on the grass.

Cathleen let go of him to start unbuttoning his shirt. He did the same for her. That intensified the kiss until they fell naked into the bedroll, stretching around each other for the covers, searching for refuge from the cool breeze that reached them off the lake.

For a little while they huddled in each other's arms, hugging each other so tight they could barely breathe, finding comfort that was enough for that moment. But the body heat that rose in them both came from desire so strong it consumed them.

"You said . . . you were . . . rescuing me," Cathleen said, gasping as she had done when they were out in the cold water, "but I can't even breathe."

She nuzzled into the hollow of his collarbone and ran the tip of her tongue along it. It left a trail of fire.

He pulled back enough to cup her breast with his hand and rub his thumb over the nipple. She made such a tiny, pleading cry deep in her throat that he felt he had a chief's power.

A chief in the olden days. She cradled his face in her hands and moved up against him so he would replace his hand with his lips. When he laved her with his tongue, she melted, helpless to move again except to slip her fingers into his hair and hold his mouth on her as if she never would let him stop.

And he did not want to stop. Until she began to caress his shoulders with the palms of her small hands and to run her fingertips down the valley of his spine.

Desperate now, he found her mouth with his again and her sweet womanhood, weeping for him, with his fingers.

*Mine. She's mine.*

Her mouth was ravishing his with a wantonness that was somehow rooted in her innocence.

*I've taught her everything she knows. She's mine. Mine.*

Then it was her small, bold hand that was

wanton—sliding down over his hip and around to touch his hard, hot manhood and then to caress it.

She tore her mouth from his and placed her open lips on his neck. They burned their shape there, moving against his skin.

"Please, Black Fox," she whispered. "Now."

He lifted himself up and over her as she held him in the cradle of her arms and thighs and welcomed him into the soft, hot refuge of her body. Almost out of control, he plunged deep, driving for her soul.

She clung to him with a passion that intoxicated him past remembering, past thinking, past breathing. But not past knowing.

Cathleen was his. He was hers. For tonight.

This night was theirs.

The next morning, when the sun was halfway up the sky, the first of the lawmen Black Fox had summoned rode around the end of the bluff and hallooed the camp. Cat, who was at the edge of the lake cleaning up the breakfast things, startled at the sound of a strange voice.

Then she silently berated herself for being surprised. She had known other people would come here today and she had reason to welcome them. Didn't she want Becker and Glass and their men to be caught? Didn't she want to try to prove her innocence in the Turner killing?

Yes, but she was sad and resentful, too, because

the only people who belonged there were she and Black Fox. She was furious at life, too, really, deep down inside—sick at heart that her time with Black Fox was at an end. She watched as somebody came riding right on up to their camp on a tall sorrel horse. It must be Rainwater or Adair— by the look of him, he was Cherokee—and he was a lawman. The very way he rode proclaimed his authority.

She turned back to her work, scrubbed the skillet with sand and rinsed it in the lake, while she relived the hours just past. They had slept late, until the sun was past rising and all the pink was gone from the sky. Until the growing daylight had waked them in each other's arms.

They had fished and built a fire and made coffee. They'd cleaned the fish and fried them with hush puppies she made from the cornmeal in Black Fox's saddlebags. Then they had sat crosslegged, facing each other across the fire, and eaten the delicious crispy fare while they talked and laughed and looked into each other's eyes.

Together. They had done everything together.

After they had made sweet, sweet love one more time in the early cool of the day.

She could still feel his gentle hands and taste his hot, spicy mouth. Remembering that last kiss wrenched her insides so hard it wrung the life out of her. She had been alone for such a long, long time and for all those weeks and months, she hadn't had any idea how lonely.

Her heart twisted bitterly as she dipped the skillet in the clear, blue water one more time and then gathered and stacked the tin plates and the utensils. She stood up and looked out at the far-away hills instead of at Black Fox and the other man talking at the campfire.

She had built a stone wall somewhere inside her between her mind and her heart when her mother died. Now what she had to do was find it and set it there again, for when she and Black Fox parted.

She had to do that. She couldn't spend her strength wishing for what couldn't be—she had work to do. Glass still roamed unpunished. Becker was wreaking havoc all over the country under the mark of her sign. Her family was gone, destroyed, and no one had paid for that.

Cathleen O'Sullivan hadn't lived in the woods like an animal for nearly a year and risked her life over and over again for no reason. Now was the time for her to pull herself together and get her revenge.

Only then would she think of the future. She might even have time in jail to get through, but she wouldn't worry about that now, either. What she had to do right now was help Black Fox prove her innocent of shooting Donald Turner in the back.

And to kill Tassel Glass in an honorable way. Or not.

Devastation filled her. She felt so desolate about the mess she was in, so sick of being torn between what she wanted to be and what she had to do, that she might even shoot Old Tassel in the back if the opportunity presented itself. She was past caring about her pride or her reputation or anything else. Black Fox was a lawman, like that other proud man who had just ridden in here, and she was an outlaw. It was as simple as that.

Two sets of ambushers waiting for an unknown number of prey—armed horseback outriders riding around the wagons to protect them and the shotgun-toting wagonmasters on the wagonseats driving the teams—would be a very confusing fight. If she got any chance at all to exact the vengeance that had ruled her for so long, she would do it and not even care if it was honorable or not.

Then she might just light out for a far country knowing that Tassel Glass would never kill or hurt any more defenseless women and *that* would be her reward. She could live with that.

The old, calm mountains, reaching into the sky with their shades of purple and blue, beckoned her from the distance like a refuge to be reached someday. Someday. Someday soon, this would all be over and she would be free of the vengefulness that had driven her for so long.

She turned and carried the cooking things back to the fire.

"Cathleen," Black Fox said, "this is Isom Rainwater, of the Cherokee Lighthorse. Isom, Cathleen O'Sullivan."

He must have already explained who she was. Rainwater tipped his hat, spoke to her politely, and looked directly into her eyes with a sharply curious look. Then he turned right back to the business at hand.

"This is your deal, Black Fox," he said deferentially, "so you decide. But my opinion is that we need to set a watch for the whiskey wagon down the road the other side of the Gap, far enough that a man can ride back to give us plenty of warning."

"Right," Black Fox said, "if nobody's spotted it before that. I told Willie to keep an eye out on his way back."

"We'll have to time it just right when we move in," Rainwater said, "so as not to spook Becker and his bunch."

He gave a dry chuckle.

"It's not an easy thing to ambush the ambushers."

The men talked on and Cat listened to them, but she couldn't really hear their plans. Her sweetly aching, sated body was already longing for Black Fox again and her thoughts were set on him. It would only be a few more days, no matter *when* the wagon came up the road from Fort Smith and rolled into the Limestone Gap.

After that, she most likely would never see him again.

Black Fox took it as a good sign when he looked up from the map Isom Rainwater was drawing of the Limestone Gap and saw Rabbit Sanders riding around the end of the bluff.

"Two men in less than a day," he said, glancing at the sun that was only beginning its downward journey. "I'm beginning to think we might get a good bunch together."

Isom followed his glance.

"Sanders has been over the Deadline hunting Akey Edwards," Isom said. "I didn't know he was back in the Nation."

"Black Fox, who is that coming in?" Cat asked.

She was walking up from the lake carrying the clothes she had just washed over her arm. A rolled red bandana was holding her hair off her face, her faded chambray shirt was spotted with water and the knees of her jeans were dirty. He had never seen such a beautiful sight.

"Another Lighthorse," he answered. "Rabbit Sanders."

She took the wet clothes to the bushes that grew along the foot of the bluff and began to lay them out to dry. Black Fox tried not to watch her but Sanders had ridden nearly up to them before he was able to force his gaze away from her and glance at the new arrival.

"Boys," Sanders said, with a nod of greeting, as he stopped his horse.

"Get down," Black Fox said. "You hungry?"

"No, thanks," Sanders said. "After I ran across Willie in town last night, I stayed at the boarding-house. He said you wanted us as fast as we could ride but I had already come from halfway to Tahlequah that morning. I was rode out."

"Yeah, sure," Black Fox said lightly, "we all know you just wanted to put your feet under Mrs. Tallman's table."

"That, too," Rabbit said, completely unabashed, as always. "Am I too late to get in on the fun?"

He stood in the stirrup and swung down from his horse.

"We'd never throw an ambush without you," Black Fox said.

"Well, I aim to make sure none of 'em gets away," Rabbit said, leading his horse over to the other mounts, who were grazing at the foot of a little curve of the bluff, and starting to unsaddle. "I've about had enough of this chousing all over the country."

"Did you get Akey?" Isom asked.

"I went after him, didn't I?" Rabbit asked.

He was always cocky, too, which irritated Rain-water mightily but it never bothered Black Fox. Rabbit was the youngest member of the Lighthorse now, a distinction that had once belonged to Black Fox. He could remember how that was.

"Yep," Rabbit called across the small, grassy meadow. "I got ol' Akey and guess what? He's the one shot the famous Federal Deputy Marshal Donald Turner in the back."

Sanders might as well have thrown a bolt of lightning. Black Fox's heart began to pound like a dance drum. From the corner of his eye, he saw Cathleen whirl around from her task to stare at Rabbit but he couldn't look at her.

He, too, was trying to see right into Rabbit's head and make sure this was true.

"How do you know?" Black Fox asked. "Did he confess?"

"Bragged about it," Rabbit said. "And after I went through his saddlebags, I knew the brag was true."

He pulled his tack off and carried it to where the other saddles stood near the rolled-up beds.

Black Fox turned to look at Cathleen and for one shining moment, happiness blazed between them. Then it went out of her face like a snuffed candle flame.

It happened so fast and was so inexplicable that it chilled him. She never broke the look between them but as her face paled, it closed to him. He couldn't read one hint of what she was thinking.

Quickly, he looked at Rabbit.

"What did you find?"

"Turner's gun, his badge, and all the subpoenas he had to serve."

"I'd say he did it," Rainwater said.

Then he looked at Cat and touched the brim of his hat.

"Based on what Black Fox has just told me, that's good news for you, Miss O'Sullivan."

Her lips looked stiff, as if she wanted to cry. At first, he thought she wasn't going to answer but she did.

"Yes," she said. "Thank you, Mr. Rainwater."

For another minute, Black Fox thought she wasn't going to move, either. She started toward the fire, where Rabbit was headed.

Rabbit was looking Cathleen over, clearly wondering who she was and why that was good news for her. He was also looking at her like a bold man looks at a beautiful woman.

Black Fox couldn't even think well enough to introduce them.

"Let me pour you some coffee," Cat said to Rabbit. "We don't have cream but we do have sugar."

"I'm Rabbit Sanders, Miss O'Sullivan, ma'am," the Lighthorse said, "and I take mine black."

Sanders turned on his powerful smile and Cathleen managed a halting one in return. Black Fox felt a stab of jealousy like none he had ever known.

"That clears her of the killing, Black Fox," Isom Rainwater said.

He was always a stickler for the letter of the law.

"There are other charges against her," Black Fox snapped.

Rainwater stared at him. In fact, they were all staring at him—he could feel their eyes on him.

"I was just thinking, considering the danger of the ambush, you might let her go on her word. For now," Rainwater said, carefully keeping his tone mild and noncommittal.

*Let her go? I can't let her go! How could I let her go?*

Black Fox glared at him.

"Miss O'Sullivan has a stake in this ambush," he snapped. "Becker has been leaving her sign at his own crimes."

"You know that for a fact?" Rainwater asked, still mildly, but Black Fox would swear that his sharp eyes now held a knowing glint.

All three of them waited for his answer.

"I do," Black Fox said, getting some control back into his voice. "She was in my custody when the sign of The Cat was left on a robbery and a shooting, plus a killing."

"You're The Cat?" Rabbit asked softly, from behind him. "I have to tell you, ma'am, I admire your bravery."

"Thank you," Cathleen said demurely.

Black Fox whirled on them. "Miss O'Sullivan,"

he said, "I'd like to talk to you for a moment."

He said it so fast he nearly bit his own tongue.

She was handing a full cup of coffee to Rabbit. Their fingers touched as he took it.

Finally, she looked up and acknowledged him.

"Very well, Mr. Vann," she said, "let's walk along the lake."

He would prefer to go around the wall of the bluff and get out of sight of the others, but with that look in Rainwater's eyes, he wouldn't suggest that now. No one else needed to know there was anything between him and Cat.

At least, not now. Especially not until he knew what he meant to her.

"So," she said, when they were out of earshot of the other two Lighthorse, "I have a big stake in the ambush, do I? And that's why you aren't letting me go, even if Rabbit has proved I'm innocent of murder?"

"You watch yourself with Sanders," he snapped. "He's a rounder."

*And he's not much older than you.*

He dragged his thoughts away from Rabbit and his charming smile.

And he would not let himself think about the fact that it was Rabbit Sanders and not Black Fox Vann who had proved The Cat did not kill Donald Turner.

He glanced back over his shoulder at the other

two lawmen who were talking there, beside the fire. This might be his only chance to talk to Cathleen alone.

So, hard as it was, he went straight to the heart of the confusion tormenting him.

"You don't seem very happy about being proved innocent," he said. "Why not?"

She shifted her gaze away from his.

"As you so quickly said, Black Fox, there are other charges against me."

Her noncommittal tone of voice gave him no hint of her feelings.

He stopped walking and stood right there, waiting until she stopped, too, and turned to look at him again.

"None of your other charges is a hanging offense," he said. "Why did the light go out of your eyes as soon as you thought about your life being saved, Cathleen?"

She held his gaze but she didn't speak.

"You looked like you'd been hit with a hammer."

She didn't answer. She didn't even open her mouth.

He tried to wait her out, he tried to keep his wits about him, but his tongue got away from him.

"I was so happy we could . . . have more time together," he said. "Why weren't you?"

She still didn't say a word. She only looked at him with her riotous curls dancing in the wind and her huge, green eyes filled with tears.

"I was so sad," she said, but she didn't hesitate and her voice didn't tremble, "because maybe I am still going to hang. I intend to kill Tassel Glass if I have to shoot him in the back."

# Chapter 17

Now Black Fox felt as if he were the one who'd been hit with a hammer. Her eyes were full of tears, yes, but they were also shining with determination. She meant what she said and she showed none of the anguish that was tearing him apart.

What was it? Did he love her?

Surely it didn't go that deep. It was just that he hadn't been with a woman in a long time. It was just that he'd been lonely.

How could he love an outlaw girl who was an Intruder to boot? One who was ten years younger than him?

Yet he had already acknowledged that she was far more than a girl; she was long past being a girl.

A strong, courageous woman was what she was, and he had always admired courage.

She was a woman he could fall in love with.

The thought stopped his breath.

Surely he hadn't already done so.

Yet whatever it was that he did feel for her was ripping his heart from his body.

She whirled on her heel and started walking away down the edge of the lakeshore. Ungrateful little jade that she was.

Hot fury burst to life in him.

"I'll tie you to a tree if I have to," he called after her.

She stopped and turned around. She looked at him so straight he actually felt she could see his heart racketing in his chest.

"You can't," she said flatly, gesturing toward the other lawmen. "They won't let you."

"This is between you and me," he shot back.

What did he mean? What was he talking about?

He had been wrong last night—they didn't belong to each other. That had not been his instincts telling him that. It had been only a wild, emotional wish in the heat of passion.

"I've been at it for a year," she said, and now there wasn't a trace of a tear or a regret anywhere about her—not in her defiant stance or her steady voice or her green eyes blazing at him. "Nothing and nobody's going to stop me from killing Glass now."

The very look of her filled him with despair. She was not only courageous, she was the most stubborn, determined woman he had ever known.

"If you do, you'll have to go through me," he said.

"Then so be it," she said. "I didn't expect you to understand but I wanted you to know. I've never lied to you before and I don't intend to start now."

He spun on his heel and left her before he could say anything more.

Cathleen didn't say anymore to Black Fox for the rest of the time of preparation except about things that didn't matter, like camp-keeping chores and food gathering. She reached deep for the strength to shut him out of her mind and concentrate on the task before her. She watched the federal lawmen and Willie arrive, she talked to them a little, and to Willie to thank him for all he'd done to help her. She told him how grateful she was and that she'd felt guilty about the wound he took when she called Tassel Glass out.

But she made no talk of feelings to Black Fox.

Willie told her about his gunshot wound and his nursing by Kinesah and her mother, plus his trip to Fort Smith and back, but something was different. The best she could tell, Willie wasn't sweet on her anymore and that was a great relief.

Black Fox had looked so miserable out there by the lake when she'd told him she was still bent on revenge that she knew she had hurt his feelings as a lawman. And as a person. Making one of them miserable was as much as she could bear. After all, both of them had tried to help her.

During the planning for the ambush, though, she had put that guilt away. Black Fox didn't care a thing about her or he would understand why she had to finish what she had started with Glass. Come to think of it, she *had* lied to him, after all, because despite what she'd told him to the contrary, she *had* expected him to understand.

She wrenched her thoughts away from him, refused to let her gaze rest on him—he was sitting on his haunches by the cookfire eating the breakfast prepared by the cook who'd come in with the prison wagon the night before—and took another sip of her coffee, leaning back against the bluff where she was standing in the shadows away from everyone else. During the past two days and nights, she had put *every* feeling away except her cold hatred for Tassel Glass and she didn't intend to let anything, like looking at Black Fox's handsome face, obscure that now.

"Rider coming," one of the Parker deputies said, and everyone turned to watch one of the night lookouts, who happened to be Rabbit Sanders, coming back into camp at a long, fast trot.

"Barring trouble on the road, the whiskey wagon will hit the Gap along about the middle of the morning," he called, stopping his horse far enough away to keep his dust out of the food. "Becker's bunch knows it, too. They're scattering into the brush along both sides of the Gap like a covey of quail."

Excitement crackled through the camp. Black Fox stood up and took command.

"Saddle up and leave here in pairs," he said. "Don't ride hard—it's not far, we've got time, and we need Becker's men settled so we'll know where to place ourselves. Wait for me at the lookout tree."

These men, except for Willie, were professionals. After the first excitement, they moved with quiet sureness to follow Black Fox's plan. Cat went to get her saddle and carried it to her own horse, trying to stay out of Black Fox's view, trying not to attract notice from anyone.

She set the saddle down beside Little Dun, dropped her tin cup into her saddle bag, then slung it over her shoulder while she saddled. That done, and the bridle on, she walked around to the other side of her mare to slide her long gun out of its holster on the saddle skirt.

One more time, she opened the breech and made sure it was loaded. It was old and temperamental, but she knew it well. If Black Fox didn't tie her to a tree, she could do the job she had to do.

She replaced the rifle, pulled her hat down tight and walked around the little mare again, mur-

muring to her as she ducked underneath her neck. Dunny snorted her desire to be off.

Cat immersed herself in her usual rituals of getting ready for a raid—she ran her hands down her horse's fleet legs to reassure herself she was sound, she checked the cinch one more time, she fastened the stampede strings on her hat. Then she stuck her toe into the stirrup.

"You and I are a pair," Black Fox's voice said.

For one crazy instant, she thought she had imagined it. She stepped on up and threw her leg over Dunny.

But then he led his gray horse up beside her and swung into the saddle.

Cathleen took a deep seat and a firm hold on the reins.

"If you're pairing with me so you can tie me to a tree," she said, tilting her head to look him in the eye, "pick another partner."

"No," he said, "I've changed my mind."

He wasn't going to say anymore right then. She knew him well enough to know that, so she rode out of camp beside him. He didn't say another word all the way to the lookout tree at the head of the gap.

Once there, he dismounted, gestured to her to do the same, and they gave their horses' reins to Willie.

"You've done your part and more with the ride

you made," Black Fox said to him. "How about if you hold the horses and watch from here to see if anybody runs?"

Willie nodded, but a little reluctantly.

"Some of Becker's men could easily slip away from us," Black Fox said, "especially the ones on the walls. I need a sharp eye to see if any of 'em try to break when we make our shout."

"Then I signal our men on top?" Willie asked.

"Right," Black Fox said. "I'll leave you my spyglass as soon as I go down to the road."

Then he turned to Cathleen and gestured for her to come with him into the brush. They lay on their stomachs at the top of the cliff on the west side of the gap while he looked over its sides and the road with his glass. Finally, he handed it to her.

"Becker's picked up some more men," he said. "There're three on the west wall, two on the east, four with Becker down there on the sides of the road and three with the wagon."

Well, evidently he was going to let her participate, after all. Cathleen scanned the gap.

"I see them," she said.

Becker's new wagon sat crossways of the road right in the middle of the gap with two men hiding in the bed of it and one out in the road, pretending he was working to fix the harness of his team. He had men on the south end of the gap ready to ride out of the cover of the trees and take the whiskey wagon. Glass or whoever was coming to meet it from the north would be separated from their prize by the fortified wagon and its team.

Cathleen studied the position of everyone.

Finally, Black Fox asked, "Ready?"

She nodded and handed the magnifying glass back to him.

"All right," he said. "Let's go."

There was no use questioning him. He'd tell her soon enough what he wanted her to do. Then she would figure out if she could do it and take care of Glass, too.

When they returned to Willie, Black Fox gave him the magnifying glass and turned to the rest of the men, who had all gathered by now. He assigned two of them positions on top and sent half of those remaining to the road at the south end of the gap to get around Becker's men.

Then he gestured for everyone else to follow him down the winding trail that led to the road on the north end. He motioned for Cathleen to go ahead of him and she did. Once all of them were down to the trees at the edge of the road, he talked to them quietly.

"We'll fall in behind Glass and his men or whoever is coming to accept the delivery," he said. "We don't know how many they'll be, so look sharp."

They took places on both sides of the road. Finally, Black Fox nodded his approval of their choices and turned to Cathleen. He pierced her with such a significant gaze that her blood pounded in her head.

"Glass is your man," he said. "When he comes into sight, draw a bead on him and don't look away."

She clamped her jaw shut—or it would have fallen open in surprise—and stared at him. His eyes were fixed on hers. They were telling her more than he was saying in his stunning words but shock kept her from knowing quite what their message might be.

However, there was no doubt about what his tongue was saying. "If he tries to turn and run when we make our shout, shoot him."

"All right," she said, her heart pounding.

Was he giving her permission to take her revenge? Was that what he'd meant about changing his mind?

"Your best place would probably be right up there among those cedars," he said, and turned to indicate a low rise at the side of the road covered in evergreen trees. "You can sight right in on his heart from there."

He held the significant look for one more long moment, then he rode away from her to speak in low tones to the other two Cherokee Lighthorsemen who were still on this side of the road, waiting for him. Without so much as a quick glance back at her, he rode away.

Her heart fluttering in her throat like a wild bird in a box trap, Cathleen tried to get her breath as she guided her mare up the little hillock, staying between the cover of the brush and the road. By the time she found a spot on top of it and positioned Little Dunny where she could hide, dismount, unsheath her rifle and rest it across the saddle to have a clear shot at the road, Black Fox had vanished.

Every one of the lawmen had disappeared. She couldn't see a one of them—the wagon driver down in the road was the only person in sight, and she had to look back over her shoulder and down to catch a glimpse of him between the juniper trees.

She turned back and faced north, the direction from which Glass would come, and took in several, long deep breaths to steady herself. What was she doing looking for other people anyhow? Just because she suddenly felt more alone than she ever had in her life, it didn't mean that having somebody else there would help that.

No, this was the job she had set out to do and she had to do it alone. Hadn't she been working at it all alone for months and months?

The sun slanted in between the trees and the walls of the shadowy gap to light the road in strips. Cat set her sights on one of them, took another deep breath, and waited. Anybody riding in from the north would pass right through that beam of light.

She had to make sure it was Glass, though. He might send only his henchmen and stay out of danger for himself, which he sometimes did.

This was it. This was what she had been waiting for. Once it was over, she'd be free of this bitter need to avenge her family and the loss of their home.

It was pretty quiet in the gap—the wildlife had fled or gone into hiding because they sensed something was going to happen. Even the birds were silent. Becker's men with the wagon talked a little bit, back and forth, but not much.

Cat closed her eyes for a minute to accustom them to the dimness of the trees. They needed rest, too, from staring at the very same spot in that same streak of light.

Against her eyelids, she saw Black Fox's face, his eyes as he had given her that look. What all had he meant by that? Permission to shoot Glass? He had set her in a position to do that and never be blamed or questioned, if she waited until the shooting started. There was bound to be shooting on both ends of the gap, when Glass and Becker realized they were surrounded.

But that wasn't like Black Fox, who was such a stickler for the law. She could hardly believe that he wasn't bent on arresting Glass and putting him on trial.

She opened her eyes and stared unseeingly at

the sunlit streak of road. Black hadn't given her permission. He had given her the *choice*.

Stunned by that truth, she thought about it. His whole life was spent upholding the law and he could have her in jail this very minute if he wanted to. Or tied to a tree, as he'd threatened. Instead, he was trusting her to quit being an outlaw and do the lawful thing.

Yet he was also giving her the perfect opportunity to do what she had to do.

He was asking her to trust him that the law would punish Glass.

However, he was also giving her a way to mete out that punishment herself and not have to pay for it with her life.

It was her choice.

Black Fox *did* care about her.

A dozen feelings at once rioted in her heart. She had lived for this for months and months, and lived in a hard, desperate way so she could get this chance.

She set her jaw. Her conscience wasn't bothered one bit by the thought of killing Tassel Glass. This was her chance. She would kill him as mercilessly as he had killed her mother.

The sound of hoofbeats—still some little way off—floated into the gap and echoed dully off its limestone walls. Cathleen's hands tightened on the rifle. It was hard to tell which direction the horses were coming from, but then she heard the high crack of a whip and the creak of a wagon. The whiskey was arriving from the south.

She looked back over her shoulder again, but all she could see was Becker's roadblock. The trees would keep her from seeing farther south past it, so she'd better look north at all times so as to get the best shot at Glass.

That was what she did, even though it was hard not to try to see what was happening, instead of just listening. There was a closer sound of hoof-beats and then a yell—from one of the outriders, probably—then more noises of the wagon. It rattled to a stop with more yelling and cursing and loud complaints about his broken harness from Becker's man in the road.

Cathleen watched the north end of the gap and prayed for Glass to come. She wanted—no, she *needed*—to get this over with.

The argument on the road was still going on when she heard hoofbeats from the north and a cold blade of realization sliced through her. Here came Glass. It wouldn't be long now.

Her whole body grew more and more tense and she took her finger off the trigger to prevent pulling it too soon. She went up on tiptoe to stretch her legs, being careful not to take her gaze from the peephole she had in the trees.

The noise of the hoofbeats grew louder and the

sounds of men's voices came with them. Then five horsemen galloped into the gap and the lead one threw up his hand, yelling out a warning about the wagon blocking the road.

A shiver ran through Cat. She was in luck. Glass was there, riding in the middle of the pack on a tall, stout horse, his big form filling the saddle and presenting her with a target the worst shot in the world could not miss.

She sighted in on his left chest, just above his right arm, still carried in its sling. She shifted her feet and Little Dunny's body to follow him with her muzzle as he and his men all bumbled down to a slow trot and began approaching Becker's wagon. If only he would stay right in that area when the action started!

It started right then. Becker's men on the walls fired a shot each and wounded one of Glass's. All of his men instantly started milling around, trying to turn back to get out of the trap, but what seemed to be a dozen of Becker's men rode out of the trees at the side of the road, some to surround the whiskey shipment and disarm its outriders, others to surround Glass and his crew.

Becker himself stood up in the bed of the fortified wagon, pointing a shotgun at Glass, who was struggling with his left hand to draw a gun. He was sideways to Cat, but she couldn't shoot anyway, until Black Fox made his shout.

"Give it up if you want to live, Tassel," Becker yelled, in a voice that shook a little bit the same way his gun was shaking.

"Take your own advice, Becker," Black Fox shouted, his voice solid as stone with an edge that cut. "You're surrounded. We're Cherokee Lighthorse and United States marshals. We have men on the walls and behind you. Throw down your guns."

Now. Now. Now she would shoot.

Both Becker and Glass turned, astonished, to see Black Fox riding out into the open and she had the perfect opportunity.

A clear shot at Glass's broad chest was right there in front of her. Her sights were set on the left side of it. She let them drop a little to compensate for the fact that she was shooting from above, slid her finger onto the trigger and began her slow squeeze.

Little Dunny stood as still as if she had quit breathing, steadily supporting the long gun as if she did that every day of her life. Perfect. Perfect.

Glass sat frozen in his saddle, either by surprise or fear, turned toward Cathleen as if she had asked him to pose for her.

Perfect. She would never get another chance like this.

The squeeze was nearly there. One more tiny bit of pressure and her vengeance was done.

But the bitterness drained out of her while she

stood with her finger trembling against the trigger of her gun. She couldn't find any satisfaction in imagining his shirt blossoming with blood and his corpulent self falling from his horse to lie dead on the ground.

Killing him wouldn't make her happy.

Killing him wouldn't give her more peace with the unalterable fact that her mother was gone and with it, her home.

So the shooting started without her. Instantly, her heart had gone to ice; she tried to see Black Fox and if he was safe, her rifle at the ready to protect him if she saw a gun aimed his way.

It was too confusing, people were moving too fast, the narrow space was in turmoil and she saw his face once, then it was gone. She might shoot a lawman, even Black Fox himself by mistake. They would have to take care of themselves.

Cat collapsed against Dunny's warm side, drew her hand away from the trigger, and wiped her sweaty palm on her jeans. The sounds of the guns below them grew more sporadic, then stopped.

"Throw down," Black Fox said, and the low, stern order carried through the gap like a shout, but it wasn't.

It was a command that he knew would be obeyed. There were no more sounds of shots.

He was all right. He was fine.

Sweat was pouring down her face, too, so she

lifted her shoulder and scrubbed it with her shirt. Then, her arms aching, she took down the rifle and walked around her mare to slide it into the sheath on the saddle.

She leaned against Little Dun's silky neck and buried her face in it. Then she couldn't even move anymore because her heart was standing still for Black Fox.

Somehow, Black Fox had done this to her. He had helped her to make the right choice. If she had killed Glass in that cowardly way, the agony would have kept driving her. Since she didn't, it was gone.

She heard Black Fox raise his voice to send someone back to camp for the prison wagon and someone else order the prisoners to sit down crosslegged on the ground, and finally she stood up and walked around Dunny again to climb into her saddle. It would be a satisfaction to see Tassel Glass's arrogant self sitting on the ground beneath a lawman's gun.

It would be great satisfaction to see him standing, shackled, in Judge Parker's court. He would have to go there instead of to the Cherokee court because this crime involved white men.

It would be an even greater vengeance to know he would be locked up for years with his pride subjugated to his jailers.

She kissed to Little Dun, rode her out of the trees and down the brushy hillside. They came out into the gap not a stone's throw from where Black Fox was tying Tassel Glass's hands together behind his back.

Cat watched as he handed the rope to Rabbit Sanders, who then tied Glass to Hudson Becker.

"I know you boys have a lot to talk about," Rabbit taunted them, "so I'm making sure you don't have nobody between you."

Cathleen had thought she would relish taunting Tassel, too. She had expected to relish the look on his face when he saw her again.

Instead, she didn't even glance at him. The only face she wanted to look into was Black Fox's.

He gave her one, sharp, slanting glance that she couldn't read, but it lit her up inside, anyhow.

They didn't talk, not one word, all the while he was busy tying up prisoners and guarding them until the prison wagon, driven by the cook, came rattling down from their lake camp. They barely even looked at each other but that whole time they were aware of each other and communicating. Every minute, each one knew that the other one was there.

Finally, every prisoner was loaded and ready to start down the road toward Fort Smith, sitting in rows in the prison wagon with the chains attached to it replacing the ropes. The lawmen conferred; two of the deputies from Fort Smith tied their horses to the whiskey wagon and prepared to drive it back to Arkansas, while two more took over Becker's wagon and team.

"Black Fox," one of the federal deputy marshals called, "you want to ride on ahead of this little cavalcade?"

"I'm not going," Black Fox said. "Rainwater's representing the Cherokees."

The marshal who had asked the question turned to stare at Black Fox in astonishment.

"That's not like you, Vann," he said. "How come you're not sticking with these reprobates 'til the doors clang behind 'em like you always do?"

Cathleen watched from where she sat Little Dun in the shade and listened for his answer with her heart standing still.

"Got business elsewhere," Black Fox said, as he turned away from the wagon and walked toward his horse.

That was when he looked at Cat and smiled.

# Chapter 18

After the wagons—filled, respectively, with prisoners and with whiskey—had rattled off to the south out of Limestone Gap to begin the two-day trek to Fort Smith, Black Fox swung Gray Ghost around and pointed his head to the north. Cathleen, on Little Dun, sat waiting in the middle of the road.

"I'm glad you stayed, Cat," he said, riding toward her.

She thought he sounded a little bit shy. But not at all hesitant. His tone was very firm.

She laid the rein against Dunny's neck as a signal to fall in beside him. "I couldn't have just ridden away and left you. After all, I'm under arrest."

He flashed her a quick, surprised glance, then grinned that grin that made her heart turn over every time.

"I wasn't sure," she said, "whether or not you would pursue me to the ends of the earth."

Her heart thudded like thunder in its yearning to know the answer to that.

He raised one eyebrow.

"I don't know," he said lightly, "I've lost a lot of sleep lately and you're pretty darn hard to catch."

The teasing tone of his voice sent a jolt of happiness through her. It made her feel silly and flirtatious and altogether foolish, somehow.

"Only when I don't want to be caught," she said.

He kept looking at her as the horses kept pace with each other.

"Cathleen," he said. "I should tell you now that you're free to go."

She gave *him* a surprised look. "What are you talking about?"

She searched his eyes, which were twinkling with mischief. Or excitement. Or happiness.

"Every time I turn around," she said, "you're telling me or somebody else that I have some kind of ridiculous charges against me."

He cocked that brow again. "True," he murmured.

She narrowed her eyes and tried her best to

look straight into his mind. "Remember, you're
Black Fox Vann. You take being a lawman very,
very seriously."

He wasn't going to let her look away from him,
either.

"I know," he said, "and that means I have to go
by the letter of the law. If there's no one to press
charges against you, I have to set you free."

"What if I don't want to be free?"

Suddenly, both their tones of voice had changed
from playful to serious. Entirely serious.

And, suddenly, they were talking about something else besides the law.

"You're not even twenty years old," he said,
"and now you have your whole life before you as
a free woman."

Her heart clutched. Was he truly going to send
her away? Was she not as important to him as he
was to her?

In that one moment of fear, which was greater
than any she'd ever known, she knew she loved
him.

No, she *admitted* to herself that she loved him.
She had *known* she loved him since her eyes fluttered open and she saw him bending over her,
staunching the blood flowing out of her.

Her heart soared, then came crashing down. Of
course, it would be too perfect to be real if he
loved her, too.

Life was hard. Life wasn't like that.

"Well, if it's my life, I get to choose how I spend it," she said.

"You're too inexperienced to make that choice right now," he said. "You've never been anywhere but the Cherokee Nation."

"I don't want to go anywhere else," she said.

"Your contrariness is rising," he said, grinning at her again.

She put her fists on her hips and Dunny looked back to see what that pull on the reins might mean.

"I'm proud of my contrariness," she said. "It has carried me through many a rough patch."

"And it's carried me *into* many of 'em," he said.

They both laughed. They couldn't seem to stop looking into each other's eyes.

Then they sobered.

"I'm seriously trying to tell you something, Black Fox," she said. "I am *not* leaving the Nation."

"Why not?"

She gulped and grabbed her courage with both hands. She was nothing if not bold, her mother had always told her.

"Because I love you," she said, and held his gaze with hers.

A shadow flashed in his eyes.

"I love you, too," he said. "It wouldn't be fair not to tell you that."

All breath left her. Her heart stopped beating. Could it be true? Could it be?

"But I'm a rigid old stick-in-the-mud lawman," he said. "You'd be sick and tired of me in no time."

"I don't see how that's a problem," she said, smiling. "After all, I'm law-abiding now."

He smiled back and his eyes burned into hers with a fire from deep inside him.

"I must say that I love you just as much now that you're law-abiding as I did when you were an outlaw," he said.

She tilted her head and looked up at him with her meanest green-eyed stare.

"I never said the change was permanent," she said.

"I never said that, either," he replied. "But I'm thinking that if you're so set on staying in the Nation that you might want to take just one more step in the right direction."

"Oh," she said flirtatiously, "and what is it?"

"Marriage to a Cherokee so you won't be an Intruder anymore."

She raised her eyebrows.

"It's a step I *might* take," she said, "if a Cherokee man happened to propose to me."

He stopped his horse in the middle of the road, stood in the stirrup, got off, and came to her side.

"Here," he said, holding his arms up for her, "come here to me."

She slid off her horse into his embrace.

"Here's a Cherokee man proposing to you, Cathleen O'Sullivan, outlaw Intruder woman," he said. "Will you marry me?"

Then he held her tight against his hard body and, for a long moment, gazed down into her eyes. She knew they were giving him her answer, but he was waiting for the word.

"Yes!" she cried. "Yes, I will marry you, Black Fox. Now kiss me, quick!"

He held her even more tightly as his eyes twinkled.

"I always do whatever you tell me," he drawled, teasing her unmercifully, "you know that. But don't you think we ought to talk about . . ."

She rose up on tiptoe in his arms, moving her body against his at the same slow pace as his words, offering her slightly parted lips, her eyes half-closed in invitation.

He made a helpless moan and he kissed her then, cupped her face in both his big, calloused hands and kissed her, long and hard and sweet as honey, until her head was dizzy and she had no breath left.

Except for just enough to say one thing. "Let's camp here, tonight."

That made him throw back his head and laugh. He held her even closer and dropped a kiss onto the top of her head.

"I don't know," he said, teasing her. "Somebody might run over us, right here in the middle of the road."

She laughed, too. "I don't mean in the road and you know it," she said. "Let's go to that glade right on the other side of those trees."

He frowned and pretended to consider. "Oh, I don't know. It's a long time until sundown."

She tilted her head and looked up at him, smiling, with her eyes full of invitation.

"On second thought," he murmured, "let me show you what we can do to pass the time until then."

# Epilogue

"**W**hoa, Dunny Girl, we're home."
Cathleen stopped her horse in front of the house and stood up in the stirrup, ready to dismount.

"What's this?" Black Fox asked, as he brought Ghost to a halt beside her. "I remember once when you said if you didn't put your horse's care before your own, you'd be too old to ride."

She hesitated only a moment before she swung down.

"That was before I had a home to come back to," she said. "And a husband to take my horse to the barn and do my chores for me."

Shaking his head in mock dismay, he answered with the low, wry chuckle that she loved.

"Spoiled you rotten, that's what I've done," he said. "I'll not make that mistake again."

"Too late," she said, pulling her saddlebags off the skirt of her saddle. "I'm used to having my way and I'm not giving in now."

Black Fox was right; she would have to give in. But she didn't have to admit that to him yet.

"Except on this one thing," he said, and he dismounted, too.

Her eyes sought his as he let his reins drop to ground-tie Ghost and walked toward her. Without a word, he took the saddlebags from her with one hand and cradled her elbow with the other.

"I can carry those," she said stubbornly. "And, for six more months, I can ride with you just the way I've been doing."

"I was a fool to ever let you start that," he said. "And now's the perfect time to put a stop to it."

They turned and started for the steps.

"Black Fox . . ." she said.

He interrupted her immediately.

"Cathleen, you cannot be riding after outlaws and helping me bring them in to jail while you're carrying a baby. It's too dangerous and you know it."

She stiffened, ready to put up a good fight, but

instead, she let him lead her up onto the porch and to the front door of the old cabin she had come to love. Home. Their home.

"I don't want to put the baby in danger," she said. "Never. But if I don't go with you, there'll be no one to back you up and *you'll* be in danger. I'm torn to pieces between you two."

In the parlor, he dropped the bags onto the leather seat of the ancient oak rocking chair and turned to face her. He took her shoulders in his hands.

He held her so firmly, yet so gently that tears sprang to her eyes.

"What's too dangerous is for me and the baby to stay here without you," she said, her lips stiff with the unshed tears. "We might just perish of loneliness."

He bent to kiss the tip of her nose, then he held her to him.

"How about you start us some supper," he said, "and let me tend to the horses? Then we'll talk."

Black Fox left her there and led the horses to the barn. He would have to tell her about his decision tonight, to keep her from worrying any longer, but first he had to think it through one more time, to make sure he could live with what he'd planned to do.

He didn't want to leave her either. Hardly ever did he feel the need to be alone anymore—he'd been too lonely too long before he found her.

But he loved his job, too, and it had been his life for many a year.

More than that, the Nation needed him. He and the other Lighthorse had cleaned out a lot of the riffraff, that was true, but there were a lot of criminals still running to the Indian Territories for shelter from the law. The native lawmen who knew the country and its natural hideouts in the rough terrain were the only ones who had a chance of ferreting them out.

He unsaddled and brushed the horses, put them into their stalls, hayed, watered and grained them. Then he walked back across the yard to the house, his heart finding its way to peace. Life had to be lived one day at a time. There was no other way.

And a man had to think of his own family and his own place once in a while.

When he stepped up onto the small back porch, he saw that Cathleen had a fire going in the stove and was setting a pot of potatoes on to cook. She had changed into the calico dress he'd bought her. It and her hair held the colors of the October western sky glowing behind the sunset.

Home. Night was coming on and he was home with the woman he loved.

He watched her through the open door while he cleaned up at the wash bench. She looked even more beautiful and feminine in a dress and she knew he liked her to wear them.

He smiled to himself. She was planning to argue some more and she was using every weapon in her arsenal.

His eyes followed her as she walked briskly back to the table, then to the meal box to take out what she needed to make cornbread. He could watch her every minute for the rest of his life and never get tired. She moved with her own quick grace and she always did what she started to do. If any woman *could* take care of a babe and capture criminals at the same time, it would be Cathleen O'Sullivan Vann. Already, she was quite a legend in the land.

He couldn't wait to watch her flat belly swell and grow round with their child. She wanted at least a dozen, she had confided in him on the way home this afternoon.

That made him shake his head wryly. A dozen children and to be a partner on the job to a Lighthorseman, that was all she wanted. Well, that was what she *said* she wanted.

She knew as well as he did that such a thing was impossible. He didn't know everything about her after only these few months of marriage, and in some ways she was an even bigger mystery to him, but he did know this. What she was really saying was simply that she didn't want to be separated from him for days at a time so soon after they'd found each other.

He threw out the dirty water, picked up the

clean towel she'd left folded beside the wash pan, and dried his face. Then he strode to the door.

"What I'm thinking," he said, as he opened the screen and stepped into the kitchen, "is that I need to take a few months off the job to work on this farm. I noticed the barn and the other outbuildings need some repair before winter and the chimney could use a good chinking."

She whirled to look at him, her face aglow.

"Oh, Black Fox, do you mean it? A few *months*?"

"I'm going to tell the council not to call on me unless it's a real emergency," he said. "Not until summer."

With a joyful cry, she ran to throw her arms around his neck.

"And then? After the baby gets big enough, we might let Aunt Sally watch him or her and I could ride with you sometimes?"

He chuckled as he pressed his cheek to hers and caressed her slender waist with both his hands.

"If I know you, you won't let that baby out of your sight," he said. "And remember, Cat, I did survive for seven years as a Lighthorse all alone."

She snuggled closer into his embrace.

"But I did save you from Becker's gang that night at the cave," she said. "So you aren't saying I can *never* ride with you again. Are you?"

He slipped his fingers into her hair to cradle her head and tilted it back so that he could look into her face.

"No, never is too long a time to talk about . . ." he said, looking into her eyes with all the passion that was welling in his heart, ". . . except when we talk about our love. It will never leave us."

# COMING NEXT MONTH

## LOVE WITH A SCANDALOUS LORD by Lorraine Heath
### An Avon Romantic Treasure

With a well-worn copy of *Blunders in Behavior Corrected*, Miss Lydia Westland has dreams of marrying a proper British lord. But while the first titled man she meets is dashing and oh-so-tempting, the Marquess of Blackhurst is anything if not scandalous . . . and he's about to teach Lydia that all rules are made to be broken.

*e ~*

## OPPOSITES ATTRACT by Hailey North
### An Avon Contemporary Romance

The last thing Jonni DeVries needs is the notorious Hollywood womanizer Cameron Scott around her recently broken heart. Lucky for him he was in costume when they first met or Jonni would have surely kicked him off her property. Now all this sexy hunk has to do is prove he's not the cad the tabloids made him out to be.

*e ~*

## THE CRIMSON LADY by Mary Reed McCall
### An Avon Romance

Fiona Byrne wants no part of her former notorious life and instead adopts the disguise of a simple seamstress. Then she is discovered by Braedan de Cantor, a dashing stranger who threatens to expose her. Braedan has no choice but to seek out the legendary lady outlaw to save his sister, though he never imagined the peril to his own heart and soul.

*e ~*

## TO MARRY THE DUKE by Julianne MacLean
### An Avon Romance

While her matchmaking mama is picking out suitably titled gentlemen, heiress Sophia Wilson is dreaming of her Prince Charming. She thinks she's found him in James Langdon, the Duke of Wentworth. But soon after the wedding the groom announces that this will be a marriage in name only!

REL 0503

# Avon Romantic Treasures

*Unforgettable, enthralling love stories,*
*sparkling with passion and adventure*
*from Romance's bestselling authors*

*Have you ever dreamed of writing a romance?*

*And have you ever wanted
to get a romance published?*

Perhaps you have always wondered how to
become an Avon romance writer?
We are now seeking the best and brightest undiscovered
voices. We invite you to send us your query letter to
*avonromance@harpercollins.com*

*What do you need to do?*

Please send no more than two pages telling us
about your book. We'd like to know its setting—is it
contemporary or historical—and a bit about the hero,
heroine, and what happens to them.

Then, if it is right for Avon we'll ask to see part of the
manuscript. Remember, it's important that you have
material to send, in case we want to see your story quickly.

Of course, there are no guarantees of publication,
but you never know unless you try!

*We know there is new talent just waiting
to be found! Don't hesitate . . . send us
your query letter today.*

*The Editors
Avon Romance*